UNFIT TO PLEAD

Also by Frank Palmer

Testimony (1992)

UNFIT TO PLEAD

Frank Palmer

St. Martin's Press
New York

The East Midlands Combined Constabulary is a fictional force. So, too, are its characters, the pit village and the institutions on which this imaginary investigation is centred.

The detective's views on missing persons, the doctor's on false confessions and the judges and solicitor's on the unfit to plead law are based on articles in the *Independent*.

An acknowledgement is also due to Fred Gettings's *Encyclopedia of the occult*.

My thanks for help and background to solicitor Paul Bacon, who successfully campaigned for overdue changes in the legislation which came into force this year.

UNFIT TO PLEAD. Copyright © 1992 by Frank Palmer. All rights reserved. Printed in the United States of America. No part of this book may be used or reproduced in any manner whatsoever without written permission except in the case of brief quotations embodied in critical articles or reviews. For information, address St. Martin's Press, 175 Fifth Avenue, New York, N.Y. 10010.

ISBN 0-312-10569-X

First published in Great Britain by Constable & Company Limited.

First U.S. Edition: February 1994
10 9 8 7 6 5 4 3 2 1

FOR MY WORKMATES

UNFIT TO PLEAD

1

'Dear Mother.' Mum. I should have said Mum. I never call her Mother.

'By the time you read this I'll be gone.' Dead. I should have said dead. Like the girl upstairs.

He lowered his head, closed his eyes and felt hot tears boiling out of them, chasing down his cheeks. Oh, Mum, I didn't mean to.

He sat, contorted face close to the note-pad, as if in a seance – but nothing made contact, just the sound of his own sobbing, the feeling of being hopelessly lost.

He opened his eyes and they went on opening, wider and wider, and he imagined giants' eyes, like white helium balloons, overfilled, about to explode.

He slashed at the words and they vanished under heavy waves of red. He stared, then gasped at the pattern. Ugly red on white. Like the girl upstairs.

Red? Why am I using red? He dropped the felt-tip as if it were electrified, and clawed the sheet from its pad into a ball. He held his breath and let it out slowly.

Start afresh. Say Mum and say dead. Use blue or black.

His agonized eyes toured the kitchen for another pen. He couldn't stand to fetch one, didn't try. His legs were paralyzed, numbed by the sight he'd seen on the bed when he got home, weakened by the vomiting that turned his stomach inside-out. Help me. Please help me.

The voice made contact then, distantly, as if emerging from deep inside a fog-shrouded forest. He had never put a face to it or a name but he knew him well.

Last night they'd been as one, joined together in the pleasure of planning, the rising, arousing, anticipation. All day, after the ghastly reality, he'd felt deserted, betrayed.

Think. How many times do I have to tell you? Think. Last time, when that girl screamed in the park, you panicked, didn't you? But we worked it out that all you had to say was that your hand slipped; an accident, her word against yours, and the police didn't come, anyway, did they?

But this is murder. I didn't mean to but she screamed. At first I thought she'd just passed out. I sort of half-expected, half-hoped she'd have gone when I came home. I was going to say she consented, her word against mine. But she's still up there, where I left her. She hasn't moved. She's dead. He started to weep again.

Think, snapped the voice.

Trying to, he wiped his eyes with the heels of both hands and sighed noisily, nasal juices bubbling, like an exhausted child.

She said she was going away for the weekend so no one will have missed her yet. He nodded slowly to himself.

Don't run away. They'll put two and two together. Another nod, more positive.

This place will have to be cleaned from top to bottom and the truck, too.

What about her body?

Get rid of it. Dump it.

She had suddenly become it but he never noticed. He sat in the darkness, perfectly still. By the early hours he'd worked out what to do.

He slid the note-pad away with the side of his hand. Not now. He wouldn't write to Mum yet. He'd hang himself if it went wrong rather than spend the rest of his life in a strait-jacket at the State Special; but not now. The feeling returned to his legs. He rose slowly and looked out of the window. From its blackness, his own face looked back, washed out, crushed, but his eyes were normal.

Never again, he vowed. He would cast out this foul, fatal fantasy, be done with it for ever. Never again.

2

Dead. He was sure of it; knew it. Every antenna was telling him so. Deep gloom descended.

Michelle Robinson gave him a confused little smile from the top of a thin file that had taken a day to compile. He ran it through his mind again, the details so vivid that he had no need to thumb through the statements.

She'd left home earlier than usual, telling her younger sister she had to meet someone before going to work, someone who had good news; but not who or where. She hadn't shown up at the office or at the home of her steady boy-friend where she'd been expected for the weekend. Only when he'd phoned her office yesterday to find out why did anyone realize she was missing.

This girl is no runaway. He'd assured her parents: 'We'll find her,' but he hadn't told them what he suspected and what he suspected was they'd find a body.

He had shared this fear with the squad chief who'd passed it on to the acting boss who'd ordered a media release and given him one WPC. One WPC from Child Protection, a semi-social worker, when he needed a dozen hairy-arsed detectives. 'Sorry,' the message came back, 'staff shortages; everyone taking time off owing now the pit strike's over.' That's police priorities for you, he complained to himself.

The black phone on his small desk rang and, with his eyes still on the photo, he lifted it clumsily. 'Major Crime Squad.'

'Detective Inspector Jackson, please.' A woman's voice, tight, gruff.

'Speaking.'

'Oh, good.' The tightness went; the coarseness stayed. He

wondered how many cigarettes she smoked and felt a pang for one himself but he'd given them up seven months ago when pregnancy was confirmed.

Her name was Maggie, she said, deputy to Colin Bates of TVE's *Crime Catchers*. He knew of it, knew of him, not her.

Her problem was that the lead item for that evening's programme about the rape of a student outside her bedsit was rogered. There'd been an arrest which made it *sub judice*, legally taboo, so they'd have to bin it, see?

Jacko thought he could see through the newspeak so he said: 'Yes.'

She was short by one minute fifty-two seconds and wanted to fill the gap by beefing up the media release, just in, on missing Michelle Robinson, OK?

'Terrific,' said Jacko and he felt it.

'It won't be Master Bates.' He laughed. He liked a bit of boss-baiting. 'It'll be a new boy, so hold his hand.'

Hold *his* hand? Jacko had only appeared on telly once before over the killing of a vice girl, but he said yes again and agreed to a meeting in the Fairways Hotel, the HQ local with a cosy, quiet back bar.

Half an hour later, he was poring over the photo and a map of the village while he dictated details from the statements to a nervous young man with shaggy corn-coloured hair, who wrote in longhand in a virgin notebook and triple-checked everything as though his career depended on it. They sipped Cokes.

On the next round table a three-man crew, dressed like soccer fans from the terrace end in anoraks and dirty trainers, guzzled pints and goaded the new boy, his initiation rites. 'The Master will be taking out a contract on you,' grinned a lanky technician.

Bates, the star of the show, the nervous newsman explained, had personally voiced the rape reconstruction and had planned to lead on it. They'd interrupted his lunch with a CID chief to break the news of the rapist's arrest. 'Superintendent Sherman. Know him?'

Jacko knew him, the tosser. Sherman had vetoed his request for a big operation to find Michelle, dead or alive, then gone off for a freebie lunch. A dumb nod.

'He wanted to run a knifeman at an off-licence. The Master's none too pleased.'

'Why?' asked Jacko, only half-interested. He had enough office politics of his own to handle.

'He reckons missing girls are two a penny,' said a heavy-bellied cameraman.

'Jobs for the Sally Army,' added the technician.

The cameraman finished his drink with a gulp. 'Two minutes of you at the station with the notice-board in the background.'

'She said one minute fifty-two seconds,' said Jacko, very knowledgeably.

'We'll cut you down to size,' said the technician.

Jacko had the feeling that they had done that already.

He turned on the squad room TV to catch the met man forecasting more rain. A boyish newscaster recapped the headlines. 'The miners go back after their year-long strike,' he said over a film clip of a proud procession behind a brass band, 'but, locally, a low-key return with union men facing the sack.'

A still picture appeared of three men walking shoulder to shoulder through the gates of a pit, past a black notice-board with MOORWOOD COLLIERY in yellow lettering.

He concentrated with a frown on the man in the middle: William Robinson, Michelle's father, short, thick-set, with a dead-eyed scowl for the camera.

He never mentioned this, Jacko thought, pondering for a second on the stress Robinson had been under, tension which could lead to temper and abuse and God knows what. He made a mental note to check his alibi about being at an early-morning picket.

He stretched out his legs on his desk and tilted on one buttock on his swivel chair to speak over his shoulder to a young woman.

WPC Heather Hurst had spent an hour reading the statements from family, workmates and boy-friend in the file. From time to time, he sneaked glances at her. She was small and dark with the erect posture of a gymnast and she had a wonderful backside which she perched on his desk every time she had a question. He nodded at the screen. 'The man in the centre was Michelle's dad.'

Her black eyebrows knitted behind big red spectacles. 'As if

11

he hasn't trouble enough,' she said, with genuine sympathy. Kind but a typical welfare worker's attitude and he knew then that she had much to learn.

The theme music – tin whistles to a kettledrum accompaniment – and the blue flashing lights faded. 'Evening all,' said a smooth Colin Bates, flicking his forefinger from his temple towards the camera in a silly imitation of Dixon of Dock Green.

He had a voice out of a chocolate advert, dark brown which lightened for the occasional cliché in the script describing a building society robbery, filmed by security cameras in streaky black and white.

'Caught in the act, then, Super?' he said, pleased with himself, as he turned to a man whose bloated features made Jacko grimace.

'In a manner of speaking,' said the studio guest with a caption across his broad chest which said DET. SUPT. ALEC SHERMAN.

Together they studied the freeze frames of the masked robbers like a panel of soccer pundits on a sports programme analysing a goal.

'Thanks, Alec,' said Bates, turning to face the camera with an over-familiar smile. 'Anyone out there who can help put names to these faces, please call Superintendent Sherman here on this number.' A six-figure number which Bates read aloud danced along the bottom of the screen. 'And, of course, any information you have will be treated in the strictest confidence. Right, Alec?'

'Absolutely.'

'Now, crime catchers.' The camera closed in on Bates so that he appeared in full face, blow-dried hair brushed forward from left to right across high forehead on which make-up had softened deep furrows. He still looked forty plus. 'A missing persons case for you.'

Michelle's photo appeared. Tousled, very fair hair, distant blue eyes, a slight cast in the left one, and that puzzled, so saddening smile. A crisp white collar and a red and black striped tie indicated a school photo.

'Michelle Robinson vanished after leaving her home in the pit village of Moorwood four days ago,' said a younger, nervous voice, off screen.

'Normally she left home on this road . . .' a long-distance shot of a dismal estate '. . . around 7.20 in the morning to catch a bus to work. Last Friday she left almost an hour earlier. She told her younger sister she had someone to meet and was hoping for "some good news" – those were her words – but didn't say who, where or what good news.'

'We're treating this as a matter of considerable concern.' A different voice, local, slow and flat, which Jacko didn't recognize, spoke over a new picture of Michelle, a seaside snap, full length, side-on, a thin body in a red shirt with no discernible bosom but a well rounded bottom in tight jeans.

'She didn't report for work on Friday morning. That evening she had arranged to travel to the family home of her boy-friend, a young airman. She didn't turn up. Her seventeenth birthday was on Saturday.'

Jacko knew the words had come out of his own mouth but they sounded as though he'd been dubbed.

The photo that introduced the item reappeared. 'And she's made no contact with her family, to whom she's very close, or her boy-friend.'

His own face now. Mid-forties, tired, with creases that seemed to push him past fifty. Hazel eyes behind steel rimmed spectacles. Dark brown hair caught in the wind exposing a receding forehead. Det. Insp. Jim Jackson, said the caption, as if he didn't know. What a mess, he groaned.

'In addition . . .' behind him was a notice-board with EAST MIDLANDS COMBINED CONSTABULARY in white letters on a blue background '. . . we have another incident in the same locality within forty-five minutes of her leaving home.'

A blown-up street map, an H on its side, appeared. Red arrows pointed to Michelle's home on the top line and the stop where she usually caught the bus on the bottom. There was a black cross on the lower road to the left of the bus stop.

'The X is where a woman cycling to work, just before 7.30 a.m., to the canteen at the local colliery was hit from behind by a speeding vehicle and knocked unconscious into a hedgerow. She didn't get much of a look at it and the driver didn't stop. She describes the vehicle as being like an army truck so it may be a khaki-coloured Land-Rover type.'

A longer view of himself, wearing a mid-blue suit with

unbuttoned jacket flapping on the March wind. On-screen, he looked cold and tentative. Off-screen, he couldn't believe how old and sick he was looking.

'Of course, these incidents may not be connected,' he added with a face that confirmed uncertainty. 'But we'd like to know more about that vehicle and any others in the vicinity around this time, particularly a white sports car. A witness reports seeing it heading west and stopping to pick up a girl hitcher dressed, as Michelle was, in denims and carrying a small bag. Most important of all, we need the person Michelle was meeting to come forward.'

A phone number flashed across the bottom of the screen and stayed there as he was replaced by Michelle's pale face.

His voice continued, disembodied, running through her description: young-looking for her age, long blonde hair, blue eyes, slim, wearing a smart blue denim suit. 'She was a home-loving girl, happy at work, a steady boy-friend, an untroubled background. She had a change of clothes in the bag and money but we can find no reason for her to run away.'

Apart from Heather no one was to see his face shadow with sorrow. He had used 'was' instead of 'is', which put Michelle Robinson in the past tense. Only last night, when he'd taken their statements, he had tried to reassure her parents in the privacy of their home. 'Keep your hopes up. We'll find her.' Now, on TV, that most public of places, he'd written her off as dead.

Heather stood and walked to the set which she clicked off. 'Very good,' she said, sincerely.

Jacko saw Michelle's face diminish into a white dot and imagined her life vanishing with it. Down the tube. He felt as he'd looked – old and sick.

'Hi.' One word from one woman and his spirits soared.

'How was I?' He sounded himself again.

'Terrible.' She giggled. 'I thought the broadcasting authorities had a rule that horror movie stars shouldn't be shown until all children are tucked up in bed.'

He laughed. 'It was the sound of my own voice that worried me. Am I always that much of a country yokel?'

14

'Always,' she said in a soft, southern accent (sensual, to him) and they laughed together.

They laughed a lot. They were friends as well as lovers. Mrs Jacqueline Cruickshank had been a witness in the vice killing inquiry. They had known each other for ten months. For seven of them she had been pregnant. Everyone down their road was prematurely calling her Mrs Jackson and one day soon they'd wed. He'd already proposed. 'To please my old mum,' he'd pleaded. 'She thinks living in sin is a sin.'

He had known Jackie would be watching, had pictured her flopped on a green couch, legs outstretched, head propped on a lace runner so she could see over the mound that was her stomach. A mound out of which a son – he was sure of a boy – would soon emerge into a world of good and bad, haves and have-nots, to do his bit, however small, to right a wrong and make it a better place. Of that he was equally sure. 'How's Horace?'

'Kicking in protest at the sight of his father.'

Heather silenced a ringing phone on her desk and started making notes.

Dinner, Jackie was announcing, was lamb hot-pot, his favourite on a cold night, but not to rush, it would keep. He had a quick vision of a long, lazy evening at home.

Heather shot him urgent glances and he cancelled the thought with a shaft of shame at another vision – of Michelle's mother sitting at home waiting for news.

He said sorry he'd be late. He knew she'd understand. Only a mother could understand that worst vacuum of all: not knowing whether someone you have carried in your womb, fed, bathed, clothed, loved, your own child, is alive or dead. They blew each other loud kisses.

'Thanks for calling, Mr Mason,' said Jacko when he took over the phone from Heather.

Like he'd just told that policewoman, Mason began, he'd been watching *Crime Catchers* and was sure he owned the white sports car they were seeking.

He'd driven his Merc through Main Road, Moorwood, that morning, bound from his home, a cottage on the edge of

Sherwood Forest, for the ring road, then the M1, to call on a client of his family's timber firm.

He'd picked up a hitcher near the colliery who had long fair hair and wore a denim suit – 'but the thumber was a scruffy youth, not a teenage girl.' Jacko bit on his disappointment.

'He stepped into the road and virtually hijacked me. He was in a real panic. I dropped him off outside the City Hospital just before the ring road. He'd had a call from the maternity wing that his girl had gone into labour.' The hitcher didn't volunteer his name, he added.

'See anyone else about the village?' Jacko asked.

'No pickets or anything. Haven't seen any for months. The early underground shift are in by six so it was quiet. The thumber had just missed a bus and no one was waiting at the shelter. There was one of those security cowboys dashing around. Almost sideswiped me. You must have seen them. Did more flying about the coalfields than the pickets. They're the new growth industry. Thank God it's over.'

Amen to that, thought Jacko with relief. The strike had depressed him. He regarded himself as a back-street boy of socialist stock and even he had come to regard it as the biggest cock-up in trade union history.

'It was bloody awful up here,' Mason chattered on. 'The locals working, apart from a handful. The strikers trying to picket them out. Strike breakers had their windows and cars smashed. A couple of Coal Board depots were set on fire.'

So, Mason continued, outside contractors were engaged – road haulage firms which moved the coal that railmen had blacked, coach firms ferrying workers through the picket lines. Private security firms were hired to protect them.

'Private armies, they are. You know, white cars and Range Rovers with blue stripes so they look like police patrols. Drivers in dark uniforms with chevrons and pips. Cones which say POLITE NOTICE so motorists misread them as POLICE NOTICE. Know the sort of thing?'

Most of the action, he went on, had moved north in the final months as the union fought to stop the strike crumbling. 'But lots of firms kept the guard on in case of attacks from flying pickets. You still see them about. This one, a white Range

Rover, shot straight in front of me as I was pulling away with the hitcher.'

'Notice anything special about it?'

'Oh, yes,' said Mason. 'It had their logo on the door. That Mountie in the hat. TVE Security. Know it?'

3

Heather wound down the window and showed her warrant card to a guard in a black Mountie hat, who made a call from his enclosed glass box, then raised a red barrier to let them in.

Jacko parked at the side of the building, four storeys high, each smaller than the one below, a roof shaped like a cocktail umbrella, giving the place a Chinese look. The bricks were deep red with the cement in the pointings dyed to match. Situated on an approach road to Moorwood, it stood out stylishly against its industrial estate neighbours which were mainly grey breeze blocks with fascias of warping wood.

The initials ran down the front of the building and, she explained, they stood for Trent Vale Enterprises, not TV East, as he'd assumed.

A white Rolls-Royce stood by the automatic sliding doors in a space marked PRESIDENT. He, she said, was Glynn Tyson. The quiet Canadian, the force's PR called him. He'd been twenty, a boy from the Ontario lakes, when his country's air force posted him to rural England, Heather went on, relaying what the force's PR had told her. He took a teenage English bride home with him.

They'd returned with a grown son and bought a run-down manor close to the riverside village where his wife was born. 'The tip,' said Heather, 'is he fled his homeland just ahead of a breaking scandal over a pyramid-selling firm he ran in Toronto.' Within two years he was a media millionaire, owner of a big group of giveaways, a money-making machine.

'One man the Mounties didn't get,' said Jacko with a smile.

Below the E in TVE was a bronze plaque with the Mountie hat

logo and, under that, his associated companies brought together under the pagoda roof less than a year earlier.

Heather rattled through the list: TVE Systems for newspapers following him into job-shedding computer technology, TVE Transportation to cut out rail and postal services, TVE Securities which had supplied the guards against the pickets and now had as many clients in the mining industry as it did among the media. There were TVE Properties and TVE Insurance, of which she knew nothing.

TVETV was the latest and lowest on the list. It had started out making promotion films and expanded into a production company with contracts to provide inserts that regional newsrooms within national networks were too busy to handle.

Crime Catchers was just one of a dozen five- or six-minute programmes it produced, the only one fronted by Colin Bates, who doubled as TVE media director.

'In return for police co-operation, he gives senior officers video coaching sessions on how to tell journalists nothing but nicely,' said Heather, concluding her briefing.

'He's not got round to me yet.' Jacko put on his solemn face as he told her that last year, on the vice girl inquiry, he'd been in trouble with the PR Department for telling a very large man from the *Sun* to fuck off. She laughed happily.

He decided to let her lead the interview but wasn't sure whether it was because she'd liked his story, was a reward for her impressive research or to find out what she was made of.

Waiting in the warmth by the reception desk was Colin Bates with an outstretched hand. 'Nice to see you again.'

Jacko, who had never seen him in the flesh before, took the hot hand in his cold one but felt no professional warmth. He had the look of a desk man who had long since stopped knocking on doors. His suit, newly pressed, was chocolate brown to match his voice. No waistcoat or pullover spoilt the view of a white silk shirt. A striped tie, claret and gold, drew attention to a well lunched paunch. 'How can we help?'

Heather told him and, as she spoke, Jacko saw his face dissolve into a mixture of relief and understanding.

'Follow me,' he said and he led the way, soundless on a grey cord carpet, along a ground-floor corridor. They went through a door with the name-plate: 'Mr L. Tyson, Director, TVE PROPERTIES, TVE SECURITIES'.

'Luke free?' he asked a brunette at a word processor who nodded them into the inner office where a man sat behind a big desk. Luke Tyson ('The boss's son,' Heather whispered but Jacko had worked out the nepotism for himself) looked up from his paperwork. Bates made the introductions.

Heather explained yet again. He swung round in his chair and spoke with only the top of his fair head visible behind its high fawn back. 'Friday, the first. Early turn. Moorwood.' A pink shirt-sleeve made its selection from a row of clipboards that hung on the wall. He was already flicking over pages when he swung back into view.

The pink sleeve went to one of two cream phones. 'Where's Mountie Bannion?' He gazed absent-mindedly at Heather as he hung on and Jacko squeezed off a smile. 'Get him in here pronto.'

'Five minutes,' he said. Bates's chatter filled them, dropping names about senior officers he knew and cases his weekly programme had solved. Heather sat next to him on a long fawn couch, Jacko on a straight-backed chair, studying Luke.

He was not yet thirty, six foot and slim with hair out of the wheat belt. Only a matching moustache and eyebrows had escaped the sand-blaster that seemed to have been busy on his flawed face. He spoke softly but clearly; only slightly transatlantic.

When his secretary knocked and inclined her head round the door, he stood and walked out with long, easy strides. A few seconds later he returned. Following him was a squat man, younger than Luke, in a white shirt and black uniform trousers of coarse material. He had short, black hair, uncovered by a Rose Marie hat; mercifully, otherwise Jacko doubted that he could have contained himself. 'Keith Bannion,' said Luke, without looking behind as he strode back behind his desk. Bannion was not asked to sit.

Heather explained for a third time, while Jacko looked into a sallow, aggressive face that reminded him of a Spanish waiter who'd not been left a tip.

Yea, Bannion said suspiciously, he'd been on that run in a white Range Rover that morning. At 7.30, he'd called at Forest

Coaches and, ten minutes later, the colliery down the main road. Both were clients. The early morning cleaner at Forest Coaches had reported all quiet. So had the man in the time office at the pit.

'See this girl on your travels that morning?' Heather handed him the full-face photo of Michelle Robinson that the BBC had used.

He looked at it for what seemed a long time, shook his head, handed it back.

'Or anyone hitching?'

Bannion frowned. 'No.'

'Or a khaki-coloured truck?'

Bannion stuck his tongue into his cheek, looked away towards Luke in thought, then back again. 'Not that I recall.'

'How about a white Mercedes sports car?'

A headshake.

'That's odd,' said Heather brightly, 'because he remembers you.'

She stood to take off her thick mustard coat which she lay untidily over an arm of the couch. She turned her back and bent to unzip her brown shoulder bag. She was wearing a tight black woollen dress. She sat down again and read out an extract from the statement Mason had given Jacko the previous night.

'Rubbish,' Bannion blurted when she had finished. 'I never had a near miss with any car.'

'Better not have done,' said Luke with a hint of menace. Bannion gave his boss a stare, bolshy, unafraid.

'We're very keen here on our road safety record,' said Bates with a beam just for Heather. He switched it off when his eyes travelled beyond her to Bannion. 'Why didn't you report this earlier?'

'Report what?'

'Surely you saw my programme last night?'

'Didn't see it.' Bannion gazed indolently at Bates. 'I was out buying a fishing rod.'

With a peacemaker's smile for both of them, Heather opened her notebook. She took down Bannion's movements while Luke cross-checked them on the clipboard.

He'd left home where he lived alone just after seven, he said. He'd seen no hitcher, boy or girl, and no one at the service bus

21

stop outside Forest Coaches. There, he'd chatted briefly to a cleaner called Sam and made a fuss of the depot's dog, which only liked people Sam liked. Things were just as quiet at the colliery.

'Where's your vehicle now?' she asked.

'Outside.'

'Can we examine it?' An encouraging smile. 'Just to eliminate it.'

'Most certainly,' said Bates, ingratiatingly. 'Anything to help the local constabulary.'

Heather unearthed a suspect next day. Michelle Robinson had been pestered for a date by a local boy. She'd said so to a girl friend from the village, a fellow-passenger who regularly caught the 7.26 bus from the stop outside Forest Coaches on the main road. A colleague at the estate agent's office in the city centre where she worked had confirmed it.

His name was Nick James, aged eighteen, living in the back streets of Moorwood with his widowed mother and working at the colliery just up the road.

Michelle had ignored him. She had a steady, her airman, who, like her father, Jacko had carefully checked and cleared. James had been a scab – working through the strike, crossing her father's picket line. 'No chance,' she'd said. A striker's daughter, Jacko mused, would not even have been seen walking out with George Michael, if he'd been breaking the code of the coalfields.

A buzz of excitement was running through her, recharged him, making him feel young and keen.

An hour later, he took James, a tall, spotty youth, into the nearest station. He complained, 'Can't I have my snap first?' – a local word for food taken to work in tins or plastic boxes. Heather went to question his mother and search his bedroom.

'Never saw that girl that morning or since,' he said firmly. 'She's just one of half-a-dozen I fancy and besides I've gone off her. She's so bloody rude.'

He'd left home on his motor bike at 7.25, his usual time, he insisted, and clocked on four minutes later in the pit-yard offices where he worked.

His mother confirmed the time of his departure. Soccer stars were pinned to the walls of his bedroom; nothing naughty, not even a page three girl. The only semen stains found were on a handkerchief in the pocket of his red pyjamas.

The lead sank. So did Heather's spirits. Jacko consoled her with a drink in the Fairways that night, explaining the facts of CID life, the straw-clutching excitement, the dead-end depression, the lot of a detective without a clue. 'Of course there'll be false leads, blind alleys, but we have to hang on and we'll get there. No matter how long it takes. We'll get there.'

Heather's brown eyes brightened behind her red specs and soon they started swapping brief biographies. She was twenty-five, almost twenty years younger than Jacko, and had volunteered for CID for experience which, combined with her Child Protection service, would eventually make her a candidate for sergeant in the Missing Persons Unit. 'Tell me,' she asked, looking deep into his face, 'why are you so convinced she's dead?'

Jacko sighed. 'The trick with missing persons is to sort out the vulnerable – the over-65s, the mentally ill and, above all, the 17s and under who have never run off before.'

He listed his reasons on his fingers. 'A close family. A steady fella. A steady job. No trouble of any kind.' He shrugged. 'Just a hunch, a feeling. I can't seem to convince Sherman.'

She prattled on about her love life, non-existent at that moment, her ambitions and Jacko sat with a fixed smile, his mind far away, on Michelle's photo. Where are you? he was asking himself.

He knew, just knew, she would never answer so he asked himself: Where is she? Who did it? He got no reply.

He had to hammer to be heard above the cries of a baby, angry with hunger. In all, Jacko had knocked on a dozen doors working his way down a list from the City Hospital. He had his opening line off pat but had to raise his voice above the din to rattle through it.

'Yes,' said a youth, immediately. 'Come in.' His dark eyes were dull, their lids and bags yellowed from lack of sleep.

His chin and cheeks had a five o'clock shadow at ten in the morning.

Tom Wright showed him into a lounge where a coal fire glowed red and low in an open grate. In front of it, stealing its warmth, was a black wire frame on which white cot sheets were being aired.

'Sorry about the racket,' said Wright with an exhausted sigh as he slumped down on to a lumpy sofa.

Sure, he remembered last Friday. A nostalgic smile for a youth lost at eighteen. 'Sound asleep, I was, when Mum woke me with the news that Julie was about to sprog. I'd promised her I'd be with her at the birth.'

Brave boy, thought Jacko. He was still undecided. It sounded a bit modern to him.

'I threw on the denims, picked up the bag Julie had already packed and sprinted out the estate, down the lane to the main road.' He was in time to see the 7.26 pulling away.

He didn't fancy a twenty-minute wait in the cold for the next bus. 'So I thumbed. This flash white job picked me up almost straight away. Nice bloke, the driver. Dropped me outside the hospital.' In good time, as it turned out, to witness little Gemma's entrance.

'Remember seeing a TVE security patrol?' asked Jacko, in a normal voice now that the crying had stopped.

'Too right. Almost pranged us as we were moving off. Always tearing around here like shit off a shovel. Think they own the roads.'

No, he said, he hadn't seen a khaki or olive-green army-type vehicle. Or a teenage girl in denims. No, he didn't know a girl was missing from the estate. He'd been staying with his Julie at her parents' place most of the week. He looked at the photo Jacko showed him. He didn't know Michelle Robinson.

'Come and see the little gem,' he said suddenly with childlike pride and he stood as quickly as he spoke. He led the way to the back kitchen half the size of the small lounge where towels and more sheets hung on a plastic frame.

The smell reached Jacko before the sight. The sourness of urine. The sweetness of talcum powder. The warm dampness of ironing which a worn woman, a grandmother at forty, was doing at a board. The smell of a new baby which would soon invade his home.

A girl, pale, very frail, young enough to be at school, was sitting, with legs apart, on a straight chair, in front of a back boiler giving out meagre heat. Her cream shirt was open. One bare breast, small and white as a cooking onion, was half-hidden. At the other, a baby sucked noisily, small face wrinkled as a dried apricot in concentration.

Jacko stopped a yard short, pinning his raincoat to his thighs with his hands, not wanting to contaminate them with his dirt. He looked down and smiled an imbecile's smile. 'Me and my lady are getting one of those in a couple of months' time.'

Tom neutralized a disbelieving look which seemed to question, with a buck's arrogance, an old stag's ability to pull off such a feat. 'Let's hope you get more sleep than us,' sighed his mother without looking up from her ironing board.

She didn't know, either, that a teenage girl half a dozen streets away was missing but expressed no surprise. They often went missing from estates like this, Jacko realized, to find a better life. They were bleak streets with concrete backyards, built in the 1930s. Some runaways ended up in juvenile court or council care and for a moment, just a second, he wondered if he was fretting too much.

Tom led the way, sure-footed as a Sherpa, through the hall, an obstacle course with a pram, high chair and a play pen, the clutter of babyhood. At the front door, Jacko fished in a pocket for a five pound note. 'Buy the kid something.'

'Thanks.' Tom took it without embarrassment.

'Did you see anyone else around that morning?' Jacko asked.

He gave it some thought. 'Only Hollis running up the main drag towards the colliery.'

'Who's he?'

'A right snotty bastard. White collar exec at the pit.' Tom flicked his head to his left. 'Lives round the corner. End house in the cul-de-sac. No point in calling this time of day, though. He lives alone.' He smiled, conspiratorially. 'Everyone round here thinks he's a bit of a . . .' he hinged his forearm upright but let the wrist flop '. . . know what I mean?'

Jacko knew. A limp wrist, a homosexual. No one would ever

be able to say that about Wright with a howling baby indoors, he thought. Or me, come to think of it.

There is something moving and magnificent about an old colliery, Jacko often thought. Like visiting the trenches at the Somme. Holes in the ground where men had soldiered side by side with only each other to rely on; where they had battled in the mud through fatigue; where many, far too many, had perished. He approached with a sense of homage.

Wet, black slime splashed up beneath his maroon Cortina from the road, potholed by heavy lorries while the railway lines to the power stations in the Trent Valley had rusted during the strike.

Only once had Jacko gone down a mine, a police PR exercise, and he'd never forgotten the cloying claustrophobia, the heat, the straps of the pads that skinned the backs of his knees, the long rutted road that made walking to the face jar his back, the alcove in which men had to defecate, the mice that scurried for scraps from snap tins, the deafening noise from the cutter, bigger than a tank, his morbid fear of being buried alive.

The twin wheels high on the sage-green lattice-work headstock were slowly spinning. Behind them, a rolling hill was being sculptured by giant caterpillars from never ending supplies of waste soil cascading from a conveyor belt.

The cables from the spoked wheels fed themselves into a red-bricked building, solid as a chapel, which housed the lifts and baths. Across the grimy yard was a single-storey brick building with a dusty door. A clerk in the wages office broke off from a soccer argument, chummily abusive, with an underground worker whose orange overalls were streaked with black, and gave him directions.

At the end of a long cold corridor he tapped on a door marked *Subsidence Inspectorate – Area Office*, and walked in.

Norman Hollis looked up from paperwork in neat piles on his grey metal desk. He was thirtyish, fair, with a rugged outdoors face, and wore a navy-blue boilersuit.

Jacko showed him his warrant card and sat, uninvited. 'We've got a girl missing from your estate and we're wondering if you might have seen her . . .'

26

'Red Robbo's bairn.' A flat, local voice, uninterested and uninteresting.

'Heard about her?'

'You keep nothing secret round here.' He paused. 'No one's surprised.'

'Why?' Jacko's eyebrows lowered in surprise behind his spectacles.

'Ever met him?'

No business of his, he decided, so he said: 'They've still heard nothing.' Hollis said nothing. 'Why is no one surprised Michelle's missing?'

'They're a rum family.'

'In what way?'

A distracted smile. 'How long have you been on this job?'

Jacko, annoyed, began speaking urgently. 'Believe me, there's reason for concern here.'

A dissenting shrug. 'Everybody here thinks she's done a bunk and who can blame her from that family?'

Jacko shook his head slowly. 'Not her style.'

'Style?' A short mirthless laugh. 'They've got no style.'

Not true, thought Jacko. He'd come to like Mrs Robinson. She and her husband had moved down from the north-east when his old pit shut in the 1960s. Both had retained their warm Geordie accents, though their two daughters spoke as locals. Their mother energetically kept the house as spotless as the Wrights' he'd just left was chaotic. She'd taken a job as a cleaner to eke out the union strike pay. Michelle had passed up a chance of sixth-form college to work as a filing clerk at a city centre estate agency.

He had not been able to get through to Mr Robinson, a bristling man with a beer drinker's belly. Mostly he'd maintained watchful silence while his wife did the chatting. Getting him to talk in more than monosyllables had been like drawing teeth. When he was out of the room, his embarrassed wife had explained that he blamed the heavy police presence on the coalfield for the defeat of his union. 'They struck me as a close-knit family.'

'Herr.' Half-snort, half cough. 'Then you don't know much. Robbo's a raving militant. He picketed every day.'

Jacko leant forward. 'Correct me, if I'm wrong, Mr Hollis,

but the strikers had to picket or they didn't qualify for union benefits. Makes sense. He needed the money.' He shrugged, non-committal. 'He seems OK to me.'

'He didn't have to do what he did, though.'

'What did he do?'

'Smashed up my vehicle. Put a brick through a headlamp.'

'Did you witness that?'

'Security did. If he comes back, I go.'

So that explains why Robinson wasn't back at work, Jacko realized. It was Coal Board policy that any striker guilty of acts of violence or damage against strike breakers or their property would be sacked. Hollis was demanding his pound of flesh.

Jacko regarded himself by nature as an appeaser, a compromiser, a bygones be bygones man and he decided he wasn't going to like Mr Hollis – ever. 'What sort of car do you run?'

'I don't want to make a police case out of it. He'll pay for it with his job.'

'What sort of car, Mr Hollis?' Jacko lengthened his words.

'A Nissan Patrol.' Jacko gave him a surprised look, so Hollis quickly added: 'I have to do a lot of on-site inspections. It can be rough work.'

'Colour?'

'Brown.'

'Did you drive it to work a week ago today?'

'Why?' A pause, then lamely: 'Yes.'

'We have a witness who reports you running on the main road . . .'

'Well, I never saw her.' Hollis spoke before the question was finished.

'Why were you on foot if you drove your truck to work?'

An uneasy look. 'A breakdown.'

'Where?'

'Going out on a job. On the ring road. What's this . . . ?'

Jacko cut in, rudely. 'So how did you get back here?'

'Got a lift.' He headed off the next question. 'A stranger.' He paused, unsure. 'In a Metro, I think it was.'

Hollis looked up in mild relief as the door swung open. Into the office came an acned youth who dropped two folders on his desk. Nick James recognized Jacko immediately and his mouth dropped.

Hollis was staring, transfixed, at the top file. Jacko read the name upside down: Forest Coaches. James tapped it. 'Shall I get round there and . . .'

'No.' Hollis cut him short.

Jacko addressed James. 'Perhaps you can help us, Nick?' Hollis gathered himself, trying, but failing, to hide his surprise that they knew each other. 'We're just trying to get everyone's timetable right for last Friday.'

'Still?' said James, puzzled but without resentment.

'You clocked on at 7.29. Right?' James nodded. Jacko turned to Hollis. 'And you?'

'I got here five minutes or so after him.' He nodded at James who took it as a signal to leave, which he did, quickly.

'What were your movements before that?'

'I was going on a survey, broke down and got that lift back.'

'So you'd be about the village when Michelle usually left home?'

'Now look here . . .'

'Where's your truck now?'

'Outside.' A suspicious glare. 'Why?'

'I'd like to take a look at it.'

'Why?'

'Quite apart from Michelle being missing, Mr Hollis, a woman who works in the canteen here was bowled over by a jeep-type vehicle, khaki-coloured, that same morning. You'd expect us to check all similar vehicles, now wouldn't you?'

'It wasn't mine. Mine was knackered on the ring road.'

'Then you won't mind us having a look.' Jacko was using his pleasant voice. 'You can have a solicitor present if you like.'

'Yes, I bloody well do mind.' A piqued face and voice. 'You question me in front of my clerk, then you turn round and accuse me of a hit and run.'

Jacko rose, smiling. 'We'll do it the hard way then.'

He waited in the wages office, arguing sport, for the ninety minutes it took for Heather to arrive with a JP's warrant, a vehicle examiner and a forensic scientist.

Hollis and James stared from their office window as Heather

bent forward into the vehicle to sort through the glove compartment.

Hollis's gaze was long and lustful and Jacko decided Tom Wright had misread him. It was not a limp wrist's look.

4

Madness. He wasn't sure who said the word or where he was but he sensed the fog lifting slightly, letting in a greyish light. He seemed to stand still, outside of himself.

Madness. That word again and a black figure flitting in and out of the trees but he still wasn't sure who was speaking.

In his waking dreams, before . . . He blanked it out and began again. This is very complicated, he told himself.

What is? a familiar voice asked.

Before, like, when I was having good dreams, I used my brain as a sort of video and if the scene wasn't working out right I'd put it on rewind and start again.

Do it now then, the voice commanded.

The misty scene faded and returned, unchanged. The black figure reappeared, stationary now, faceless, bottom-heavy like a filled bin-liner, and he addressed it. 'What were you saying?'

'Only that it's going well. It's been a week and . . .'

'It's been an awful week. I haven't slept.'

'You're sleeping now.'

'How can I be sleeping when I'm talking? Leave me in peace.'

A moment's peace and the forest grew lighter as though day were breaking and he could no longer see the black figure.

'She was lovely, wasn't she?' That voice again. From nowhere.

'I'm not listening.'

'What an arse.'

'I'm not thinking of women.' His own yelling echoed round his head. 'And she's a policewoman. It's madness. Do you hear me? Madness. *Madness.*'

His eyes opened wide. His head ached. His mouth was coated

and foul. The sensation at his groin was stilled. He was sweating and shaking again.

A nightmare, he told himself. Just another nightmare and not as bad as the rest. And it was you telling him he was mad, not anyone accusing you. You're not mad and no one is saying you are. So it wasn't even a nightmare. Just a dream. Now try to sleep. Sleep.

5

He'd been on it a week now, getting nowhere, frustrated, depressed, and his annoyance increased when the squad's controller told him: 'You're wanted on the flight deck.'

Normally Richard Scott would come to him, if to do no more than stretch his legs and escape the boredom of office routine. Scott's rank and title, Detective Chief Superintendent and head of CID, carried with them an office on the flight deck one floor up from the pine-panneled reception hall at HQ.

He was a hands-on chief, out in the field for the big operations, dropping in unannounced. They were close, he and Jacko. They thought alike, and Jacko knew he would have got his dozen detectives had Scott been here.

His deputy, Detective Superintendent Alec Sherman, was sitting in striped shirt-sleeves behind a desk, cleared of its usual chaos.

He nodded to a straight chair, not the long wall bench where Jacko usually lounged beneath Scott's framed collection of anti-police cartoons. Jacko's favourite was drawn three years earlier after the inner-city riots. A terrified young bobby was fleeing from the front line on which petrol bombs and bricks rained, passing a wall behind which the senior officer in charge, scrambled eggs on his epaulettes, was cowering. 'Christ,' the deserter was saying to himself, 'I didn't realize I'd run this far.'

'Heard from Richard?' he said, sitting stiffly.

Mr Scott, he was formally informed, was likely to be away for a further month investigating an internal corruption complaint in a distant force. All detectives seem to do these days, thought Jacko, moodily, is investigate each other.

'And, I'm afraid, I've had a complaint about you.' He looked down at a note-pad, the only loose document on the desk. The rest were neatly stacked in a triple-decked tray. Odd bits of paper were on a spike with a round wooden base such as butchers and newsmen use. A paper hoarder, Jacko decided. 'On behalf of a Mr Norman Hollis, of the NCB.'

Jacko nodded, unconcerned. Operational detectives are used to fielding complaints. Some regard them as a badge of honour, a virility symbol; others as slander on their reputations, putting their careers and pensions in jeopardy. Once Jacko had belonged to the latter school, working himself into a sweat at the first sign of trouble. Now, in an age that had become increasingly and sometimes understandably distrustful of authority, he accepted them as occasionally unavoidable. 'What about?'

'Two-pronged. His solicitor says you ordered a search of his vehicle in full view of his working colleagues.'

'True.' Jacko nodded positively. 'He wouldn't give me permission to take it away so I got a warrant to do it there.'

'Was that necessary?'

'His vehicle tied in with a description on the hit and run. I didn't want any quick repairs done on it.'

'Isn't that a job for Traffic? There were only minor injuries after all.'

A surprised look. 'We need to eliminate it from the missing girl inquiry.'

'Did Forensics find anything?'

'No.' Jacko shook his head glumly.

Sherman pulled a sour face. 'Secondly, there's an allegation that you showed political partiality. Says your action followed expressed sympathy and admiration for the strikers.'

'Balls,' said Jacko without anger. 'Who's saying this?'

Sherman's dull brown eyes returned to his notes. A face that had once been handsome but his black hair was greying without distinction at the temples. Pink skin slackened at the jaw and his stomach wobbled beneath a cotton shirt forming a fold over the belt to his midnight-blue trousers. All, Jacko suspected, due to desking in charge of admin and public relations. Or maybe long lunches with Colin Bates of *Crime Catchers*. 'A Mr Hill of Gemmell and Co.'

Jacko had heard of neither. 'Tell Mr Hill it wasn't that way. We were discussing the finances of the Robinson family, not union loyalties. I was questioning the bum background Hollis was trying to give me. That's all.'

Sherman pursed his lips into a thin smile. 'He's not making a formal complaint.'

'I should think not,' said Jacko, feigning indignation, privately pleased he wouldn't face the time-consuming hassle of a disciplinary hearing. 'I told him he could consult a solicitor.'

'Perhaps he didn't want to run up the expense.'

'Then why bother now? WPC Hurst phoned him this morning to tell him his vehicle was cleared.'

'It would have been better if you'd called him.'

Jacko stayed silent. Fair enough, he conceded.

'You see,' Sherman went on, 'everyone in the coalfields is still a bit, well, sensitive. The chief wants no hint of politics, of taking sides on our part.'

Not fair enough, Jacko thought. Michelle Robinson's dad was right. The police did take the government's side. The politician in him seized on a debating point. 'My point exactly. Hollis was shitbagging Robinson just because he went on strike. I was pointing out that we don't care whether he's a striker or a worker, but we do care about his missing daughter.'

'Fine,' said Sherman, soothingly. 'Then I'll back you all the way. A bit of friendly advice, though. Steer clear of the subject until the dust settles.'

'Of Hollis, you mean?' Jacko stirred in his hard chair.

'Well,' said Sherman hurriedly, 'I assume in the light of the forensic report you've no further need of him.' Jacko bit his lower lip and kept quiet. 'On the subject of the dispute, I mean. Don't be drawn. Then we'll avoid misunderstandings like this.'

A conciliatory smile was acknowledged with a curt nod. Sherman looked down, as though embarrassed by having to hand out the mildest of reprimands. Normally – or so they said in the squad room – he could be a lot harder than this.

He tore the top sheet from his pad and, with the first two

fingers forming a V, hooked it on to his spiked collection of bits and pieces to show Jacko that the subject had been closed.

'How's that Missing Persons inquiry going? I've read your reports but what's your feeling?'

Jacko relaxed, briefing him fully. He ended with: 'Like I said a week ago, I'm worried.'

Sherman had listened intently, mounting concern on his flabby face. 'Abduction and murder, you mean?'

'It's ten or eleven days now,' Jacko answered ambiguously.

'Mmmm,' said Sherman, uncomfortable. Worry was written on his face as clearly as on the paper he hoarded. He had read and filed the daily reports without detecting the foreboding that Jacko tried to inject into them. 'Let's involve Division and set up an Incident Room. Flood the village for a few days. Get some publicity for a reconstruction on Friday. Put out some posters and questionnaires.'

He returned Jacko's steady gaze. 'I wish you'd expressed your fears a bit earlier.'

'They were in my reports, sir,' he replied, coldly.

Sherman phoned the divisional chief inspector with orders to set up an incident room and detach a dozen detectives to the inquiry.

Jacko sat, trying to work out his change of mind. Maybe he wanted to prove he could be Action Man, not just a pen-pusher, watching his back, protecting his career with a capital C. Next month Sherman was being promoted out of plainclothes and HQ to take charge of a division as a chief superintendent, so if there was glory to be grabbed, he'd take it. If there was a can to be carried, Jacko would be left holding it; the way it is in the police service.

The Robinson home was quiet and as cold as death. The polished grate was empty now there was no perk of concessionary coal from the colliery. The fawn phone in the hall had lost its trill to an unpaid bill.

Mrs Robinson looked from the sofa, a beggar's look, hungry for news. 'Anything?'

Jacko shook his head. He sat beside her, keeping on his

raincoat. He told them of the plan to enlarge the inquiry. She and her husband were only half listening, eyes on the TV set flickering in the corner.

Jacko felt clammy. The reason, he knew, was in that corner. The TV set had been on so long that it seemed to be giving off heat; always the same, in his experience. Families like this, in desperate trouble like this, are mesmerized by it. They watch every news programme in some sort of absurd hope that an announcer will break in with a news flash to tell them that it's all been a big mistake so that they can come out of this void, this vacuum, and go on living, happy ever after.

He watched in silence with them. The coal strike and its aftermath were well down the running order on the regional news behind a £20-million plan to build a holiday village in Sherwood Forest, home of Robin Hood. The weatherman predicted wintry showers with bright intervals.

Then the blue lights flashed, and pipes and drums played, and Colin Bates gave his annoying little salute and said: 'Evening, crime catchers.' A reconstructed smash and grab was followed by a DCI warning about current confidence tricks being worked on pensioners.

Bates hogged the camera again. 'Now for our clear-ups.' This, as every regular viewer knew, was a slot in which he bragged about his detections. A shadowy still of the building society job appeared behind his right shoulder as he recapped last week's item. 'Two men are being questioned,' he said, chirpily.

Michelle's face, with that puzzled little smile, filled the screen. Her mother gasped, very faintly, just a soft hiss. Her father pitched forward in his armchair.

'No positive news yet of missing Michelle Robinson, I'm afraid, but, thanks to you out there, we have traced that white sports car . . .' Bates reappeared on the screen '. . . and not one but two Land-Rover type vehicles in connection with the hit and run in the same locality which can now be eliminated. Vitally important still are sightings of Michelle. Keep those calls coming. In confidence, of course.'

With a sigh, Mr Robinson pulled himself up by the arms of his chair, stepped over a half-moon carpet in front of the empty fireplace and turned the set off. As he backed into his seat his wife turned to Jacko. 'No connection then?'

Jacko studied the blank screen. Something was wrong but nothing came immediately to mind. 'Sorry?' He turned his attention to her.

'The hit and run has nothing to do with Michelle?'

Jacko was concentrating now. 'I'm still not sure.'

'Gave that impression,' said Mr Robinson without looking at him.

That's what it is, Jacko decided. Sherman had updated his old mate Bates over a boozy lunch and between them they've got it wrong. Robinson's right. It did give the impression we have lost interest in the hit and run.

'We've traced the driver of the white car. He picked up a hitcher but it wasn't Michelle. We've also traced a security van and a Nissan Patrol but nothing to tie them in with Michelle or the hit and run.'

'So there could still be a connection?' said Mrs Robinson, confused, exhausted.

'We honestly don't know,' said Jacko, bleakly.

'What the hell do you know?' Mr Robinson spoke with bewildered bitterness at the empty grate and did not see surprised glances shooting towards him.

Jacko spoke quietly. 'We'd like to trace that hit-and-run truck even if he had nothing to do with Michelle, just in case he saw anything of her or anyone else.'

'Amazing, isn't it?' Mr Robinson was looking hard at him now. 'You flooded the coalfields with police when it suited you. Eight thousand at one demo alone.'

'Bill.' His wife slightly raised her voice, gently, pacifying, not scolding.

'Thatcher's army. That's what you are.' His voice was harsher, angry. 'Pull out all the stops when it suits the government.' Cracking now. 'But you can't find my little bairn.' Suddenly he was sobbing, face buried in his hands, broad shoulders shaking.

'Oh Billy.' Softly she spoke, slipping off the sofa to her knees before him, laying a cheek on top of his dark hair, tears seeping from the one eye still visible.

Jacko looked away, at the fireplace, hotter than hell despite its emptiness. No point in telling them to expect the worst. They were already prepared for it. They'd come to feel what he'd feared for days. Michelle was dead. Gone for good. Jesus, give up her body, he prayed. Don't keep them in suspense. Knowing the worst has to be better than not knowing at all.

6

A phone call interrupted a conference Detective Superintendent Sherman convened next day in the newly established Incident Room in Divisional Headquarters a few miles from Moorwood.

Scientists at the forensic laboratory reported they had found strands of blonde hair in Keith Bannion's TVE Securities vehicle during the examination WPC Heather Hurst requested. The hairs corresponded exactly with samples Jacko had removed from a brush in Michelle Robinson's bedroom.

A charge, exciting, thrilling, much more than a buzz, ran through him after Sherman dispatched detectives to search Bannion's home, his locker at work, and bring him in for questioning.

He killed time, rereading his file, much thicker now after a week's work, concentrating on the statement Heather took from Bannion in the presence of his boss Luke Tyson and the omnipresent Colin Bates.

Within the hour, Bannion was escorted into the interview room by two officers who had arrested him at his home, an end-terrace house in a back street close to the city centre. He was dressed off duty in lime-green slacks and red sweater, as though he'd just come off a golf course. His face had been blanched of all colours but grey.

He was told of the the forensic findings and asked to explain them. 'I can't,' he croaked, veins in his thick, muscular neck visibly throbbing. 'It's impossible.'

'Try again,' said Sherman with a sickly smile.

'I've never had a woman in that truck. Never. Honest. That's a hanging offence at our firm.'

'Let's try again,' said Sherman, very patiently.

He had the statement Heather had taken on the desk between them and he read from it. Yes, Bannion agreed, he left home just after 7 a.m. All patrolmen were allowed to keep their Mountie trucks outside their homes when they were on the early run. First call in Moorwood, he confirmed, was Forest Coaches, then the colliery. 'But I never saw that girl.'

He insisted, protested almost, that he didn't know Michelle, only what he'd read about her in the *Evening Post*, and had never seen her, only her photo in the paper and on the TV last night.

The longer the interview went on, the more colour returned to his face. No, he told Sherman, he wasn't suggesting that someone had stolen his truck from its overnight parking spot and returned it. No, he said with the beginnings of indignation, he hadn't picked up a hitcher, male or female, seen a white car or another jeep-like truck.

'So explain it,' asked the superintendent, his patience beginning to evaporate.

'I can't.' Bannion was speaking clearly, in control of himself now.

Scowling with frustration, Sherman backtracked. 'Who did you see at Forest Coaches?'

'I've already told him . . .' he nodded at Jacko, taking the note. '. . . and that policewoman. Sammy, the young cleaner.'

'Did you let him have a drive – round the yard, maybe?'

'Him?' Bannion gave Sherman an incredulous look. 'He tapped his right temple with his forefinger. 'He can hardly talk, let alone drive.'

'See anyone else there?'

He started to shake his head, then, with a thought dawning, said: 'Only his dog. The guard dog in the compound.' A smile, like the sun rising. 'He may have jumped in the back.'

'Who?'

'Max, the dog. Always makes a fuss of me.'

'A guard dog?' Sherman's turn for incredulity.

Bannion shrugged. 'If you're a pal of Sammy's, you're a pal of Max. I've already told him.' Another nod towards Jacko who scribbled a note and, with a jerk of his head, summoned a guard

41

on the door who handed the folded paper to another constable waiting outside.

'I leave the truck doors open sometimes when I'm scouting round or having a quick cuppa with Sammy. The dog sometimes jumps in and has a sniff around.'

'Did the dog jump in that morning?'

Another shrug told him that Bannion didn't know or couldn't remember.

Sherman called a break soon afterwards and the uniformed guard was ordered to escort Bannion to a cell where, he was informed, he'd be held, pending further inquiries. The search teams returned from the TVE building and Bannion's home, surprisingly neat for a young single man's, they reported. They had found nothing of significance. Neighbours could neither confirm nor disprove the time he'd given for his departure.

'Do we know any other caller at Forest Coaches who might demolish this ludicrous tale about the friendly guard dog?' asked Sherman, looking round the long conference table.

'My old friend Norman Hollis might,' said Jacko mischievously. 'He had a file about the firm on his desk.'

Heather tapped on the door and walked into the meeting, dark face flushed with a wondrous look of discovery. She was still clutching Jacko's note which had sent her to Forest Coaches to chase up Sammy, the cleaner.

He'd gone off duty, she said, but she'd got his last name and address from the foreman and fed them to Records. She read the results from a print-out.

Samuel Pattinson was twenty-three. At sixteen, he had been committed to a State Special Hospital under the Mental Health Act for an admitted offence of attempted buggery on a young girl. He had been transferred a year earlier to what they call a half-way hostel which acclimatizes patients for their return to society. He had been found a job at Forest Coaches at Moorwood. He was the duty cleaner when Bannion was on his early morning rounds.

Sherman rubbed his hands with renewed glee and turned to Jacko: 'Go with WPC Hurst and turn him over.'

*   *   *

42

Sam Pattinson's eyes, grey-blue and bright, lit up a face that was big, an open space filled with innocence.

A strong, square jaw dropped wide open to display large regular teeth at his first sight of Heather. Not surprising, Jacko cheerfully concluded. She had much the same effect on every man. It was the way the look hung there, suspended, inane, long after all of them had sat down.

Oh, Christ, he thought, immediately depressed. A child's mind in a man's body, a mental case. He hated interviewing mental cases. Too many detectives had secured statements from mental cases only to have them blow up and blow away their reputations. He resolved to proceed with caution.

The warden, a slim, tense man, hovered just inside the open door to a room that was small and artificially tidy. Coloured posters were fixed to faded flowery wallpaper. All were of Cliff Richard, a sign, in Jacko's musical view, of a cosseted childhood. He looked up from a soft chair. 'We'd like you to stay.'

The warden shut the door and sat beside Pattinson on a single bed, made with barrack-room precision. Heather perched her bottom, its shapeliness hidden by her loose mustard coat, on the top of a dresser. Jacko let her do the early talking.

Yes, Pattinson said with a vigorous shake of the head, he worked at Forest Coaches. And, yes, he cycled there every weekday for a 7 a.m. start. No, he said proudly, he had never been late or had a day off sick since he started.

He spoke in a dull dialect, vowels decapitated as well as strangled and h's drowned as well as dropped. Every sentence was exclaimed with juvenile enthusiasm and accompanied with slight rocking and swaying that made the bed creak under his sizeable bulk.

Yes, he nodded, he did know a security patrolman called Keith and, yes, he did work with an alsatian dog, and his eyes lit again.

'Is it friendly?' asked Jacko, grinning.

'Depends.'

'Does it like Keith?' He nodded, delighted. 'Does it jump up at him?' Another nod. 'And jump into his truck?'

'Looking for chocs.' A harmless little giggle.

Stop. A warning bell rang in Jacko's brain. Stop and think, and he did so as Pattinson burbled on about tricks he'd taught

43

it. This dog could have somehow picked up those hairs and transferred them to the TVE truck when he jumped in. How? Where? He didn't know but he did know he was confronted with a possible suspect, not just a witness, and he knew his duty.

He cautioned him, formally at first, then explained that he didn't have to talk if he didn't want to, and the warden went over it again, but Pattinson kept smiling and nodding and saying, 'Don't mind,' and he looked happy enough to go on talking about the dog all night.

Jacko changed the subject, slipping Michelle's photo out of an inside pocket of his brown jacket. 'Do you know this girl?'

'Yer,' he said immediately.

'Did you see her on Friday, March the first?'

Pattinson looked for guidance at the warden, who said: 'That's not last Friday. The Friday before that, Sam. Almost two weeks ago. Understand?'

'Pay day?' he asked doubtfully.

'Not last pay day; the pay day before.'

Pattinson gave it obvious thought. 'Dunno,' he said finally and genuinely.

'When did you last see her?' asked Heather.

'Today.'

She cocked her head to one side. 'Today? Where?'

'Bus place.'

'The bus stop?'

'Sometimes.' A mysterious shadow passed over his big face. 'Did you talk to her?' A heavy shake. 'What was she wearing?' 'Not much.'

Jacko and the warden exchanged anxious glances. 'She must have been wearing something,' said Heather.

'Like t'is.' Pattinson pulled on his shirt, heavy blue denim with button-down breast pockets, and Jacko felt his mouth parch.

'Who was she with?' No response so Heather rephrased it. 'Was she with anyone?'

'Max.'

'Who's Max?' Heather asked.

Pattinson gave her a look of total disgust.

Max, explained the warden, expanding on what Jacko already knew from Bannion, was a guard dog which ran loose at nights behind the barbed-wire-topped fencing of the depot. They had started at Forest Coaches together around the same time, Sam as a cleaner, the dog as anti-picket protection. They were inseparable. Sam fed and watered him every morning and the dog followed him from bus to bus as he went about his job. 'He wasn't allowed a pet at the State Special, you see. He never stops talking about him.' Pattinson signified agreement with everything the warden said with energetic nods.

'Oh, how, lovely,' Heather gushed. 'I love dogs.' Pattinson gave her a smile of forgiveness.

'Were you taking Max for a walk when you saw the girl?' asked Jacko.

Pattinson pulled both feet off the threadbare carpet, hugged his knees and rocked backwards and forwards in demonic laughter but all he eventually said was: 'No.'

Jacko made up his mind in that instant. 'We'd like to meet Max. Let's go for a run in my car and pay him a surprise call and take him a bone or something nice. OK?'

'Reet,' he said, happily.

'Rather you than me,' said the mid-shift foreman at Forest Coaches, handing Heather a padlock key tied with pink ribbon to a cotton bobbin.

Pattinson's first job in a morning, he said, was to clean the insides of five buses on regular school runs. 'He's three sheets to the wind, as I suppose you've noticed, but a likeable lad and a good worker.' He shot a worried look at the car where he sat in the back. 'Not in trouble, is he?'

'No,' said Heather a little too firmly, so she added: 'He's left an address we need.'

'Watch the seat of your pants.' Heather smiled wanly.

The car's beam cut a path of light through the asphalt yard, picking out the wire mesh of a compound. Behind it Max waited, tail down, chiselled head held high, barking, high-pitched. Jacko parked in front of a locked gate. The barking became hysterical. The dog pranced eagerly, angrily, kicking up dust from loose cinders behind the wire.

45

Pattinson climbed out clumsily, a strapping young man, broad-shouldered, thighs like tree trunks. 'Maxie,' he called, childlike again. The dog still pranced, still barked, but lower, interspersed with whimpers and whines, joyful and welcoming.

Heather wound down the window and handed him the key. He unlocked the gate, knelt on one knee and grabbed the dog by the neck with both hands, scratching his mane roughly. The dog licked his face noisily.

She pulled a tin of Chum and a flashlight from the glove compartment and passed it across the steering wheel as Jacko slid out. 'Wanna come?' he asked.

'No thanks,' said Heather, with a thin smile.

'And there you were claiming to be a dog-lover.'

She giggled. He looked over the driver's seat. 'How about you?'

'What are you looking for?' asked the warden.

'Don't know. Just checking really.' The warden shook his head.

Jacko straightened, turned and walked slowly to the gate.

'Friend,' said Pattinson firmly, gripping the dog's mane. The dog rooted with a moist nose at Jacko's trousers and the loose hem of his raincoat, sniffing up the scent of his own dog. He delved into his store of happy stories to ease inner fear. What do you get when you cross a guard dog with Lassie? he asked himself. A dog that eats you up and then runs to fetch help. No smile came to his clamped lips.

Max's tail wagged and he looked up at him without suspicion, then back at Pattinson, growling amiably. 'Here, boy. A nice prezzy.' He loosened his grip to point to the can in Jacko's hand.

The compound was dimly illuminated by the lights from the admin block and appeared to have none of its own. Coaches stood in two lines, all with olive-green livery, a white oak tree above the firm's name.

Beyond the buses was a collection of dilapidated buildings, single-storey, brick-skinned wartime prefabs, Jacko guessed. 'Where do you feed him?' A nod towards the distant buildings. 'Got a tin-opener?'

Pattinson, a thick dark anorak over his denim shirt, nodded again and set off in a rolling, ungainly sort of walk. The

46

dog leisurely padded at his side, Jacko two paces behind. Half-way there darkness settled like a sudden sea-fret over the large, looming figure ahead and Jacko thought of Lurch from *The Addams Family*, a horror spoof series from the 1960s. He switched on the flash, pointing its beam on to the cinders which crackled into crumbs beneath his brown shoes.

In single file, Max leading, they reached an uneven path of grey slabs in front of the buildings which had crumbling brickwork, seeping salt, and windows boarded up. The dog stopped at the end door, looking up at the flaking green paintwork.

Pattinson lifted the latch fastener, pushed and turned on a light in a small, cold storeroom. Shelves were fitted to two walls, stacked with bottles and tins of cleaning material. Curtain rails and cords hung from hooks. Against another wall was a small square table with a blue plastic cover, and on it a kettle, teapot, mugs and an almost empty bottle of milk. Next to the table were two kitchen stools and an ill-fitting door which, Jacko judged from the disinfected smell, led to a lavatory.

Pattinson walked to the table and picked up a yellow-handled can-opener. Jacko put the tin on the table. It sissed when the top was pierced. 'Where did you see the girl?'

Pattinson did not look up from cutting open the can with neat flicks of his wrist. He pecked his head in an undefined direction. 'In the junk room.'

'Outside?'

Deep in concentration, he spooned a thick cylinder of dark brown congealed meat into an orange plastic bowl. Jacko backed towards the open door. 'Mind if I take a look?'

'Why?'

'Her mum and dad are worried about her.'

'Don't wake her.' He was kneeling, back towards him, and Max's nose, twitching like the Bisto Kid's, was over the bowl before Pattinson had placed it on the cracked lino.

Jacko stepped outside. His gut rumbled. His bones ached. He shuddered, acutely aware that the night chill was not the reason. His burning breath misted, thick and grey as cigarette smoke.

This is it, then, he told himself. He knew it; had known it all along. He felt stirrings of sickness in his stomach.

He shone his torch round the corner of the building into the darkness. Its round beam stopped at the door of another building no bigger than a domestic garage. He looked through a small dusty window but saw no further than a half-burnt candle with a blackened wick fixed upright in its own wax on a saucer on the inside sill.

He opened the door. The beam roved round the fusty room. That gut-wrenching smell. Like no other he knew. Old furniture, rusting steel cabinets, broken desks and chairs, haphazardly piled and thick with grey grime and cobwebs, lined the wall to his left. There was a gap down the right. He steeled himself and took it. His footsteps, echoing louder than a battalion on the march, could not drown his heartbeats, heavy and irregular. So cold his breath froze on the air; so hot his underwear stuck to him.

Beyond the pile of furniture was a tiny alcove. In the alcove was a bed with a black steel frame and springs on which was a damp, pink mattress.

On the mattress she lay. On her side. Face away from him. Her flaxen hair seemed to have been doubly bound in the middle like a sheaf of wheat. Then he saw why. A blue scarf was in her mouth and a black belt was round her neck.

She was naked from the waist down. Her buttocks had been so badly mutilated that an inhuman thought occurred to him.

Either Pattinson or his wolf had turned cannibal.

He about-turned, gagging, heaving. Hand over his mouth, he ran back the way he came. He charged open the door, hung on to it with one hand and vomited on the cinders with noisy splashings. He thought of the news he'd have to break to her parents. And he was sick again; sick until his stomach seemed to cry out in pain.

7

They were sitting in the sparse interview room at Divisional Headquarters, a 1960s hodgepodge of square buildings. Pattinson was wearing a loose white boilersuit. His own clothing was awaiting collection by forensic scientists. He looked like a spaceman.

'You have been arrested on suspicion of murder,' Jacko began.

'Murder!' Pattinson's open face sealed in a scowl, more angry than frightened. 'What murder?'

'Do you know what murder is?'

'Yer.' A brief nod. 'Lots of 'em at State Special.' He gave the warden a knowing look. 'People who've killed people.' He shook his head sadly, then added crisply: 'Not me.'

Jacko put Michelle's photo on the table between them. 'You told me at the hostel that you knew this girl.'

He twisted his head as Jacko turned the picture towards him, so his eager eyes met the face half way. 'Yer.'

'Is that the girl in the junk room?' A positive nod. 'What's her name?' An uncertain headshake. 'We think this girl has been murdered.'

A firm headshake. 'Naw. Sleeping.'

'She's dead, I'm afraid. Has been for almost two weeks. The doctor says so.'

Pattinson straightened out of a slouch on his armless chair. Fright replaced anger but only for a moment. 'Know nowt about that.'

'How well did you know her?'

'Never seen her before.' He gave Jacko a truculent look.

'Tell us the truth, Sam.'

49

'Can't remember.' He looked appealingly at the warden. 'Can't remember.'

'Tell us what happened.'

He thrust out his chin. His ever-mobile face switched to defiance. 'You saying it were me?'

'Was it?'

'Naw.' Then, mumbling: 'It were Mac.'

Jacko frowned. 'Max?'

'*Naw.*' He banged a fist on the table. 'Where is he? Where is he?'

Jacko flinched. 'Sleeping in our kennels.'

'You promised you'd take us for a ride.' He leant forward, angry face close to Jacko's. 'You promised.' He looked left to Heather sitting at a smaller desk by a cream wall, taking the note. 'She promised. You lied.' He looked back to Jacko. His breathing was laboured. '*Liars.*'

He crashed both fists down on the table, which jumped. Two plastic glasses rolled on their sides and water from a jug splashed Michelle's face.

'Arhhhh.' He held his fists stiffly on the table, two feet apart and smashed his forehead between them.

He jerked up his head high and awkwardly. 'Arhhhh.' Jacko shot his hand forward on the table, palm up, to cushion the second head butt.

The warden, sitting opposite Heather, leapt up and across the room. 'Sam.' He arm-locked his rocking head, pulling it into his side, caressing his hair. 'Sammy, please, Sammy.' Pattinson's body shook as he sobbed.

Superintendent Sherman, observing from a seat next to a door, had jumped up. 'Don't worry, Sam. Have a rest. We've got a nice little room here for you.'

A veteran uniformed constable on guard outside had burst in. Sherman nodded to him. He moved towards Pattinson. 'No. *No. No.*' It was his first sight at the station of a policeman in uniform and he seemed terrified, suddenly aware of his surroundings. The constable tactfully stood aside as the warden lifted Pattinson to his feet and guided him to a cell.

'Phew,' sighed Jacko, wringing his hands.

'That bloody bump will show,' said Sherman, deeply agitated.

'Let a doctor see him, then bed him down. We'll talk to him tomorrow when scenes have finished.'

Meantime he wanted Heather to see Pattinson's parents and Jacko to take the Robinsons to the City Hospital to do the formal ID when the pathologist and the photographers OK'd the removal of the body to the mortuary at the City Hospital.

Which meant Jacko would be seeing her again. And he had to be sick again. He rose quickly with a noisy scraping of chair legs.

'Oh, no. Please, no.' Mrs Pattinson was fighting back tears already. 'Not again.'

She turned from a side door half way down a dark passage and led Heather into an overcrowded back room in a small terraced house.

'What's up?' Mr Pattinson spoke through stained teeth which gripped a rank-smelling pipe. He was in a low chair beside a gas fire.

'Sam.' His wife had a chubby face and a short, plump body. She lowered herself on to a chair next to a table littered with clean washing which awaited ironing.

Heather sat opposite Mr Pattinson and noted the bottles of coloured pills on the mantelpiece above the fireplace. She wondered who was ill. Mrs Pattinson was an overweight mass of nerves; understandably so. Her husband had skin the texture of worn-out leather. Both, she guessed.

She addressed him, repeating and expanding on what she had told his wife on the doorstep. 'Nothing's decided. He's just helping our inquiries. You might like to visit him.'

'Can I?' Mrs Pattinson had watery eyes, dark and deep-set, like two currants in a suet pudding. She sat with feet wide apart so Heather could see up her tight blue dress to the insides of her white thighs. 'We've had nothing but trouble with him.'

'You should never have let him go.' Her husband spoke with tinny harshness. There was unconcealed hostility in the look he gave his wife. Heather broke the bristling silence. 'It would help if I could see his room.'

Mr Pattinson screwed the seat of his brown trousers tighter

51

to the chair and puffed stubbornly on his pipe, ignoring her, washing his hands of it.

With a martyred sigh, his wife rose and led the way, puffing and blowing, up a narrow set of stairs covered by a worn carpet held taut by brass rods.

Pattinson's back bedroom was smaller than the one at the hostel but just as neat. Cliff Richard smiled sugarily from one wall on to a coloured poster with soldiers in khaki uniforms with badges of rank from field marshal down.

Heather nodded at the singer. 'Fond of him, I see.'

'Both of us.'

She looked across the room at the other poster. 'Does he want to be a soldier?'

Mrs Pattinson shook her head sadly. 'His dad's doing. Civilian staff at the end of the war.' Which, Heather calculated, would make him about sixty, late thirties when they had their only son.

Heather glanced over the polished dresser and a white, woven basket chair beneath a window which looked down on to a backyard. 'Does he have a nice thick woolly blue scarf?'

'Auntie Margaret bought him one for Christmas. He should be wearing it this weather.'

'And a black leather belt?'

'Two or three here or at the hostel.'

Mrs Pattinson lowered herself slowly on the top blue blanket of his single bed and talked as Heather searched the drawers.

Sam had been a beautiful baby, she said. A real beauty. Then, at about six months, his head started to loll alarmingly. Doctors told her tests disclosed brain damage. 'We thought it might have been his jabs,' she said, uncertain, 'but no one ever found out.' Or genetic, thought Heather.

He grew up big and strong and happy as a day boy at the occupational therapy centre. In his early teens, he'd thrown a tantrum when refused the use of a chisel in the woodwork class and smashed up the stool he was making.

More pent-up rages exploded into damage and threats of violence at home. One day she signed papers consenting to his admission to Roselands Hospital on the outskirts of Moorwood. 'His father's never really forgiven me,' she said.

The rift grew worse when Sam was accused of what his mother

called 'that sad business' over the little girl at Roselands. 'First he said it was him. Then he said it wasn't. Now he can't remember. I can't understand it. He never looks at girls when he's home. Only dogs interest him. He's so happy there at the hostel with his little job and dog.' She started weeping quietly. Heather sat beside her, putting an arm over her podgy shoulder.

In the five years he'd been away at the State Special, isolated in desolate countryside, she'd taken three buses to the middle of nowhere for a monthly visit. Her husband never accompanied her. 'He can't bear to see him locked up.'

Over the last year, Sam had been allowed home from the hostel every fortnight and on alternate weekends she'd made the much shorter trip across the city to see him. But never his father.

'Don't they get on?' asked Heather.

'Oh, they love each other very much. It's just that, well, Ernie hates them places. You see, he was brought up in them himself.'

S: 'The girl sleeping in the junk room – did you know her?'

P: 'A bit. Not well, like.'

Jacko was scribbling, using initials to save time and space, and Sherman, lead man at the second interview, paused between each question to give him the chance to get it down.

Pattinson looked rested and relaxed. Sitting beside him in the interview room was a silver-haired solicitor, senior partner in a law firm with a good record in legal aid cases.

S: 'How did you get to know her?'

It took several starts and stops to finally establish that he had seen her now and then waiting at the service bus stop outside the coach depot.

S: 'Did you ever speak to her?'

P: 'Oh, yeah. But she never said nowt back.'

S: 'Did you like her?'

A shy nod.

S: 'How did she get into the junk room?'

He leant forward, confidentially. 'Mac.'

S: 'Who's Mac? Is he a friend?'

No reply; just a staring silence.

Sherman went through all of this again. The answers became

less and less intelligible. He reached into a cardboard box and put three plastic bags on the desk. He pointed to the smaller one which contained a can of cleaning spirits. 'Seen that before?'

Pattinson studied it casually. 'Yer.'

More patient probing confirmed that it was used at the depot to rub greasy spots off upholstery but he said he couldn't remember ever using it. Then he more or less contradicted himself by saying he'd never sniffed it, not deliberately anyway, because he didn't like the smell.

'You see, Sam, the doctors tell us that she was . . . knocked out, gassed, put to sleep like at a dentist.'

Pattinson poked two fingers in one corner of his mouth, prising it open, to treat Sherman to a close-up view of a gap in his top gum to confirm he understood.

'Did you put her to sleep with that cleaning stuff?' Sherman asked.

'She were asleep when she came.'

He was adamant the black belt produced from the second bag wasn't his and flushed when the blue scarf was pulled from the third bag. Only reluctantly did he confirm he'd been given it for Christmas.

'What's it doing tied round her mouth?'

'So she wouldn't wake up and make a noise.'

Sherman knew by now that the wounds that had so shocked Jacko had been inflicted in a frenzy by something like a plastic curtain cord. 'So she wouldn't scream when you smacked her bottom?'

'She were bleeding when she came.' Indignant.

'How did she hurt herself?'

'Don't know.' Then, conciliatory: 'Could have been the barbed wire.' Without prompting, he added: 'She's been very bad, you know.'

Sherman framed several simple questions round that unsolicited answer but Pattinson steadfastly denied smacking her for being naughty and had convinced himself that Michelle's injuries had been caused when she climbed over the razor wire to break into the bus depot.

They stopped for a tea break, Pattinson putting three heaped spoons of sugar into his mug and talking amiably to Jacko about dogs.

54

Suddenly he said: 'I had to keep her quiet, you know, or there'd be trouble.'

'Who from?' Jacko asked.

'Mac.'

'How did you keep her quiet?' he asked, resuming his note-taking while Sherman stayed quiet.

P: 'With the scarf.'

J: 'Why did you do that?'

P: 'She'd been punished and might have cried.' He closed his eyes as if at some bad memory and, when Jacko asked him what was the matter, he told him of a slippering he'd received at Roselands Hospital before he was transferred to the State Special.

J: 'Was that for touching that little girl's bottom?'

P: 'Weren't me.' A blunt answer.

J: 'Did you touch this girl's bottom?'

P: 'Might have.' He sighed. 'By mistake.'

J: 'When?'

A black mood overwhelmed him. 'There's danger,' he said mysteriously but he refused to explain or say any more at all, and soon Sherman called another break.

Humming now. Everyone in the Incident Room busy. Not a decent night's sleep between them but Jacko felt no exhaustion, only exhilaration at a job well done, a mystery about to be solved.

He and Sherman reinterviewed Bannion, unshaven and bleary-eyed after a night in a cell, as a witness this time, no longer a suspect.

Forest Coaches, he said, had been clients of TVE Securities for almost a year after suffering minor vandalism in the early days of the pit strike.

All that time Sam had been the cleaner. 'Pickets used to taunt him through the wire. You know . . .' he cupped his right hand in front of his groin and flicked it to and fro '. . . called him a wanker and things.'

The long absent colour flooded back to his face when he suddenly remembered Heather was sitting silently at his side, taking the note. She gave him a sweet smile.

'Did he ever lose his temper with them?' asked Sherman.

'Er. I. No.' A shy spluttering. 'He's harmless.'

'And the guard dog?'

'When you get to know him.'

Bannion gave a reasonably accurate description of the cleaner's cubicle where he and Sam sometimes had a quick cuppa but said he hadn't noticed the junk room.

'What did you talk about over your cuppas?'

Bannion sat back, smiling. 'It's a bit difficult to have a conversation with him. He rambles on quite a bit. Those pickets scared him. They realized he was simple, like, and took the mickey through the wire. Never lets the dog leave his side. Says it's his protector.'

'Against what?'

'Pickets, I suppose.'

Norman Hollis, in a light-grey suit, arrived straight from home, on a day off, he grumbled, anxious about a practice session he'd booked on the dry ski-slope at a leisure centre.

He'd been to Forest Coaches half-a-dozen times surveying a claim for alleged subsidence damage to the old buildings in the compound but not, he said, on the morning Michelle vanished. He'd inspected the junk room a month earlier. 'There was no body inside then.'

'How do you get on with the dog?' asked Heather. 'Makes a fuss of you, does it?'

'It remembers you, yes. Jumps up to greet you.'

'On your visits there has it ever jumped into your Nissan Patrol?'

A quick, angry quiver. 'That's been cleared. You said so. My solicitor says . . .'

'Speak to him, if you like,' said Heather, acting on Sherman's instructions.

Hollis was allowed use of a phone. He returned to the incident room, more at ease. Yes, he said, the dog had leapt uninvited into his vehicle on a couple of occasions. 'It loves motor vehicles, apparently. Spends all his days in and out of parked buses.'

'Ever had a talk with Pattinson?'

'Now and then. He and his dog tend to follow you around like lost Jews. He's got a bit of a persecution complex. Reckons people are after him. Those pickets, I suspect. Shit-houses.' He stopped there, open-mouthed, and had to fight to stop himself throwing a hand up to it, but Heather smiled her sweet smile. He shook his head, half in apology, half in emphasis. 'Fancy picking on a headcase.'

Jacko collected Nick James from his office at the colliery. He limped to the car. A soccer injury, he said.

'What's going on?' he asked when he saw the police activity and the waiting press cars around Forest Coaches.

In the Incident Room, James said he'd only visited the depot once to help measure up. 'There was a bit of a row over a claim. My gaffer reckons damage could be normal wear and tear and the boss of the firm created hell.'

On his one visit, James played ball with the dog and talked to the cleaner. 'He's a religious crank. Like those bible-thumpers in the streets. On about good and evil.'

He, Bannion and Hollis were asked to attend an identity parade. 'You only know the cleaner either by sight or first name and we have to be sure,' Sherman explained.

Jacko organized it. No problem, he said with a grin. There was no shortage of young men at any police station who look big and gormless. He ordered them out of the canteen and into white boilersuits.

One by one, the witnesses walked down the line. All picked out Pattinson, who gazed down at them without the slightest trace of recognition.

Sherman chaired an evening conference when the experts had reported back. Michelle was vagina intacta. In addition to the sadistic beating, an attempted anal rape had left bruising. At some stage she'd been tied hand and foot. There was plenty of material in the cleaner's cubbyhole that could have been used as bindings.

Hairs and fibres from her clothing and Pattinson's inter-matched. His prints were on the can containing cleaning fluid similar to the noxious substance used to KO her. Her blood type was on his semen-stained underpants.

'Enough to charge him, isn't it?'

Everyone in the room nodded, including Jacko, who said, in

afterthought: 'Let's ask to see him again and put this scientific stuff to him.'

He and Heather rehearsed their question line as her steel-heeled black shoes echoed down the corridor. They entered the interview room, she smiling. Before they could sit down, Pattinson put a question of his own. 'Can I see Max?' he said, with a melancholy face, sitting behind the desk, his solicitor next to him.

'He's at the vet's – the animal doctor, you know,' said Jacko.

'Is he poorly?' An alarmed look.

'Oh, no. He's having his hair brushed.' He decided not to add 'by our scientists'.

'I brushed their hair,' he said with a pleasurable smile. He nodded to confirm in follow-up questions that he meant both the dog and the girl.

'When did you brush the girl's hair?' asked Heather.

'While she was sleeping.'

'Who put her to sleep?'

Another long detour followed but, finally, he was certain she'd been sleeping when she was put to bed. 'Been naughty, see.' He couldn't explain in what way, except that she was trespassing. He'd bathed her bottom because it was bleeding, see. 'From the barbed wire, I expect.' But he repeated that he hadn't hit her.

He wouldn't admit to tying her up, apart from gagging her with his scarf so she wouldn't cry. 'Mac told me to.' But he wouldn't describe Mac except to say that he was dark.

'Did you touch her, apart from bathing her and brushing her hair?' asked Jacko.

'Might have done.'

'In what way?'

'Cuddled her.'

'On the bed?'

He nodded. 'To make her warm. She was cold.'

'Did she tell you she felt cold?'

He looked surprised. 'She felt cold.'

'Did you love her like you loved that girl at Roselands?'

'Never did.' But it soon became clear that answer was specifically about the little girl at Roselands, so Jacko asked again.

'Might have done.' He was talking to his chest. 'Must have

58

done. If you say so.' He looked up, defiant again. 'Don't remember it, though.'

'Did you get undressed down to your underpants and get into bed with her?' A numb nod. 'Why?'

'Told you. To keep her warm.'

Tentatively, tactfully but steadfastly, Jacko turned to a subject that males never discuss among themselves, let alone in front of a woman. Masturbation. He used a variety of street terms, crude from the pit yard, coy from the school yard, before obtaining the painful confession that he sometimes played with his Johnny.

'Did you do that while you were cuddling up to her?'

'Might have done.'

'Is there a chance that it, your Johnny, I mean, might have . . .' He couldn't find the right expression.

Shamefaced, Pattinson helped out. 'Must have slipped.'

There was no point, the solicitor told them, in reducing their final interview into a written statement for him to sign. Sam couldn't read or write.

It made little difference to their case now. He wasn't admitting murder, not in so many words, but he was virtually a self-confessed necrophile.

Jacko looked at him with a gentle smile that hid the revulsion running right through him. He could no longer target his ineffable fury towards Pattinson, an infant mind in a grown body, so inwardly he railed against the doctor who had turned a homicidal maniac loose from the State Special. Wanker, he thought, with deepmost bitterness.

8

Click. The machine in his mind whirred. Black letters swam on to a white screen: 'Man Held on Michelle Murder Charge.'

He'd read the front-page story so often that he'd memorized every word but he still read from the screen in his mind, as slowly as a student at the public library researching back issues: 'Bus depot cleaner Samuel Pattinson, 23, appeared in court today, accused of the murder of Moorwood teenager Michelle Robinson.'

He waggled the back of his head, comfortable in the palms of his hands and stared at the ceiling. Not quite out of the woods yet, but this week had been much better and some mornings he awoke with the sheets only slightly tangled and damp and he knew he had refound the knack of sleeping.

Once he'd felt himself turn over and put out a hand which had rested on her bloodied buttocks and he'd woken up too shocked to scream. There'd be occasions when, uninvited, she'd leapt out of the dark, floodlit. Not the picture viewers and readers had seen. Her white face was twisted to one side like his father after his stroke. Her fair hair was darkened, matted, wet with fear. He'd had to turn his head away.

Over and over, he'd seen himself, in a strait-jacket, in a padded cell, screaming: 'I'm not insane. I'm not mad. Please, please, give me my noose.' There'd been times when he saw his mother, as clear as if she was on a big screen, weeping as she read his suicide note but, when he looked over her shoulder, the notepaper was a pulpy mass of red and white and he saw Michelle again and he'd wet the bed.

The shame of that, worse than he felt over Michelle or Pattinson, forced him to dredge through memories in search of some rationalization, to sort himself out, and he went through it again as he lay with head in hands.

Naturally, he'd read the porn passed around the school and wondered why they made such a big thing of bosoms, tits, boobs, though he'd guffawed with the rest. He'd thumbed through a different magazine. 'Girls. Taken from the west facing east,' it said, puzzlingly, on the cover. And, oh, my, my, my, he knew what it meant then as he feasted his wide-opened eyes on them, scores of them. Bums, beautiful bums. Shapely backsides. He'd felt a thrusting at his groin that swept aside every other feeling he'd ever experienced.

OK, what's so wrong? he'd asked himself. Some men are tit men; some leg men. He was an arse man. Next question? So what went wrong?

She'd been fifteen, a year older than him, a plump, silly girl. After school, she'd asked him in for a drink of Tizer while her mother was out. She flopped on a sofa and said to him, quite brazenly: 'I'll show you mine if you'll show me yours.'

What he saw were like the blancmanges his mother tipped from their basins and the black wire wool she used to scrub the frying pan in the sink. And the belittling look on her face at what she held in her hot hand told him she had not found it a thrilling sight, either. 'Call that a cock,' she'd mocked. 'It's no bigger than my thumb.'

He slapped her and, as she turned away, arching her backside, slapped again, harder, and something stirred for him then into a size that he thought physically impossible.

He stuck to sport for the rest of his schooldays, never mixed with girls of his own age outside the safety of a crowd.

When he biked round the park to escape the sight of his stroke-stricken father in his chair, he would let girls, much younger than him, have a ride. He always left his hand, palm up, on the saddle, for a fraction of a second, as they sat down. That gave him what he called a crossbar and, to one or two, he showed it until that ten-year-old cried and ran off.

He had lain in bed, mind in the sort of turmoil of these last few long nights, thoughts blundering around, until a voice from nowhere said: Think. And he thought and had a statement practised to perfection for when the police came, and he was annoyed, in a strange way, when the police never called to put it to the test; a waste somehow.

A long, long period of inactivity followed until he started work where more porn, much harder, was handed round and some of the magazines were about black magic featuring ritualistic beatings, fevering his imaginings.

And then, she came. His fantasy. In real life. A familiar vision then. Her, naked, helpless, arched . . .

Click. Off. A blank screen until Michelle appeared, this time the photo in the paper downstairs and he addressed her: It was your fault, you know.

For a month, no more, she had replaced his departed fantasy girl. At the bus stop she looked so young and it had come as a surprise when he first gave her a lift to hear that she worked for a property firm. He'd assumed she was still at school – a special school, perhaps, for slow learners. He liked younger, withdrawn girls. They were more trusting, pliable, and used none of the bad language he'd heard in pubs. He disliked bad language. All he'd wanted was to get her back to his place. Just for half an hour. He was sure she'd co-operate, enjoy it. The dream girl always did.

Her father was the bait. Doted on him, she did, and worried that he wouldn't get his job back when the pit strike ended. 'I'll see what I can do,' he said, trying not to sound too important. A few days later, he was waiting for her as she stepped off the evening bus. He knew her movements. The planning, the anticipation, had been part of the pleasure. 'Meet me up the road tomorrow at 6.45 a.m. I've got photographic evidence that will help your old man. My job's on the line so don't tell a soul.'

Submissively – or so it seemed – she did as she was told. 'Where are they?' she asked when they entered the cold kitchen.

Well, there weren't any actual photos, he said, stuttering at first, but he was prepared to make a statement clearing her dad. Everyone knew, he added, getting bolder all the time, he'd done the damage he'd been accused of, so there was a penalty to pay. She could pay it for him.

She asked what it was and when he told her she bad-mouthed him, the foulest language he'd heard from a female, and called him a pervo. God, how she'd screamed. He put a hand over her mouth. She struggled and kicked and fought like a pit-yard cat.

He didn't mean to kill, didn't want to kill her, and he wasn't sure whether she was dead or alive so he didn't dare remove the belt from her neck in case she awoke as he carried her upstairs to bed, this bed, and there he'd . . .

And there he stopped, with the other picture of her sidling into his mind, showing what he'd done, here on this bed, and blinked to blank it out.

Strong thoughts he needed now, brave thoughts, to prove to himself how clever, how cunning he'd been, so he returned to that loony at Forest Coaches. Every time he saw him, he'd rambled on about some janitor called Mac who'd got him locked up at the State Special for some sex crime he'd never done.

Of course, he must have done it. The police don't make mistakes like that and he smiled, broadly, bravely.

The timing had been perfect, leaving home with it wrapped in black plastic sheeting after the neighbours left for work, arriving after the early shift had gone into the colliery.

He'd given him strict instructions. She'd been naughty, been trespassing, had been punished and would get it again if she made a noise.

If he didn't want that to happen, he'd better keep her quiet. He pointed to a can of cleaning fluid that would make her sleep, told him to use his scarf to gag her and say nothing to nobody or he'd shop him, like that janitor.

Worked like a charm, except, except . . . There was something he couldn't understand; not so much alarming but puzzling, nagging. That truck, bowling over a woman cyclist on the opposite side of the road and not stopping. What was all that about? He can't have been drink-driving. Not at that time of the morning. Or could he? He could have been on the juice all night. With the bloke in the passenger seat. He recognized him, too, but it took longer to work out from where. Why hadn't they come forward in response to the police appeals? What were they hiding?

He shook his head in the dark. He didn't know and it didn't really matter. What mattered was that he'd rationalized the rest.

It wasn't his fault. Right.

It was that neighbour's fat bitch of a daughter for taunting him. It was the bitch mother of his dream girl for taking her away. And that silly bitch from Moorwood who screamed when all she had to say was no. And, as for that loony at Forest Coaches, he was a proven sex criminal, better off where he was.

'So you're out of the woods then?'

'Not until the trial,' he answered before it dawned on him who had asked the question.

'Will you have to give evidence?'

'Don't know.' He was mildly surprised to find himself carrying on with the conversation.

'Then we'll see that WPC Hurst again. Good. She's gorgeous and so approachable. I'm sure . . .'

He could not believe what he was hearing, shocked to feel a throbbing at his loins. '*Go away.*'

9

On a cold, bright spring morning they buried Michelle Robinson. The detectives from Division and HQ clubbed together to buy a spray of lilies. All white. Somehow it seemed appropriate.

Jacko, as the officer who had liaised with the family, was deputed to represent them. He didn't have religion and disliked (hated is too strong a word) funerals because, from the departed's point of view, prayers and songs made no difference to their destination. They were going nowhere. Neither to heaven nor hell. In his view, heaven and hell are here on earth, in the memories of the living. And if they had given time for a kindness here and a helping hand there and had never done harm, they were in heaven in people's memories and all the prayers and hymns, or lack of them, would not change that.

Funerals, he had long since decided, were not for the dead but for the living, for those left behind, to bring them some comfort. And so, as in most things, he compromised. He attended funerals as an act of solidarity. He bent forward in his seat at the back but did not kneel to pray and did not even mouth the words to the hymns.

The small United Reformed chapel, a warm, light, quite modern place with cream walls and plain teak benches, had none of the cold, carved grandeur of Establishment churches built in mediaeval times. It was well filled but by no means full. Relatives had come all the way from the north-east but most of the neighbours had not made it from the estate down the road and the colliery was not represented. This, he recognized, was not to be regarded as unfeeling. It was just that they were unsure of what reception they would be given.

In the aftermath of the strike, some fathers and sons who

had come to different decisions were no longer speaking and workmates who had been side by side together, on their knees together, in the hot earth, were drinking in different bars, avoiding each other. The strike with its sights of proud men with begging bowls in the streets and its soup kitchens and food parcels and its violence was bad enough. The averted eyes in the years to come would be worse and these depressing thoughts added to the gloom that flooded over him as he sat by himself in the back row of the chapel.

He tagged on to the small procession for the slow drive to the council cemetery and walked across the grass, whitened with frost, to the grave which had been dug in the sandy soil and in it, ashes to ashes, dust to dust, she was to find the peace denied her in the last horrendous day of her short, harmless, blameless life.

Jacko, in his heavy dark blue overcoat, felt the stiffened blades of grass snapping beneath his frozen feet as he walked towards her parents to say his goodbyes. 'Oh,' said Mrs Robinson, forcing a smile, 'you must come back for a bite to eat. You've been so kind.' And he went because he didn't know how to refuse.

As soon as he walked in, he knew he had made a mistake. The small lounge, where the home-made sandwiches and cakes were laid on a table covered with a Sunday-best white linen cloth, was full of strangers, many speaking, singing almost, in lyrical Geordie.

The kitchen was packed with willing volunteers to brew the endless pots of tea poured out in a forlorn hope that they would lubricate conversation.

He kept on his coat and walked into a small garden enclosed by woven fencing, bleached pale brown, ragged holes here and there. The grass was long and tufty. A narrow bed at the bottom had been neatly filled with wallflowers planted like soldiers on parade, sturdy and bushy and heavy in buds soon to break into a Persian carpet of vivid colours.

He felt a broad presence at his shoulder. 'She put 'em in.' He didn't have to look to know it was Mr Robinson. 'Bought them outta own wages in the autumn. Said I was neglectin' the garden.'

'They'll make a fine show,' said Jacko softly, without looking up.

'Aye.' A painful pause. 'Perhaps I was. Too busy. With the strike and the union. Neglected many things.'

Jacko sought to ease his pain. 'A man must stand up for what he believes in.'

'Suppose so,' said Mr Robinson with a hint of doubt, immediately cast off. 'Gotta fight for jobs in this damned day and age.' He shook his head.

Jacko turned to face him. He was jacketless – black tie, white shirt, a sleeveless navy-blue pullover that matched his trousers. He did not appear to notice the cold. 'Will you get your job back . . . now?' He wished he hadn't added 'now'.

'Nar.' Another headshake, resigned. 'Union says the board canna set precedents or everyone they outed will claim reinstatement. It's the law.'

Silence, so just for something to say: 'Why did you lose it in the first place?'

'Smashed a car headlamp. A white-collar man's, scabbing. A daft thing to do. Lots of daft things were done.' A trace of regret and they lapsed into longer silence, nothing at all left to say. Jacko's gaze returned to the wallflowers.

'Why?' Mr Robinson spoke suddenly and angrily. Jacko looked back at his face. A face-worker's face. A year on the surface, outdoors on the picket line, had weathered it a healthy colour but had not tanned over the tiny blue scars where dust had sealed cuts caused by flying splinters of coal. 'Why her? Why did this happen?'

Jacko bided his time, uncertain where he was being led.

'Why did they let him go?' Agony now in that pitted face. Jacko knew the magistrates' merciful decision to return Pattinson to the State Special, instead of holding him in prison to await trial, had fuelled local gossip, most of it accurate, about his mental background. Pattinson's parents, whose grief was just as deep, had received threatening letters, all anonymous. 'They did let him go, dinna they?'

Jacko gave a neutral shrug, anxious to avoid discussing the case with someone who might be a trial witness, but it was confirmation enough for Mr Robinson. 'They should string up the bastard . . .' he was shivering; not with cold, but white-hot rage '. . . and the bastard doctor who let him out. Bringing back hanging is the one thing Thatcher and me are agreed on. If I ever git mar hands on him, I'll kill the bastard.'

Jacko wanted to nod agreement with his opinion of the doctor whom he privately blamed for Pattinson's freedom and, by extension, Michelle's death. He wanted to shake his head in disagreement with the rest. He was anti-hanging; not on the grounds of a religion he did not possess but because, in his view, capital punishment reduced the state, his country, to the level of the killers they were exterminating. So he compromised and kept his head still.

He turned on the long grass. 'I'm cold. Let's go and have that cuppa.' And soon afterwards he held up a hand in a goodbye salute across the crowded kitchen because he didn't want to talk any more.

He drove his car along the ring road, slower than was usual and that was usually slow enough. He felt a curious light-headedness, a sickness coming on: in his heart, not his stomach where illness always began in him.

He sought to diagnose it as he drove by rows of terraced houses off the northern, unfashionable end of the tree-lined dual carriageway. He grew up in a terraced street like these, from socialist roots, like Mr Robinson.

Such streets were full of people who shared Robinson's view. Some of them would still have public hangings, where the condemned man was swung from the back of a horse-drawn cart and left to dangle and slowly strangle in a dance of death until someone had compassion enough to step out from the cheering crowd and pull on his legs to break his neck and end his agony.

Maybe, if he'd gone through what Robinson had endured, lost a child to such senseless slaughter, he'd pull the lever on the trapdoor himself.

You don't know you're born until your child is born, until you're a parent. He raised his eyes skyward and sent up a prayer towards a God in whom he didn't believe. Don't let Horace be a girl. Do you hear me? Don't let him be a girl.

On a warm summer's evening a sweating Jacko came in from an overdue stint of weeding in the small back garden.

68

He grumbled mildly about his nettled hands and aching legs but got the uninterested grunt he always received when Jackie was deep into the *Guardian* crossword.

As he washed them, he heard a steady scratching sound like his dog made when she demanded a closed door be opened. He followed the sound out of the kitchen across the small hallway and into the back bedroom where the setting sun lit a backdrop of crimson behind the closed blue curtains.

He was three months old now. They had given him his first break by calling him Mark, not Horace. He had his mother's bright blue eyes and pensive mouth and her brown hair, much softer and finer, as delicate as a spider's thread. He had her curiosity; her calmness in the face of new experience; her low boredom threshold and the same streak of venom when denied his own way. Once Jacko complained there wasn't an ounce of Jackson in him. 'What about his ability to drink and then snooze in the garden?' she replied, venomously.

Jacko had proved himself far more keen and competent as a father than a gardener. He rushed home from work whenever he could to bathe his son in a small yellow plastic tub, took his turn in changing and feeding him. He would brief him on the progress of televised cricket matches and sing off-key railroad songs to him. He had cut down his drinking to one wild night about once a month in the Fairways. Jackie understood his need for shop talk and never objected. 'Besides,' she told Heather Hurst, who popped in now and then when she was dateless, 'it spares us those awful Lonnie Donegan songs.'

She had often spotted him, late at night, standing at the half-open door to the nursery, staring down at their baby with a look of absolute astonishment.

Tonight he followed the sound right into the nursery, walking lightly on a thick blue fitted carpet. Just recently flakes of dry, transparent skin had begun to appear on the top of the baby's head. 'Cradle cap,' the nurse at the health centre said. 'This hot weather makes it worse. Nothing to worry about.'

To ease the itching Mark had found the strength and the will to wriggle his plump, pink body up to the top of the cot. There, working his neck rhythmically, he scratched the itch, rubbing away his fine hair into a bald patch that made him look like an infant monk.

He was doing so now, lying on his back, fists clenched, eyes shut, his face filled with a gummy grin of sheer contentment.

Jacko looked down on him.

Unspoken, but loudly in his own mind, he said: If anyone ever touches a single hair on this child's head, I'll kill him. Hear that, you perverts lurking out there. One hair and you're fucking dead.

That autumn Samuel Pattinson, in a new dark blue suit, climbed the steps into the dock at the Shire Hall, a Victorian court-house that was forbidding and a bit seedy and had not aged with elegance.

His big open face looked bewildered and frightened, which, Jacko realized, was the exact effect the authorities had in mind when they commissioned the grim building more than a century ago.

They designed their courts with marble columns, echoing flagstone floors and carved oak, and dressed their dignitaries from the last act of the *Damnation of Faust* to scare the living shit out of people in the dock, to let them know they were in the presence of higher and mightier beings who were about to lord it over them. Jacko himself was sometimes awed by courts and sometimes angered by them.

Over the years, miscarriages of justice have taken place in such courts. Just how many is impossible to estimate. When an inkling of a mistake surfaces, the legal Establishment, he suspected, closes ranks to bury it again. Such admissions, they tell themselves, destroy public confidence in the system. What they really mean is that it leaves them with dirt and, in the days of hanging, death on their hands. Oh, British justice can be blind all right.

But not today. This was copper-bottomed, he thought, sitting on a bench behind the bewigged, black-gowned barristers. On a ledge in front of him was Michelle's file, four inches thick in the end. But a nutter in an open-and-shut case wouldn't make a short story, let alone a book, for him to write, with Jackie's help, when he retired. He was ready to file it away in the back of his mind.

When a prison guard took Pattinson's arm to make him stand

as the red-robed judge entered, he snatched it away, more frightened than angry, and sat down, head hanging.

And that was how he sat through a fairly short hearing that even Jacko, with all his previous court experience, found strange. When the jurors raised their Bibles to be sworn in, they took oaths not to give a true verdict on the evidence but to decide whether Pattinson was fit to plead.

'Your role,' the judge patiently told them, 'is rare but not unique. Your duty is to decide, having heard medical evidence, whether the accused is capable of instructing his legal representatives so they can give him a proper and professional defence and of giving evidence himself in support of it. You have to be certain that he understands the charge and the proceedings and the difference between right and wrong.'

The Crown's QC gave a brief summary of Michelle's disappearance and discovery. Extracts from Pattinson's interviews were read and not challenged by his own QC who seemed to be fighting with both hands tied behind his back.

The rest of the hearing was given over to doctors. All of them said Pattinson's brain was diseased as well as damaged from birth. There was no possibility of recovery, they said.

At this, Jacko (the only police witness on standby to give evidence which, in the end, wasn't required) looked up into the tiered public gallery. Mrs Pattinson, sitting alone at the back of the half empty court, was silently weeping. So was Michelle's mother who gripped her husband's hand tightly.

The judge, an ageing man with a benign style, asked the one question of real interest. 'He was in your care without limit of time for the offence against the young girl at his previous hospital, Roselands, so why was he released a year before Michelle's death?'

He addressed it to a diminutive doctor with white hair all over except where it should be, on the top of his head, and Jacko half-expected him to answer in a German accent but he replied in standard BBC. 'Because he made good progress in his five years with us, adapting to the regime, learning basic skills, never showing signs of violence towards female staff or patients. Now there are additional signs of cerebral degeneration and life expectancy cannot be put beyond forty.'

71

Which meant, everyone in court could work out for themselves, more than half his life had already been lived. Mrs Pattinson wept more tears. Mr Robinson audibly groaned and his wife gripped his hand tighter still.

The judge did not ask the obvious follow-up question: 'Was it a mistake?' But the revelation, Jacko speculated happily, was already enough to ensure the headline in the tabloids: 'Bungling Doc Frees Madman to Kill'.

The only mild disagreement between the medical experts was over his mental age. They put it variously at seven and ten – too young even to appear before a juvenile court for cycling without a light or breaking a greenhouse window.

The eight men and four women on the jury did not retire to their room. They went into a whispering huddle in their box. Their foreman, portly and smartly dressed, rose from their midst to announce their verdict:

'Unfit to plead.'

10

Two years later

Not tonight. He needed all his strength to think. So not tonight. He was doing it every night again, automatically almost, after dropping the latch and putting out the milk bottle. He never gave it a name, not even 'it' and certainly not the terms they used in the pit yard or the school yard.

Not tonight, he told himself firmly. Apart from a few unconscious lapses, his resolve had been maintained until the hearing; eight long months of abstinence, a total blockage.

He had mixed memories about the court case. Sweet, because he wasn't required to give evidence. Bitter, because that meant not seeing her. Oh, how he'd longed to see her. Just once again. A side-on view.

The night he read of Pattinson's committal to the State Special Hospital, he'd celebrated by setting up a meeting with her in his mind. Her brown eyes sparkled behind her red specs at her first sight of him. She'd been very co-operative – no, more, enthusiastic – about the sex games he'd suggested and they played together every night, improving on them, refining them. Sometime he would imagine her in a police uniform, then order her out of it and, passively, she would obey; a willing slave, submitting to him. He still wasn't quite sure why she faded out. It was, he supposed, because she was out of reach, unattainable, and he needed an edge of reality to his fantasies. He had to believe he could make them come true.

He replaced her with his old dream girl, a reality. Her image sprang at him: naked, helpless, rounded buttocks arched towards him, eyes on him, pleading with him. A stirring now, a throbbing, a hardening.

No. He lifted up his head and slammed it hard down into his pillow. *No.*

He'd never had a steady when he met her, out looking for lost balls on the municipal golf course. She was slim and flat-chested, as secretive and solitary as the neighbour's fat daughter had been open and coarse.

He had seen her, on and off, always alone, for a month before he found the courage to talk to her. It was another month before he walked her home in the twilight and was asked in. She lived in a council flat, had no dad, and her mum worked every night as a barmaid. 'Fancy a little session,' he eventually said because he thought it the thing to say, not really knowing what a sex session on the sofa entailed.

'Don't mind,' she said and she put her arms round his neck.

Nothing moved within but after a while his fingers found the gap between the waistband of her jeans and her blouse because he thought it was the thing to do.

'*No,*' she said crossly and, to his relief, she grabbed his wrist.

'Don't you want to?' he said, feigning annoyance.

'No,' she said, quieter. She wasn't on the pill, she said, real grown-up. Did he carry anything? she asked but only, he suspected, to find out if he went with other girls. He shook his head.

Good, she said, she wasn't sixteen anyway. 'No harm in a bit a of slap and tickle, though,' she said with a serious smile. When he frowned, she stood, unbelted and lowered her jeans and turned.

Stirrings then. Such stimulus. Delirium. Even before they laughed and rolled together on the settee, he had reached his first climax in any sort of company.

Once or twice a week, there was much laughing and rolling together and tears from her, too, as slaps became spankings and slipperings and, coaxed by magazines he saw at work, full-blown flagellation and during that time he lost his virginity in an act of sodomy.

It ended quite suddenly when her mother married a pub regular whose work took them to Tyneside. The girl only ever wrote once, all about her new home and friends, with a veiled hint of a new boy.

74

He allowed her back into his make-believe world because he was convinced she would return, knocking on the door, begging him to take her back. He would play hard to get but she would plead with him to punish her for hurting him. And, only after a very slow build-up, teasing her, torturing her mentally, would sentence be ritualistically carried out.

These rituals were adapted from the magazines and books he was reading. So many books, with words he had to look up and line drawings that made him feel hot, just seeing them. Sometimes, unexpectedly and just momentarily, WPC Hurst worked her way into a scene. He would freeze-frame her, study her. Too smart, too dangerous, he always decided. One day maybe. The ultimate night. The Night of the Super Sabbat. Not now. And he would rewind and rerun the scene, exorcizing her, replacing her on the rack with the regular girl.

Everything he did, everything he read, seemed to be shared by the dark figure from the forest of his mind. He was fully developed now, flesh on his bones. A face like his, meaner, a body like his, leaner, stripped to the waist, oiled and gleaming, the slavemaster from the Arabian Nights.

He had a name for him, a strong, powerful name – Makatiel, one of the Seven Angels of Punishment, the plague of God – taken from one of his books, along with exciting, exotic, erotic words and phrases: the left-hand path, morning star, prickings and unctions.

Downstairs, in the cellar below the kitchen, he had created what he and Makatiel called the Dark Room, walls painted black and lined with drawings he'd copied from his books.

Naked, a white sheet over him, he looked at the ceiling which reflected clumps of weeds, grey in colour, swaying in time to rippling curtains drawn across a half-opened window.

He wondered if the movement was hypnotic. Hypnotic things like the Black Glance and the Evil Eye were real to him; grey the colour of this twilight world. He was a Brother of the Shadow.

He turned his head away, heaving his body after it until he rested on his right shoulder and hip. He began to conjure up the kind of girl he wanted to initiate, a sort of female equivalent of that loony; obedient, simple, unquestioning.

A face came into focus. A face he had seen for the first time that day. He studied it. He turned her over, inspected her flip side.

'Will she do?' Makatiel asked, quite suddenly.

'I need to check her out. I want no mistakes.' He stopped himself from thinking: 'This time.'

'No rush. Half the fun, isn't it – preparing?' A few seconds of nothing. 'But if she seems . . .'

He didn't wait for the question to be completed for he knew what was going to be asked. 'Yes,' he told himself, 'yes, yes, *yes*.' The urge engulfed him and could no longer be controlled.

'Missing Persons, Sergeant Hurst.' After twenty months' CID experience, Heather had made it. She finger-tipped her big red-framed spectacles higher up her small nose. Then she started making neat notes.

Angie Stevenson, aged seventeen, had not been seen for three weeks. Child Protection had a bulky file for her.

At ten, Angie had been taken away from her divorced mother and placed in council care. She had lived with her for less than a year after the death of her grandmother who'd raised her. In that time she had run away twice.

Firemen had rescued Angie from a first-floor council flat after a neighbour had spotted smoke seeping under the locked door. She had set fire to a tattered sofa when she fell asleep with a cigarette between her fingers. 'She's always left alone,' said the neighbour. Her mother did not fight the custody order.

At twelve, after three attempts at fostering her had all ended in her running away, she was transferred from a council home to a probation hostel on conviction for shoplifting. She already had some experience of sex and drugs.

At fourteen, she fractured a hip in a fatal road crash. A car stolen by an absconder from the hostel hit a lamp standard while being chased by a police patrol. He died at the wheel. She was thrown out of the passenger seat. The injury

76

left her walking with a slight twist that made her bottom protrude.

At sixteen, she left the hostel, dossed here and squatted there until she found a semi-permanency in a crumbling terraced house rented by an older girl with a string of convictions for prostitution. Within six months, Angie had received a caution for soliciting kerb-crawling motorists.

It wasn't the landlady who raised the alarm. She'd been away in London during one of the periodic blitzes by the Vice Squad against kerb-crawling.

A Labour canvasser had knocked on the door on a drizzly June evening. No reply. He pushed in the letter flap to slip through his party's leaflet. The stench was overpowering.

The beat man broke in and found a rotting cat. He bounced the case off to the RSPCA. 'Nothing to do with me,' protested the landlady. 'It's Angie's. She adored the scraggy thing. I just can't understand it.' The RSPCA bounced it on to Missing Persons.

Heather, in a fawn two-piece suit, collected up her notes and walked down the corridor to the Major Crime Squad office. Jacko had his down-at-heel black shoes on the desk, white shirt opened at the collar, two-toned grey tie pulled down, reading, catching up on his case-load.

'Hallo, stranger,' she said, over his shoulder. He threw his head back and beamed. A room always lit for him when she walked in.

They had seen little of each other for some time. He'd spent the early part of that year away from the office, on the murder of a private detective, an absorbing case. He was certain there was a book in it to write when he quit.

They'd grown close, he and Heather, a bond formed two years earlier on the Michelle Robinson case, drinking chums in the Fairways when he was between inquiries and she was between romances and she still popped round to his home, though Jacko recognized that his toddler son was the attraction, not him. In love, he'd noticed, she wore her contact lenses. Out of love, she reverted to her red specs. She was wearing them today, so he wouldn't ask after her love life. 'What you got for me?'

She perched on his desk and took him through her note. 'Can you give me an afternoon?'

'What ya got in mind?' He smiled salaciously.

She put on a bored expression. 'I mean, are you busy?'

He threw his head sideways. 'Am I busy?' he asked the squad collator, a sergeant with dull dress sense and a sharp brain. His answer was directed at Heather. 'All he's done for a month is bask in glory over that private dick. Take him, for christsake.'

Heather took him in her brand-new red Fiesta, lovingly polished, to Nottingham, a twenty-minute drive. She drew up in the red-light district. At the turn of the century, this had been a posh part of the city with a huge playing field as its focal point, the site of Britain's biggest travelling fair for three glorious days each year, a part of the city he adored, especially the wide main road up to it with crowded, happy pubs and restaurants with cooking from every continent and travel agents who advertised trips to colourful places.

In his down-at-heels shoes he felt uncannily at home in the terraced streets, with their Victorian bays, but even the romantic in him accepted that there was nothing exotic living in the shabby street where Angie had lodged.

'Fifteen nicker a trick,' said her landlady, thirtyish, with bags under her eyes. 'She wasn't full time. Just now and then for food and stuff' – by which, both realized, she meant dope.

'Any regulars?' asked Heather

'Only one. Once a week in his truck. A bit of a weirdo, apparently.'

'How do you mean?'

'Rough like, and well . . .' A struggling face for a second, then a knowing one. 'Heard about the admiral's daughter marrying the matelot?'

Heather shook her head while Jacko perused the damp patches behind the wallpaper which gave off a fusty smell.

Well, she said, the admiral had told his daughter on the eve of the wedding: 'I know sailors so if he ever asks: "Let's do it the other way," refuse point-blank.' One night six months into the marriage, curiosity and the spirit of adventure got the better of her. 'Let's do it the other way.' 'What?' exclaimed the sailor. 'And risk having a baby?'

Jacko laughed out of politeness. The look on Heather's

face told him whatever turned her on (and even happily married men idly wonder about such things sometimes) that was not it.

'No risk of Angie falling for one, either, not with him. Know what I mean?' added the landlady.

Heather knew. 'What's his name?'

'Mac something. Never clapped eyes on him.' She lit a new cigarette off the old. Filthy habit, thought Jacko. He'd just broken with it again after a four-month nicotine binge. 'I was expecting her to flit but not that sudden.'

'Why?'

'The landlords don't allow subtenants. She had to go or I'd have got notice to quit. But not overnight. Not that sudden.'

'Who are the landlords?'

'TVE Properties. Charge the earth and never do any repairs.' She pointed to bare electrical wires on a wall behind peeling paper, a cracked window pane and a door that wouldn't shut. 'Subsidence, they reckon it is. From the pit.' She yanked her neck in the vague northerly direction of Moorwood. 'They're penny-pinching bastards. They even fine you a fiver if you're a day late with the rent.'

'So where could she be?'

'Search me,' said the landlady. 'That Mac was offering to set her up but she was a bit chary of him. I don't think she'd go anywhere without the cat.'

They checked the neighbours and got lots more moans about the landlords but no sightings of Angie.

'What's your feeling?' asked Heather, driving back.

'She's hardly a vulnerable. She's run away half-a-dozen times.'

'Odd about that cat, though.'

Jacko had lost interest and didn't even respond. 'Just keep her on the Active List. She's not Priority, is she?'

A week later the landlady phoned. She'd received a postcard of a green-spired clock tower at Skegness, a cheap and cheerful seaside resort eighty miles to the east.

'On the front with Mac,' it said in careful, rounded writing. 'Day off from new job. Found a flat with poss of winter accomodation. Look after cat. Love. Angie. X.'

79

Heather collected it and showed it to Jacko. 'She's spelt accommodation wrong,' she pointed out.

'Yea,' said Jacko, whose wife regarded him as the world's worst speller. 'They get no education these days, these kids.'

11

Another year . . .

And material for another book. Jacko was basking again, the wounded hero, not long back from a long spell of sick leave. He'd muddled his way through a web of corruption to uncover an armed jailbreak plot and ended up in hospital with a fractured skull.

'Your brain unscrambled yet?' A cultured public school accent, a waspish delivery, and he did not have to look up from his reading to recognize the Little Fat Man. Detective Chief Superintendent Richard Scott was a friend as well as the CID boss who had pulled his strings on the jailbreak job.

'Just about.' Jacko looked up anyway, grinning, pleased to see him.

'Then run the rule over this.' Scott dropped a memo on his desk and ambled away.

'Missing Person – Priority,' he read. A teenage girl called Barbara Brown was on the run from the State Special Hospital. Only two items in a long description caught his eye: an expensive gold bracelet and the phrase 'well developed'. Big knockers, he thought. A sugar daddy on the outside, perhaps?

He checked Records who had no fingerprints because there were no convictions. Not everyone at the State Special, he discovered, had been sent there by the courts, so he phoned the hospital. 'All I need is background.' The medical superintendent said he'd help but it had to be in confidence and Jacko readily agreed.

Barbara Brown had been admitted on the say so of her mother. A normal girl till puberty, problems overcame her with the speed of her physical development. She'd started to imagine herself as a film star, harmless enough day-dreams, which turned nasty with allegations that she had been abused by her stepfather, a solicitor. Mild schizophrenia was diagnosed.

She went as a private patient to Roselands, a grim mental hospital converted from a Victorian workhouse. She made satisfactory progress away from her home environment and the superintendent as good as said, in modulated best Oxford, that doctors there were beginning to conclude that there may have been some substance to her allegation.

Jacko could hardly believe his ears. Most medical men won't tell you if a patient has a cold, unless you've got a court order, and this one was spilling the lot. The relapse came, he continued, when she complained that she had been sexually assaulted by a member of Roselands' staff – a caretaker in his mid-thirties with twelve years' trouble-free service and, before that, an impeccable record in the army which had invalided him out because of a leg wound suffered in a Belfast ambush.

Three other girl patients, present at the time of the incident, condemned her at an inquiry as a liar living in a make-believe world. She flew at them, wrestling them to the floor, biting and kicking.

He was running through her case history effortlessly, in complete command of all the clinical facts, but Jacko was no longer impressed. He had recognized those modulated tones now. This was that daft dwarf of a doctor who had freed Samuel Pattinson to kill.

She was transferred to the State Special, the psychiatrist went on, as a difficult and dangerous patient. Her recovery was again speedy and she was soon moved from the maximum security wing to a row of big villas outside the walls where patients lived in small, self-supporting communities preparing for their release. Supervised shopping trips followed, but, out of character, she never returned from her first solo shopping trip. 'Naturally, we're very disappointed.'

'Why?' asked Jacko, moodily.

'She was doing so well that we were hoping to let her go.'

'Is she a danger?'

'Not to the public . . .'

Heard that before, he thought, acidly. 'But she is, well, a striking-looking girl, easily led, very vulnerable. The risk is to her.' Probably conned you, he groused silently.

The doctor promised a photo, via a police dispatch rider, but when it arrived Jacko felt a twinge of disappointment as he studied a straight-on head shot. She was surprisingly young-looking, no make-up, blonde hair down to her shoulders, bold eyes and a chin that was a little too masculine. He prepared a press release with copies of the photo and asked the PR department to circulate it.

The phone rang next morning. 'Mr Jackson. Colin Bates here. *Crime Catchers.*' Clipped voice, busy, busy. 'This missing girl of yours. Well worth twenty seconds. But she doesn't look very dangerous.'

'Nobody is saying she is, Colin.'

'Still, Mr Jackson.' A pause, sharply pointed, then, as if he were trying to sell the story to himself: 'Nutters on the run always provoke a spark of passing interest.'

Got it, now, thought Jacko. Missing girls are two a penny, jobs for the Sally Army, unless there's an element of danger in them to make his viewers tut-tut about lax security. 'Haven't you got something more up-to-date? I'd like an extra frame for a bit of on-screen movement. This pic must be two years old. A full-length or a side-on would be ideal.'

'Only wish I had,' said Jacko truthfully. 'That's how long she's been in institutions.'

'In that case,' he snapped, 'she's only worth fifteen seconds.'

He put down the phone without a thank you or goodbye, which Jacko, when he'd finished his fuming, accepted as fortunate. He'd taken such a dislike to him that he'd probably have signed off by calling Chief Superintendent Sherman's favourite journalist Master Bates.

12

High above the heads of the shuffling crowds hung white helium balloons. He imagined giants' eyeballs floating out of their sockets and couldn't think why.

A flash from the past, a faded memory, a bad dream perhaps. He had a proven technique for blocking out bad memories. He dismissed it and looked about him.

He seemed to be in a forest. A forest of lights, static, then turning. A towering, dense forest of lights. Yellows, so many yellows, and reds and blues and green and whites, hanging from a hundred rides and decorating two hundred stalls; so bright, so many, that the night cloud held rainbows.

He breathed in the smells. Of candyfloss and frying onions and roasting chestnuts and gingerbread, of mushy peas with mint sauce and steam from the engines and sweat; above all, the sweat. He liked the smell of sweat.

That noise. Such noise. The side-show barkers, the hammer blows and bells from Try Your Strength stands, the crack of wooden balls on coconuts, the ping of pellets on the rifle ranges, the popping of balloons, the jangling discord of pop music, amplified and competing with restful melodies of barrel organs, the sound of thousands of feet in slow step, and, above all, the squeals of fear from young girls on stomach-churning rides. He liked to hear girls squeal in fear.

He'd read that geese used to be sold at this fair, flocks of them, to fatten for Christmas eleven weeks hence. The rides and the stalls came to cash in on the flocks of people. Tastes changed to the whiter meat of turkey but the rides and stalls still came and so did the flocks of people, bigger every year, a million over the three days, so that now Goose Fair was the biggest travelling funfair in England.

To the lyrical writer of an article in one of TVE's free newspapers, the sounds, the smells, the sights, the slow-moving, almost aimless masses gave the place the magical feeling of a Far Eastern city – 'Hong Kong with a nip in the air' – and the night chill that October brings is known as goosey weather and parents get pimples of cold while their children are prickled with excitement.

He felt both sorts of goose bumps as he wandered around. Every time he saw a policewoman he hoped she'd be WPC Hurst. Three years now and still she wouldn't go, refused to vacate his mind. All he wanted was to follow her for a while and take the vision home with him, home to bed.

Crack. He stopped in his tracks, turned and followed the sound to a side-show over which purple flashed out the words: ARABIAN NIGHTS.

Crack. A man in a black leather suit without sleeves to display his bulging muscles lashed the catwalk with a bullwhip, kicking up dust and dirt. 'Two minutes to the the next performance.'

He'd witnessed this scene a thousand times in his mind and he felt a pulsing at his loins.

A busty, leggy girl, bold face lathered in heavy make-up, stood in profile in a very short, very tight, pale green gauze wrap which showed off a skimpy white bra beneath. A gold bracelet jangled on her wrist, a vaguely sexy sound, but her chest was much, much too big and the pulsing stopped.

Her back to the gathering crowd, in a blue diaphanous skirt that reached down to her bare feet and swept the catwalk, another girl swayed woodenly to a slow movement from *Scheherezade*.

He stood and stared, unblinking. And he saw through the long skirt finger-shaped marks which, he knew, would have been red, then black and were now no more than a deep tan spreading from beneath her white bikini pants.

More than a pulsing now; a pounding.

Crack. The bullwhip came down again. 'One minute to the next performance,' barked the slavemaster. He joined the end of a small queue, eyes never leaving her until the music stopped and she skipped through a dusty golden curtain.

85

Inside a big, square tent with a small raised platform, he stood slightly apart from the crowd, thirty or so, no more. And the show reached its climax, for him, when the slavemaster's whip curled with a slapping sound round her bare midriff and pulled her across the stage like a spinning top towards him.

Afterwards he walked among the crowd, seeing, hearing, smelling nothing. I must have her, he kept telling himself. She likes it. You can tell from the look in her eyes that she likes it. She'd pass the test.

Not like the last one. She'd lasted more than a month. Good at first; great. There'd been the panic over the cat she'd left behind but he'd sorted that, cleverly, and he congratulated himself. But rewards. She was always demanding rewards. That wasn't supposed to be part of the Pact. He was giving her board and her own bed in the Dark Room. Drugs, she demanded. Lived on them. Chance after chance he took to buy them, to please her, to keep her quiet. Cost a fortune. The stupid bitch refused cheaper stuff like aerosols of fuel and glue.

He'd worked out why she needed so much dope, of course. To kill the effect of the Silver Cord. In the end it was like flogging a dead horse. The method of her disposal gave him a greater thrill than dictating that seaside postcard to her with the deliberate spelling mistake.

The street in which he lived had backyards. At the bottom of each, ten strides from the kitchen door, was a row of single-storey buildings in which every home had its own outside lavatory, coalhouse and wash-house, museum pieces from the 1950s. All the tenants had converted their smallest bedroom into a bathroom and the outhouses became storerooms, but he had cleared the rubbish out. Half-filling the coalhouse with high-grade domestic was easy and cheap with his contacts and he used it in the grate beneath the square brick-built boiler in the far corner of the wash-house.

And bit by bit he boiled Angie Stevenson down to the bone. He panicked for just a second when a neighbour popped his head over the wall and inquired: 'What's that awful smell?' But he remembered the loony and his dog, just clutched them out of thin air, and said: 'Sorry. Horsemeat for my mate's dogs. Won't take long.'

He skimmed off the fat when it cooled in the deep, round

basin. He put it into jam-jars. The residue he disposed of down a backyard drain and he remembered the case of mass-murderer Dennis Nilsen, caught because too much evidence never made it to the main sewers, and plenty of sodium hydroxide followed it down. He reheated what he saved and poured it into plastic cylinders to make candles which he coated with tar.

On nights of Sabbats, they lit the Dark Room where the bones of Angie Stevenson, rewired together, hung in star formation, the front of her skull to the wall. For over a year, uncomplainingly, she took and passed the Test of the Silver Cord. And no one, not a single person, had missed her.

Now Makatiel, Angel of Punishment and the Plague of God, needed a fresh woman, a living woman. She's the one, he told himself as he mooched, round-shouldered, hands in his trouser pockets, among the ceaselessly moving crowds. I must have her.

Think, a voice cautioned from the forest. Control yourself. Remember Michelle Robinson. And with that the emissions which had continued to seep long after he left the show stopped and soon he felt himself dry and calm and a plan came into place.

He played the side-stalls closest to the tent, eyes on the exit throughout the two last shows, spending more money than he intended, winning a cuddly dog with six ping-pong balls in a goldfish bowl.

He recognized her as she came out, dressed in black hipsters, high-necked mauve sweater and a green anorak. She walked slowly through the thinning crowds. He fell into step behind, picked up pace and cannoned his right shoulder into her left as he drew level.

He looked round at her with a frosted frown, which he allowed to melt almost immediately into a smile of recognition. 'Oh, you. Sorry.' She looked at him with a mixture of surprise and suspicion. 'Enjoyed the show,' he said with a nod.

'Really?'

'Yea. Good that. You dance well.'

'Not really.' They fell into step. She looked down at the toy he was holding in front of him. 'See you've had a bit of luck, then.'

A casual shrug. 'On Test Your Weight.'

'For your girl-friend?'

Another shrug. 'Don't have one any more. She's gone to live in Newcastle.' He grinned and offered it to her. 'You have it.'

'No. I couldn't.'

'Please. I feel such a fool carrying it around.'

He pressed it into her reluctant grasp. 'Thanks,' she said, looking down at it, fingering its ears.

'Walk you home?' She looked back at him, suspicious again. 'I won't try anything, honest.'

She nodded ahead of them. 'I'm in a van on the park just up there. The boss's. Me and the other girl. Just temp.'

'That's show-biz,' he said, man-of-the-world, and they both gave short laughs. He was heading that way anyway, he said. The conversation continued in stops and starts up an asphalt drive with a dark backdrop of tall trees until she nodded to her left to a battered black Commer van which stood in a row of vehicles inside a roped-off area with a hanging notice: PERMIT HOLDERS ONLY. 'I'm down there.'

They stood facing each other. 'Don't that whip hurt?' he asked, sounding concerned.

'Not really.' She rubbed her stomach in afterthought. 'The tip catches a bit sometimes but not really.'

The seepage started again and his breath billowed like a cloud of steam from the Cockerels and Horses on the cold air. He closed his eyes and seemed to sway. She touched his right arm lightly. 'You all right?'

'Tired. That's all.' He pulled himself upright.

'Me, too.' She paused. 'Coming tomorrow?'

Don't rush this, he told himself. 'Busy,' he told her. 'But Saturday I'll come to see you.' He paused. 'I'll win you a big teddy bear.' She smiled an engaging smile. His face remained serious. 'Seriously. And afterwards maybe we could have a nosh – Italian, Chinky, Indian, whatever you fancy. Would you like that?'

She seemed to take a minute to make up her mind. 'Sounds nice. Thank you.'

They arranged to meet by the boxing booth straight after the last show and waved each other good-night.

He called after her. 'What's your name, by the way?'

'Jill,' she said, turning.

'I'm Mac. See you Saturday.'

Heather flounced into the squad room, plonked herself on his desk and demanded: 'What the hell's going on?'

Jacko saw she was wearing her red specs again. Having no man in her life was bad for her ego and made her a touch tetchy. 'What's the trouble?'

'This.' She thrust a red Missing Persons file into his hand. The tag said: JILL FISHER. The name meant nothing and he said so. 'That's odd,' she said, cooling down.

Jill Fisher was missing, she went on. The last sighting of her was as a dancing girl at Goose Fair. Heather had tracked down the owner of the Arabian Nights show. The man who'd answered the phone had said Detective Inspector Jackson had already been in touch.

'That is odd,' he said, thoughtfully. He explained he'd been chasing up Barbara Brown, an escapee from the State Special. An *Evening Post* reader had reported seeing her performing in the same show. The owner had told him that a girl answering the description and calling herself Beverley Beaumont had worked for him for three nights in Nottingham and three in Hull, the fair's next stop, and then left, London-bound, she said.

'Sorry,' said Heather, regretfully. 'We seemed to have been chasing each other's tails.'

With a smile, fond but sly, he opened his desk drawer, fiddled to find a folder – red again, for Priority – and handed it to her. She read his file; he hers.

A social worker reported Jill Fisher, aged seventeen, missing after she failed on two successive Sundays to visit her baby daughter in a foster home.

'She's never missed before,' she'd told Heather. 'She's got the makings of a good little mum. Once she's settled down, there's no doubt she'll get the baby back.'

Her father, embittered by the desertion of his wife long ago, had turned her out when she returned with baby from the maternity home six months earlier. 'You made your bed,' he'd said. 'Now go lie on it.'

Heather had quizzed her boozy boy-friend. He'd admitted

back-handing her. She left a tearful note and packed her small blue suitcase the morning after a final thrashing. His flat was searched. They found Jill's crumbled farewell note in a dustbin. Two women officers from the Child Protection team canvassed neighbours and old schoolmates. They found one who had seen her on the catwalk at Goose Fair.

A sad story, he thought, tragic and disturbing. 'Two girls missing from the same show.' He was shaking his head. 'Too much of a coincidence.'

They travelled to a desolate smallholding on the misty banks of the River Trent. He knocked on the tinny door of a white caravan, streaked with green moss and black soot. 'You again?' said a weedy youth in a stained T-shirt and dirty unzipped jeans.

Inside was the showman, a craggy, dark-haired man, mid-thirties, in a single bunk. He sat up, stripped to the waist, but didn't get out of bed. Heather sat in a fraying canvas chair and Jacko, standing, no place to sit, felt a pang of jealousy as she eyed his rippling muscles.

They asked him about Jill Fisher first. She'd just appeared, he claimed, the day before the fair opened while they were setting up. That was the way he hired all his girls. She'd seemed so desperate that any job would have done. She would have settled for the ticket desk on his Arabian Nights show, and looked surprised when he'd made her a £15-a-night dancing girl.

'She had this lovely arse, see,' and Jacko noticed that he had not stolen a glance at Heather, as most men did, when this subject was on their minds.

'She took off after the final performance in Nottingham on the Saturday.' He looked up at Jacko. 'Told that other girl she had a date with a punter. Shacking up, I expect.' He'd offered more work in Hull, the show's final fairground stop of the season, but she didn't travel with them.

'The other girl, Bev Somebody with arthritis . . .' he made claws of both hands and held them in front of his smooth, strong chest to show that he meant a big bosom '. . . she came.

'She pulled out after Hull 'cos there was no more work. Said she was heading for London. Talked non-stop – a posh accent, too. Reckoned she was going to be a page three girl, get a job with a chorus line, then Hollywood. Potty . . .' Not half, thought

Jacko. 'But nice; no trouble. She'll be on the game now, I expect. All do in the end.'

'Did Jill leave anything behind?' asked Heather.

'A small bag with a few belongings. It's stored in the shed with the costume basket.' He flicked his head in a direction beyond the filthy small window.

'And Bev?' asked Jacko.

The showman shot the youth a worried glance. 'She took her things.'

'All of them?' An unhappy look. 'I asked you a question.' No response still. 'We have a search warrant.'

He tossed off ancient striped blankets and heaved himself out of bed. He was completely naked, a Charles Atlas of a man with a seven-stone weakling's manhood. Heather looked away – masking her disappointment, thought Jacko, in secret glee.

He padded barefoot to a tiny work-top, a battered black phone above, drawers below, one of which he slid open. He returned with a bracelet, solid gold, delicately woven, which he dropped into Jacko's opened hand. 'She lost this,' he said, climbing back into bed. 'In Hull. You can see the safety-catch's bust.'

Jacko looked down to confirm it. Even he knew it was an expensive and tasteful piece. 'Why didn't you give me this when I called last week?'

'You didn't ask.' His handsome features were disfigured by an aggressive glare. 'She lost it, I said. I didn't nick it. Helped her to look for it.' He looked at the silent youth who nodded. 'Searched everywhere. She was very upset about it. In tears. Said it was a present from her dead dad. I found it in the grass when we were breaking down the tent. I was keeping it for her. She said she'd do the full tour next season unless she got a better offer.'

Carefully, Jacko slipped it into an inside pocket. Heather unashamedly ordered the showman out of bed again and he stood, unconcerned, as they searched under his mattress and then in every corner of the caravan.

They went outside and retrieved the blue case from a shed, untidier than Jacko's own, and looked through the pathetic contents. A pair of jeans, a pair of flat shoes, two changes of sweaters, three sets of underwear, a few pairs of white socks and a string-topped toilet bag with cosmetics that smelt as though they'd only ever be worn by the brave and the broke.

'No handbag,' said Heather. 'Must have taken it with her.'

'What are you looking for?' asked the showman, still in bed, when they returned to the caravan.

'Evidence,' said Jacko, crisply.

'Of what?' A few seconds for the dawning. 'Surely, you don't think . . .'

'Two girls missing in a week. What do you expect us to think?'

'But they all take off after a week or two. On the run from somebody or something. Most of them use false names.' His face registered a thought which he helpfully shared. 'They were good mates. Jilly probably went ahead to find a place and Bev joined her with another forty-five quid stuck down her bra.'

'Without taking her good mate's suitcase?' asked Jacko sharply.

'With Jill leaving behind a baby she loves?' asked Heather, just as sharp.

'But you can't possibly think . . .' Silence.

'Think what?'

'That I . . .' His eyes travelled to the dumb youth who stood by the opened door. They exchanged tiny amused smiles.

Jesus, thought Jacko, closing his eyes for a second. A limp wrist with a commercial eye for erogenous zones.

He asked the PR Department for maximum publicity when they got back. He phoned Colin Bates of *Crime Catchers*, blatantly oiling up to him. 'See that latest release, Mr Bates? We're very worried about her. We'd appreciate your help.'

'A waste of time and space. I ran that State Special runaway and not a peep. It's always the same. There's hundreds of them. Sorry. Full.' The line went dead.

Jacko visualized him screwing up the press release on the missing Jill Fisher and tossing it away. Where her sad goodbye note to her baby's father had finished. In the wastepaper bin. Along with other discarded rubbish. Among the crap. Thrown away. A throwaway life.

'Bastard,' he said, addressing his replaced phone.

The Hull daily ran a picture caption on Barbara Brown (aka Bev Beaumont). A middle-aged motorist made contact on the same night. He thought he recognized the face but recalled the figure more vividly. 'A better pair than that first streaker at Twickers or was it Lord's? Erica what-ever-was-her-name?'

He'd given her a lift westbound for a few miles and dropped her near the Humber Bridge. She kept rubbing her left wrist with her right hand and, when he asked if she'd strained it, she said no, and added something about losing a bracelet that was precious to her.

And then the trail went cold . . .

13

Nine months later

The sloping lawn was mottled with big patches of brown, bare and cracking. Jacko, gazing out of the kitchen window, lived and worked and thought in simple equations and, to him, green equals growth equals graft in the garden, and he just wanted to loaf on his day off. He couldn't understand why everyone was complaining about the heatwave. Droughts kill weeds; no weeds equals no weeding. Simple.

He'd stroll up with his dog to playschool and collect Mark and they'd all play in the spacious garden that came with the three-bedroomed house bought when the bungalow became too small.

Jacko cherished his days off and Jackie reckoned he deserved them. Earlier that hot summer he'd been on the murder of a government minister's sister; a long, worrying inquiry, a domestic in the end; but a dazzlingly different domestic and more source material.

What a run, he told himself. Is there no stopping this superstar? He ought to go up to the den and peck out a few hundred words on Jackie's portable while the details were fresh but, sod it, it was such a beautiful day.

The cream phone rang on the kitchen wall. 'Scott,' said a plummy voice. Jacko groaned inwardly. The Little Fat Man only ever rang on a day off to take him off it. 'A big one. Abduction in the forest. There's a lot more to it than a missing girl.'

He told him where and when to report. No sorry or please or thank you, but that was Scott's style. Jacko rated him more highly than days off. He would work himself into an early grave for Scott.

He changed into his light-weight check suit, scribbled a

note on the kitchen table for Jackie and drove his silvery-grey Cavalier up the ring road to Divisional Headquarters. He had not set foot in the Legoland building in four years and a bit, not since he arrested Pattinson. Sometimes he thought of Sam. Not with doubts, merely wondering how he was getting on at the State Special and if he'd ever be fit to face trial. He supposed not.

The overcrowded car park confirmed the size of the operation about to be launched and there was standing room only at the back of the lecture hall. Scott, at the front with a blackboard and maps behind, started his briefing as soon as he walked in.

Tracey Smythe, on holiday from her boarding school, had taken her horse for their usual morning outing, he began. She'd saddled up in the stables behind the family's rambling old house on the edge of Sherwood Forest. Her father owned Forest Coaches at Moorwood and was a magistrate.

Her mother expected her back for breakfast. An hour later, worried that she might have taken a tumble, she had driven and walked over the route Tracey usually rode. In a clearing, beside a broad bridle path, she found the horse, still saddled, contentedly munching grass in the shade of birch trees.

There was no sign of Tracey. She phoned her husband who raised the alarm. A sweep by tracker dogs of the immediate area yielded nothing. Mounted police were being drafted in and Scott was pointing with a ruler towards the map and the ground to be covered.

The missing girl was fourteen, a junior champion show jumper, wearing a pink blouse, knotted across her bra-less chest and shortie jeans. 'She has what's called in equestrian circles a comfortable seat which isn't surprising because she could ride before she could walk. Now . . .' Scott stopped for effect and attention. 'While Mrs Smythe was out looking for her daughter, their au pair took a phone call – a Filipino, so her English is only passable and there were, of course, no tapes on the line then. She's done her very best and reports that the caller, a man, told her . . .' he looked down at his clipboard to get it verbatim '"If you want to see her alive again, put ten thousand in small notes in the roots of the Major Oak and don't tell the police."'

A murmur rumbled through the packed room. Kidnap f

95

ransom is a much rarer crime in Britain than murder. Jacko had only come across one and that turned out to be a financial squabble between two overseas businessmen. Kidnap, every detective knows, requires deft handling. Ever since a hostage was allegedly fed to a herd of pigs, the media have always agreed to complete news blackouts. In return for their co-operation, they get regular briefings but promise not to use a line until the embargo is lifted. There is, however, a drawback in making such a request: the absence of publicity means members of the public, passers-by, dog-owners walking their pets, don't come forward immediately with sightings and other clues.

It is an awesome decision for a CID chief to make and Jacko was pleased it was up to the Little Fat Man, not him. 'In the interests of trying to secure the release of the girl unharmed, I'm applying a news blackout,' he went on.

There were some brief nods and some single shakes from heads in a divided audience. Jacko was among the nodders. Without debate, Scott doled out the jobs: 24-hour listening posts and surveillance teams at her home and in the forest, dressed as tourists, rangers and campers, road blocks to find regular travellers, house-to-house inquiries in the nearest villages, a team to her school to see if there was a boy-friend in her background with an eye for a quick buck, 450 acres of woodland to be searched, a huge job.

He gave Jacko Moorwood because, he said, he knew his way round the village and assumed he still had good sources there who might point to someone who had it in for the Smythe family, a malcontent with a motive.

Who does he think I am, thought Jacko, memory man? It was so long ago, so much had happened since, that he had to flip through the Michelle Robinson dossier, on file in Divisional Records, to refresh himself on the names and addresses of local contacts he'd made during that fortnight's inquiry.

He lowered eyebrows at a certificate, signed by Chief Superintendent Sherman, sanctioning the destruction of the exhibits, Pattinson's clothing mainly, to free much-needed storage space, on the assumption that he'd never be fit for trial; that he'd have to stay, technically unconvicted, at the State Special until he died. He wondered how it would affect the

outcome if Pattinson made a miraculous recovery. Still – he shrugged it off – Sherman was the boss at the time, titularly, anyway.

He started at Forest Coaches, the family's firm, working through past payrolls to see if any employees had been sacked and denied compensation, looking for that malcontent with a motive. He found none.

The cluster of decaying buildings inside the compound had been pulled down. (His memory was not so easily demolished and, in his mind, he saw Michelle again. Queasiness returned.) In their place stood a smart set of green single-storey offices, like super Portacabins, a common sight in coalfields, with flexible foundations and hinged walls which won't sink if the disturbed earth moves beneath them.

Early one morning he saw Keith Bannion, whose firm, TVE Securities, still held the contract, arriving in a white Range Rover, a broad-brimmed Mountie's hat sitting unhappily on his head. Jacko waved through the wire.

Inside the compound lived a colony of feral cats but no Max. He had bitten Pattinson's replacement and had been destroyed, said the foreman. Jacko hoped no one had told Pattinson.

There was no Moorwood Colliery any more, either. The gates where workers and police had battled with strikers were locked and rusting. The headstocks had been demolished, and thin, thirsty weeds pushed through holes in the pit yard where more wild cats scavenged. Sheep grazed on the grassed-over slagheaps. The surface buildings were crumbling behind the advertising hoardings as they awaited developers to convert the derelict site into an industrial estate. A moving sight still, much sadder.

He drove into the estate, no coal dust to grime the windows these days, but no less dreary. He called on the two ex-miners who had been sacked, along with Michelle Robinson's father, because they threw bricks at a Forest coach on the picket line. It had cost them heavy fines and compensation, which, he reasoned, they may have wanted to recoup. Both were well alibi-ed.

At a loose end on a balmy evening he dropped in on the Robinsons with some trepidation, fearful his presence would reopen old wounds, but they made him feel welcome. They sat in white plastic chairs drinking shandy in the back garden, neat and tidy, its fencing renewed.

'Told 'em it would happen,' Mr Robinson said when Jacko raised the closure of the local colliery. 'Scabs wouldn't listen.' Four years on, thought Jacko, still not healed.

He was suntanned from his job as a window cleaner. Michelle's sister was at sixth-form college now, he said with sheepish pride, and he laughed good-humouredly as Jacko poked fun over the relegation of Newcastle United, his home town team, and they jointly bemoaned England's performances against the Aussies, armchair sports buffs chatting.

Only his distant, dull brown eyes hinted at hidden pain and they hardened when, apropos of nothing, he asked: 'That madman still locked away?' Jacko nodded but made a mental note to check. 'I begrudge every penny tax I pay to keep him.'

His wife shook her head to silence him and Jacko changed the subject. 'What happened to that bloke Hollis up the road? Did he lose his job when the pit shut?'

'And there's another bastard. Not him. Transferred to another pit. Promotion. A place of his own now in town. Doing well, him. Not a penny redundo for me, though.'

His wife shook her head more severely. 'We manage.' They fell into a shocked silence when Jacko told them of the inquiry he was on. Because of the news blackout, it was the first they'd heard about the missing Tracey. 'Poor soul,' said Mrs Robinson. She was thinking of Tracey's mother, Jacko realized, with understanding and insight that mercifully few parents share.

There was warmth in their farewells and Mrs Robinson said: 'Don't make it so long next time.' He was pleased he'd called, felt good about it.

He dropped in on Norman Hollis, unannounced, at his office in a big pit which mined rich seams under rolling farmland. His outdoor face aged as he told him: 'We're talking to everyone who's had business dealings with Forest Coaches and its MD Mr Smythe.'

'So?'

'So, you had. Four years ago. Over a subsidence claim which, as I recall, was somewhat acrimonious.'

'Rubbish, ridiculous. They bung in a claim one day and expect payment the next. It was settled in full within a year which is the norm. Who told you such nonsense?'

Jacko avoided answering. 'We're checking on everyone who regularly uses the main road from town up here.'

Hollis visibly smouldered as he checked his work sheets. He'd passed within a mile of Tracey's home and an hour of the time she vanished, on his own *en route* to a site inspection, but no, he said, he had not seen a girl on horseback. Yes, he could and did provide the names of the people he was meeting and, to Jacko's mild surprise, yes, they could take a look at his newish, grey Nissan Patrol.

'Want your solicitor?' Jacko couldn't remember his name.

'That won't be necessary,' he said, affably.

No further ransom demand was received. No attempt was made to collect the decoy money from Robin Hood's hide-away, the Major Oak, so contorted with age that it had to be held up by timber poles that looked like a huge wooden Zimmer frame. After a week Scott lifted the news black-out.

A tidal wave of words and pictures flooded across the front pages and the screens. It produced nothing other than criticism from a backbench MP demanding to know why the public had not been warned earlier.

Tracey's parents appeared on TV tearfully pleading for her safe return. It was all too much for Mrs Smythe who broke down with the cameras trained unremittingly on her.

The wave turned into a stream and then a trickle as the inquiry became bogged down in the unnewsy grind of the routine but swept back again with the discovery of the body.

Firemen found her when they were damping down after one of many blazes that destroyed acres of tinder-dry under-growth.

She had been buried in a shallow grave in a patch of what had been waist-high bracken. Forensic scientists and pathologists spent weeks working on the remains, blackened by decomposition as well as flames.

There was clear evidence that she had been tied hand and

foot because the bindings gave some unintended protection to the skin. There was some evidence that she had been buried in her skimpy top but none to suggest she had still been wearing her shorts. Inside her had been found minute traces of tar and a form of foreign fat.

'What's your thoughts on that?' Scott asked the Home Office pathologist at a briefing with his senior aides.

He paused. 'A back passage dildo, maybe. A home-made candle which melted down.'

'Made from what?'

He looked down, grave-faced. 'Human fat, we think.'

Everyone looked down, eyes screwed shut as they took in with short, sharp breaths the horror of what he was saying. Jacko had seen and heard much in his career but he was unprepared for that. Every cell in his body seemed to curl up. He could barely concentrate as Scott ordered a new news blackout on the medical report.

Colin Bates devoted the whole of one *Crime Catchers* programme to the hunt which he ended on location with microphone in hand, putting on a nation-mourns voice: 'No woman is safe here while this case is unsolved.'

Privately Jacko had always fancied Hollis as the hit-and-run driver who'd somehow got away with it, so, with sex the confirmed motive, he dropped him from his thoughts and put Samuel Pattinson in the forefront of them because of the Forest Coaches connection, the nature of both crimes and the age of the victims. He wondered angrily if that daft dwarf doctor had let him out for a seaside or shopping day trip. He checked and double checked but found incontrovertible evidence that he'd been working on the hospital farm, enclosed by high walls, topped with electrified wire and scanned by security cameras, from dawn that day. A dozen guards could prove it.

Soon the autumn rains came and a green balm soothed away the brown burns and the black scars in the forest and tucked them up for winter under a blanket of golden leaves.

'Oh, God. Help me. Help me, God.'

There were two separate and distinct voices in his head:

Makatiel, the Plague of God, and Adam, the heavenly man, the one who had not sinned.

In the throes of sexual delirium, he was Makatiel, scornfully sweeping aside Adam's slightest doubts. On sterile nights like this he was Adam blaming everybody but himself for his torment; that recurring vision of capture and a strait-jacket at the State Special.

'It was an accident,' Adam said. 'She shouldn't have screamed. She frightened me. It was her fault.'

They would debate, often aloud (or so it seemed), one voice tenor, the other baritone. Sometimes he would quote these conversations in exercise books in writing so manically fast that it was indecipherable apart from words written in capitals, in different coloured inks, underscored and followed with a string of question and exclamation marks. These jottings he kept in the Dark Room in a pile of books and magazines so dog-eared that some pictorial pages were held together by Sellotape. 'All I wanted to do was flash her.'

'Child's play. You gave up flashing in the park and moved on to better, blacker things,' Makatiel reprimanded.

'But it had been so long,' said Adam. 'Nine months since the Goose Fair girl and it was a disaster. She begged and pleaded when I got her back here. Why does it never work out the way you planned? She failed the Test first night. Blubbering over her kid. If it isn't cats, it's kids. What's wrong with them?'

'Relationships. And we must avoid them.'

'I didn't want a relationship with the girl in the forest. I don't know what came over me. I didn't plan it. Just being there. In the forest. Among the trees. I thought I'd been there before.'

Adam knew that Makatiel would understand and would not reply so he went on: 'I had no idea who her old man was. I just wanted her to see and hold Phallus. Why do they scream? I can't think straight when they scream. I had to keep her quiet.'

'Had our way with her, though,' said Makatiel, darkly. 'Afterwards. And we got away with it.'

'I was thinking, though, wasn't I? I'm getting better at it. That ransom demand. To give us time. All those cars and tourists about. I had to do something to stop the publicity. Publicity almost caught me first time.'

'Brilliant!!' Makatiel enthused. 'They hardly mention it any more in the papers.'

'Not so brilliant. They're still working on it and I haven't got an alibi.'

'Maybe we'll see that WPC Hurst again.'

The mention of her name used to be enough to thicken the juices that ran though the body these two voices inhabited but there had not been a flicker of interest in any woman for week upon impotent week.

'Are you crazy?' asked Adam, astonished. 'I don't want to see her or any police officers. Didn't you hear me? I haven't got an alibi.'

'Get one.'

'How?'

Both voices lapsed into a lengthy silence, then said in unison: '*Blackmail!!*'

'The hit-and-run truck,' said Adam, excitedly.

'Go and see him. Tell him . . .' Another long silence while he pictured the confrontation. Slowly, he began to see himself standing in front of his desk. He'd say he had a problem but mention nothing about murder or about the corruption taking place. He'd say very politely: 'I had a slight prang up on the forest road that day. Nothing serious. I paid for the repair to the truck myself. I didn't stop because I'd been to an all-night party and wouldn't have passed the breath test.'

He'd look him straight in the eyes and say: 'The trouble is the police might get on to me and I don't want to lose my licence. That wouldn't be fair, would it? I mean, I'm not the only hit-and-run driver in the world, am I?'

He would be bound to ask: 'What do you mean?'

And he would simply say: 'Moorwood, 1 March 85. You scratch my back; I'll scratch yours.' Something like that. He'd have to agree to put him in the clear. There were thousands, millions perhaps, at stake, plus a stretch inside.

'Brilliant,' Makatiel repeated. 'Next time we must plan more carefully.'

'There won't be a next time.'

'You've said before.'

And he lay on his bed, replaying the scene, rewinding, honing his words.

These nights his dreams were as dry as the bones of Jill Fisher and Angie Stevenson who had hung, unmolested for weeks, each side of an inverted cross above a black-clad altar in the Dark Room.

14

Nine more months on

'Snap,' said Heather, that astonished look of wonder on her face. In their haste to find each other, they almost collided in the corridor which linked their offices. Both were holding buff paper torn from a telex machine and Heather waved her copy in triumph.

The machine had just chattered out details of an incident at Skegness, a resort so popular in the East Midlands that it is sometimes known as Nottingham-by-the-Sea.

A police patrol car had been summoned to photographic studios. On the pavement stood a customer, a hand swathed in a blood-stained towel. 'She stabbed me, the cow,' he told the patrolmen. Inside was a teenage girl, naked, apart from a G-string, with a knife and smashed equipment scattered about the floor. She went quietly; too quietly. At the police station she wouldn't say a word and refused to see the duty legal-aid solicitor.

The complainant, married and big in local business circles, had met her at a hotel where she worked behind a bar and was known as Bev. He'd engaged her, he said, to model for respectable art publications. The hotelier gave the police her home address, a tiny attic room in a tall house, where no documents, no personal letters, nothing, could be found to confirm her identity.

A WPC on desk duty had scanned through the Priority List of Missing Persons and noticed the name of Barbara Brown who sometimes used the name Beverley Beaumont. Though the photo was out of date, she had the same square chin, bold eyes and blonde hair.

Jacko turned and led the way back to his room and desk. 'He's bloody lucky,' he said, over his shoulder. He was thinking about the last ex-patient from the State Special he'd investigated and what he'd done. He sat on his swivel chair and fished the red file out of his top drawer. 'Not dangerous, eh?' He shook his head at the note he'd made during his phone conversation with the State Special superintendent about the girl's mental state.

Heather, unusually, did not perch on his desk. 'Well?' Jacko looked up, puzzled. 'Let's go.' He shook his head sadly. 'Don't you want me to come?' Heather did not hide her impatience and irritation. 'Look, she may be your case but Jill Fisher is down to me. She could help me. I'd like to come.'

'Go for us both then,' he said, raising his voice.

The collator looked up from a file-strewn desk. 'I'm trying to concentrate here.' He saw them glowering at each other and offered mediation: 'What's wrong?'

Heather began to tell him. Jacko answered privately. What's wrong? What's fucking wrong? Everything's fucking wrong. He felt so, so tired. One blow after the other, he'd suffered.

He saw himself as a team player who needed sidekicks to spur him on. The young one he had nurtured through the vice queen killing had been promoted back to uniform. The woman sergeant who had worked with him so well on the private eye murder had been shunted off to admin after some lesbian liaison upset the chief who preached liberality and practised discrimination. The smartarse who replaced her and helped crack the case of the government minister's sister had gone off round the world.

Each parting had left a void which he could have filled with the Little Fat Man to lean on. Scott had taken charge of the forest kidnapping at the outset but the workload of CID chiefs is too heavy to concentrate on a single inquiry for long.

A superintendent took over till early in the new year when he was switched to a fresh murder case. He'd been replaced by a chief inspector, a sound operator, an extrovert, never a day's illness in his life. After a month in the chair, he'd been found late one night sitting in his darkened office, weeping over a picture of Tracey Smythe. Exhaustion, they called it. A breakdown, they meant.

It all landed on Jacko's plate. He'd been on it, day and

night, without a break for nine months. He was depressed and drained.

He was smoking again, heavily, and had worried away a stone so that the check suit he was wearing hung off him. To cap everything, that spring the Little Fat Man went to Scotland Yard as a commander. There was a boozy farewell party at the Fairways, at which they had presented Scott with a majestic captain's chair.

'And talking of my love of antiques . . .' he said in his thank-you speech and he told affectionately abusive Great Failure stories about Jacko (the con man clergyman who got away because he hadn't recognized him without his dog-collar; the prisoner he'd uncuffed so he could go for a piss and who'd pissed off) but he ended: 'I am losing a fine friend,' and Jacko, standing at the bar, had to turn his head away.

Scott's old No. 2, Alec Sherman, had been transferred from Divisional Command back to CID as the new chief. He had a completely different style; hands off, keeping them clean for eventual promotion to assistant chief, keen on budgets and discipline, leaving on-the-road inquiries to his deputies.

Everybody thought Sherman would switch Jacko to a different inquiry to give the forest job new impetus, fresh eyes and a younger pair of legs. But all he'd used was a silly catch phrase of his: 'Put it in a bag, Mr Jackson, and shake it up' – whatever that meant. He'd called him Mr Jackson because they didn't really know each other but then hardly anybody really knew Chief Superintendent Sherman. They called him the Olympic Torch because he never went out.

And Jacko had stuck at it and was down to checking out convicted buggers whose files were piled high on the collator's desk and everyone knew that was rock bottom. Not once had Sherman called him in to kick it around, toss out a few ideas, because everyone knew he didn't have any.

He had toyed with the idea of taking his ticket two years ahead of time. But what could he do? He couldn't write books now, crowing of successes, with this Greatest of All Failures hanging over him, haunting him.

It was a low point in his life that ranked alongside the days that followed his father's death, when he was a young PC, and he'd mourned over words he'd never spoken, things he'd never said to him and now never could. He was that low. What's wrong? I'm a fucking failure; that's what's wrong.

'Go.' The collator offered his adjudication. 'Both of you.'

'How can I?' Jacko nodded at the mountain of files.

'You're not the only detective in CID.' The collator switched on a conciliatory smile. 'We'll cover you with the Olympic Torch. Have a trip. Wrap it up quickly and snooze in the sun on the beach. You look as though you need it.'

The collator gave him a shrewd smile and Heather's was forgiving and inviting. He unlocked his bottom drawer, sorted through the chaos to find a white envelope, put it in his inside pocket, patted it from the outside. 'Thanks.'

It was a warm, sunny morning. Summer had begun where last year's left off, only earlier, and grass was already browning in unaccustomed heat for May.

Heather had dressed for the weather in a yellow loose-fitting two piece which showed off a golden tan from a spring holiday in Cyprus with a travel shop manager. She was wearing her red specs so Jacko knew he had since travelled on and out of her life. 'How's your love life?' he asked anyway, to get a conversation going.

'What love life?'

'Can I be of help?' She raised her eyes. 'After my nap on the beach, maybe?' And they laughed and the tension was gone.

She drove her prematurely ageing Fiesta, badly dented on the driver's door and dirty all over these days, east along the undulating A46. They swapped gossip until the ruined castle at Newark and then Jacko started to read aloud extracts from both red files on his knee.

Beyond the foot of the gently rolling wolds they lapsed into a contented silence and he began to purr with innocent pleasure. For a mile or so he kidded himself that it was simply the thought of finally catching up with a runaway whose disturbed mental background had kept her file sitting in his drawer for eighteen months.

Anticipation grew as Heather drove by a black-bodied wind-mill with five white sails on to the long straight run into the resort with its lines of poplars assigned the hopeless task of shielding the road from the winds off the North Sea.

Now he knew why he was excited. This was the road he had

travelled many, many times on the green Lincs Road Car bus on day trips with his mum and dad. This was revisiting his childhood when violent death was unknown to him and happiness was a paddle and a donkey ride and patiently building a sand castle and sucking a lollipop and holding his father's hand when he was grubby and tired and sleeping all the way home.

Never go back, they say, but that's nonsense. You are what you are because of days given to you by people who loved you without question and returning revives and refreshes that love. And suddenly he found himself telling Heather things he had never spoken of before, not even to his father; of happy times together, his love for him and the missing he still felt after all these years and she listened in respectful silence and he felt much, much better.

Before she reached the next landmark, a crossroads pub, white all over, with flat, railed roofs, like a cruiser washed up on an extra high tide, he was deluding himself that he could smell the tang of the sea. Sometimes a travelling man gets an uplifting feeling in his heart as he approaches a place which is dear to that heart.

He knew, just knew, that this was going to be one helluva big day in his life.

'Still not talking,' said the WPC who greeted them at the town's police station and court-house which stood on concrete stilts as if worried about the next tide.

He peeped (let's be honest here: leched) through the spyhole in her cell door. The girl was sitting side-on at a tiny table, smoking, head down, her long blonde hair half-hiding her pale face. She was in sandals, black slacks and a loose white cheesecloth top that couldn't disguise her full figure.

'Behave yourself,' said Heather, as she led the way in. The girl did not look up. 'Can we talk, Bev?'

'Should you not be cautioning me?' A husky voice, an elegant sound.

She's given it away, straight away, thought Jacko, delighted. She comes from a legal family, all right.

'Why?' asked Heather. 'We're not interested in what happened at that studio.'

'I'm making no complaints against anyone,' said the girl, firmly. 'They only land you deeper in the shit.' It sounded so out of place with that articulation that Jacko smiled.

'I'm from the Missing Persons Unit,' Heather went on. 'And you are missing. Why in God's name did you run away? You were making such good progress. You'd have been home by now.'

A remote look at the mention of home. She bit her top lip, bloodless almost, without make-up, and said nothing.

'Got something for you.' Jacko pulled the white envelope out of his inside pocket. He poured the gold bracelet into his hand. Her eyes seemed to reflect its brightness. She held her palm out and he dangled it, then let it drop. She stared at it, grasped it, closed her eyes, raised her clenched hand, lowered her forehead to meet it and began to cry. He lit a cigarette and gave her a few moments before saying, very quietly: 'We recovered it from that travelling show.'

'Thank you.' She knuckled her eyes dry.

'Our pleasure. Contrary to popular belief, policemen have fathers, too.' They smiled warmly at each other. 'The safety-chain's broken. You ought to get it fixed.'

'Difficult from here.' The smile had gone.

He shrugged. 'Let's go for a run and drop it off at a jeweller's, have a walk on the beach and a chat.' The girl sniffed and smiled again, weakly this time, and accepted an offer to help herself to toiletry in Heather's shoulder bag.

They drove along the front, only moderately busy at the start of the season. Jacko was smiling nostalgically. 'Used to come here with my folks as a kid. So bracing.'

'Especially in the winter,' said Bev from the back seat. And they laughed together at a joke always made about the 'Skegness is so bracing' motto advertised with a high-stepping Jolly Fisherman, the resort's mascot. A toytown castle, a pleasure park, all concrete and no grass, and a theatre whose pier had been blown out to sea on one winter's winds blocked their view of the big beach to their left.

Yes, the girl said, she was Barbara but she preferred Bev or anything that wasn't BeeBee and she stopped talking again.

They turned at a green-roofed clock tower, a monument to Queen Victoria, with a weather vane pointing down the main street with shop windows offering bargains which were Amazing, Super, Fab. They stopped at a jeweller's where Jacko dropped off the bracelet.

'An hour,' he said as he climbed back into the passenger seat. They headed back for the clock tower which prompted Jacko to ask Heather: 'Did that missing Stevenson girl ever show up?' She shook her head.

From the back Bev was saying she'd never set eyes on Skeggy until eighteen months ago but she quite liked it. Mostly, as a kid, she said, she'd been to places on the Med and those memories silenced her once more.

Heather parked in front of a putting green and took a tartan picnic rug from the boot, handing it to Jacko with her saucy smile. 'For your sleep.'

They walked, Jacko puffing, more than 200 yards across dry, flat, stony sands and climbed, heavy-legged, up deep dunes topped with tufts of pale, wispy grass for their first uninterrupted sight of the sea. No illusion now, that salty smell mingling with the acrid dampness of washed sand that settled on his face. The sea, still 300 yards away, was more grey than blue, its waves so gentle that they stirred the sands without whiteness, the breeze so soft and warm that he closed his eyes to its caress.

He spread out the rug in a hollow among the dunes and stretched out on it. 'Wake me when the tide comes in.' He ceremoniously folded his hands on his chest, crossed his ankles and closed his eyes.

It was true, Bev began, what she'd told her mother but Jacko was only half-listening, letting his mind drift, to find a peaceful place in which to rest so sleep would come.

'From thirteen, whenever she was out, he'd come to my room and cuddle up. "How's my petite BeeBee?" he'd say. "You'll be a star one day." I played up to him at first. I think he is some sort of fucking French film freak.' What lovely alliteration, thought Jacko, drifting back, paying full attention. Just rolled off her tongue, effortlessly; not in an exhibitionist attempt to shock; just naturally, and he realized that Roselands, the State Special, the fairground and a bar had been her finishing school and who was he to complain about foul language anyway?

Eventually, her stepfather was making her do acts which Jacko made a one-word mental note of: fellatio. 'When I complained, it

110

was me who got locked up, not that bastard.' He opened his eyes and saw she was shaking her head. 'I didn't lie, either, about that caretaker at Roselands,' she eventually went on. 'But those three bastard bitches did.'

'Why?' asked Heather.

'He was smuggling in drugs for them.' A sage shrug. 'They were bending over for him, weren't they? He was doing it with lots of girls.'

Roselands was closed soon after Bev's transfer to the State Special. The staff were dispersed, too. 'And you'll never guess where they sent that turd burglar?' Heather guessed right. 'I came off the bus from a shopping trip, my first outing alone, saw him standing outside my villa in his uniform, ogling me.' She sighed. 'So I got right back on the bus and I've been going ever since. He's not going to slap his mutton dagger in my hand again. Never again.' She set her face and shook her head determinedly.

'What's his name?'

'McPhain.' She spoke it with hate, real hate. 'Uncle Mac, the younger kids call him. Poxy pervo.'

'Where did you learn to express yourself so colourfully?' asked Heather, with an amused smile.

'My old man was a journo. Smoked and drank himself to death. Blame him.' A fond smile, for the first time affection in her voice.

Jacko sat up, pulled out his cigarettes, lit two and handed her one. First stop, she said, breathing in smoke in a way Jacko wished she wouldn't, was Nottingham, the Goose Fair and a job with the Arabian Nights show.

'That's one of the reasons I'm here,' said Heather. 'Did you happen to come across a girl called Jill Fisher?'

'Bunked with her. Nice girl.'

'She's missing.'

'You seem to misplace an awful lot.' She laughed lightly, but stopped when they did not join her and she became very serious. 'She was always droning on about her little girl. She wouldn't run out on her.'

'That's what Social Services say. What happened?'

Bev stared out towards the sea in concentration. 'The last night, a Saturday, I kipped on my own. She had a date for a late meal with some customer and never came back.'

111

'Did she tell you his name?'

'Mac,' she said, looking down.

The name on the postcard Angie Stevenson had sent to her landlady, Jacko thought with a start. 'Mac,' he repeated out loud and it seemed to echo across the almost deserted beach. 'You don't think it could have been McPhain?'

Bev didn't know because she'd never seen Jill's date but the thought had crossed her mind. 'He's the sort of back-scuttler who would haunt fairgrounds.'

Jacko's heart pounded, much harder than the distant waves on the flat shore line. From every direction thoughts swooped in and wheeled around his head like flocks of crying gulls. Mac and Angie. Mac and Jill. McPhain was at Roselands before the State Special. Mac and Sam Pattinson. Was McPhain at Roselands when Sam was there? Was he up to his tricks then? Could it have been him, not Sam, with that little girl? Too far fetched. Or is it? Let's look at it another way. 'Up at the State Special,' he said casually, 'did you ever meet an old client of mine – Sammy Pattinson?' The name meant nothing but the description did.

'You mean young Dr Doolittle.'

'Don't answer this if you don't want to, but did you hear anything about him on the grapevine?' A nonplussed look. 'I mean, on the same lines as McPhain and young girls.'

Bev answered with a three-second burst of bright laughter. 'Who, him? He doesn't know how. He might fancy a few sheep on the farm but that's all.' She looked up, still smiling. 'He's harmless. Honestly.'

Doubts, mounting guilt, swamped him like an inrushing tide.

Bev looked at him, the brashness, the boldness gone. A little-girl-lost look. 'Will I have to go back to the State Special?'

He emptied his mind. 'Off the record, what happened last night? What have you been up to?'

Bev left Hull after the last Arabian Nights show and was bound for London. She picked up a lift on the Humber Bridge in a lorry that was going to Skegness. The fairs there were laying off, too, at the end of the season but she found a job as a barmaid and a little place of her own where she'd stayed through two bracing winters and one summer season.

'Sure, I pose topless if I get a cash offer. It's the only

112

asset I've got. It's look, don't touch. This freak last night took some standard stuff for twenty-five pounds. Then he offers double for S and M shots. "Piss off," I said. "I'm not into porn."

'"OK, OK," he sez. "Just this little one." He pulls a silver dagger out a drawer, tilts back my head and sez: "I just want you to stick your tongue out and hold the point to the tip." I flipped. I admit it.' Her blue eyes burnt, angrily. 'But I don't want to complain about it. Like I said . . .' Her voice trailed. 'It's just more trouble.'

'We'll get you a lawyer,' said Jacko.

'No thanks. They all piss in the same pot. He wouldn't believe me.'

'A woman lawyer, then,' he added, firmly. 'Talk to her first. Then put into writing what you've told us. But tone it down a bit.'

'Lie, you mean?' A mouth-open, eyes-wide look of shocked innocence.

'Only a little bit. I mean, weren't you frightened for your life and acting in self-defence? Didn't he get his cut accidentally when you were trying to disarm him? Wasn't the equipment smashed in the struggle?'

'But that's perjury.'

'We'll show him your statement and, a pound to a pinch of shit . . .' Jacko had succumbed '. . . he'll drop all charges before his wife finds out. You may not have to give evidence so there won't be any perjury.' A shrug that said: Simple.

'You'll have to go back to some sort of hostel till the McPhain thing's sorted out. But I'll insist not the State Special. You give us a full statement about Uncle Mac with the names of all the girls he's assaulted. We'll have a crack at stepdad, too, but that will be difficult after all this time and without back-up.'

'Corroboration, you mean,' said Bev, very ladylike. She looked down and then, very sincerely: 'You two are shit hot, you know.'

If only you knew about the mistakes I think I may have made, thought Jacko, gloomily. I could be responsible for one of the biggest cock-ups in police history. He got up and folded the blanket. In the car, outside the jeweller's shop, he fastened the repaired bracelet to her wrist and she gently laid a soft warm hand on his. 'Thanks, old man,' she said with a smile of such affection that his heart was stilled. He smiled a fatherly smile.

15

William McPhain, bachelor, sat in a sound-proof interview room at Divisional HQ. A slight, nervous man, wimpish really, neat, dark brown hair, face pinched as though he had made a conscious effort to stay out of the sun. Across the desk sat Jacko in shirt sleeves and a WPC from Child Protection who monitored the tape recorder.

McPhain was not invited to take off his black tunic top or offered a cigarette from a packet of twenty Bensons which emptied as Jacko smoked one every fifteen minutes. 'You have been arrested following complaints of gross indecency and other sexual offences against young girl patients.'

'Like who?'

Jacko opened a manila folder and took a statement from the top of a thick pile which had taken a week to collect. 'Barbara Brown, who was . . .'

'A pathological liar.' A shifty smile. 'Caught her, have you? She's blaming me, I suppose. Been expecting this. She's raking all this up again to excuse her escape.'

Jacko began to read extracts but McPhain interrupted again. 'I've been through all this before.' A local accent, a reedy voice. 'She's a liar. I was cleared at an inquiry. I had witnesses.'

'Like who?' Jacko stole his question with an icy stare.

He named the three girls who gave evidence for him and against Barbara Brown (aka Beverley Beaumont) at the inquiry at Roselands.

'How very odd,' said Jacko, smiling, as he slowly slipped three more statements in front of him. 'We've talked to them all again, you see.'

He read extracts from new interviews which gave details of

what had occurred in the caretaker's flat at Roselands, grim things, vile things, to a father unthinkable things, all the more graphic by the matter-of-factness of the prose. McPhain's face froze. 'It's a conspiracy. That cow Brown has got at them.'

'They've not been in contact with each other since your old hospital closed.' Jacko leant back and strummed the desk with his fingers. 'Well, now, Uncle Mac. Explain yourself.'

He stuck out his stiff leg beside the table and rubbed it. Slowly, the confession came. That's nearly always the way with child abusers, Jacko found. Few ever face up to it first time round. Well, yes, he conceded there may have been a bit of horseplay ending in tears, so there may have been a few let's-make-it-better cuddles. 'I was only larking about.' For a while he stuck to a story that whatever happened was their idea, their way of saying little thank yous for the sweets and treats he bought them.

Finally, he was confronted with cannabis and hard porn, mostly paedophile, magazines found by the officers who'd stayed on to search his quarters after his arrest at the State Special. In a stream of tears names, approximate dates and most of the details flooded out.

He blamed variously an ex-fiancée who ditched him, shift patterns which made a normal social life impossible and his leg which, Jacko concluded bitterly, was not the only part of his anatomy which suffered permanent stiffness.

Jacko placed a photo of Tracey Smythe on the table. 'Ever seen her?'

McPhain studied the face with a look that changed from mild puzzlement to sweaty panic when he recognized her as the girl in the newspaper stories about the kidnap and murder in the forest. 'Oh, no. You can't blame me for that, surely? Not me. Never.'

He was asked where he'd been that day. 'Working,' he said without thinking.

Jacko shook his head, bottom lip over his top, pouting. 'Day off. We've already checked.' He asked for time to think. 'Certainly,' said Jacko. He stretched out the word, easy-going, be-my-guest, then suddenly leant forward, elbows on the desk. 'Ever been to Goose Fair?'

It took Jacko two cigarettes to pin him down to the fact

that he'd been to the fair on his own the Saturday night Jill Fisher disappeared. He claimed not to have noticed the Arabian Nights show or he'd have noticed Barbara Brown ('and I'd have reported her').

Another cigarette was spent on trips to Skegness which he claimed not to have visited during the summer Angie Stevenson vanished. And he hadn't a clue after all this time where he'd been the day Michelle Robinson went missing.

Never in his life, he protested, had he ever seen any of the four girls in the photos which, one by one, were placed before him.

'What are you saying?' He was fighting now, a rearguard action, the ex-soldier in him coming out. 'That I'm a mass murderer or something? I've harmed nobody. I've told you everything.'

Harmed nobody? thought Jacko, heartsick. The man's a fucking animal but he merely asked: 'Everything?'

'Everything.' Flat, final.

'Then what about Sam Pattinson?'

They had gone back twelve years, yet McPhain remembered the name instantly. 'You can't trust a word he says.'

'Ah,' said Jacko, 'but we have also interviewed the girl concerned.' This was true, a long, painful interview, but the girl was severely mentally handicapped and made no more sense than Pattinson. 'She's an adult now, you see,' said Jacko with an ambiguous smile. 'Old enough to vote.'

The stifling, fuggy room went silent except for the whirling of the tapes in the machine. McPhain looked from Jacko to the WPC and back again. 'Oh God, my God.' A wailing, a calling to prayer. 'I'd do anything to turn the clock back.'

They turned the clock back those twelve years. He was just out of the army, the wounded invalid, in his first civvie job as junior janitor at Roselands. Lots of patients from the juvenile ward came to his quarters when he was off duty. He read to them, told them stories, taught them simple card games. Good therapy, he claimed.

He'd given piggyback rides to this particular girl. A real tomboy, she was, so they'd reversed roles and one day, well, he couldn't help himself. 'I didn't go all the way. I stopped myself.' Premature ejaculation, Jacko guessed. An attempt, not the full act. Same as Michelle. A wave of excitement within swept aside all feelings of disgust.

Sam had been there in the room when it happened, sticking soldiers he'd cut out of a magazine into his paste book. He'd taken no notice, not a blind bit, of what was going on until the girl cried in pain. McPhain thought as he'd been trained to think in the army – fast. He ordered Sam from the table where he'd been sitting to the bunk and made him lie down with the girl.

He smeared wet, white paste with a brush from the paste pot on Sam's trousers. He showered, hid his underpants and changed back into uniform. All the time through the open door he told ghost stories – about devils and demons and what they could do to people who didn't tell the truth. 'And the truth is, isn't it, that you were playing and it slipped?'

'I slipped?' asked Sam, confused.

'No. It slipped. It. It. It slipped. Get it right.'

'It slipped,' parroted Sam.

'Remember. Get it right or the bogeyman will have you.'

McPhain left the room and made a noisy show of returning to find them side by side. Sam responded as coached and repeated it to the charge nurse whom McPhain summoned and eventually to the police and his solicitor. 'It slipped,' he told everybody who asked.

'God but it's weighed on my conscience. Never had a proper night's sleep since. I panicked.' He rubbed his leg.

A slight smile of justification through self-pitying tears. 'But I was right, wasn't I? He is dangerous. It was right to lock him away. He's back at the State Special, you know. In the security wing. They should never have let him out in the first place. I'm on outside villas and never see him. I haven't seen him since he left Roselands. But I know he's here. I read about him in the papers years ago. He killed that girl at the bus depot when they let him out, didn't he?'

'This girl, you mean?' said Jacko, pointing to Michelle Robinson on the table.

Gobbets of sweat broke out on his furrowed brow. 'You mean . . . It wasn't . . . You think . . .' It was all occurring to him very slowly and when it finally did he threw the top half of his puny body forward, his head on one side, his eyes pleading. 'No. No. You're wrong. Please believe me. You've got to believe me.'

He was always uncomfortable in the presence of psychiatrists; a mental hypochondriac who suspected at some time or other that he suffered from every symptom ever described in every diminished-responsibility hearing. The doctor added to this doomed feeling when he peered through round spectacles and pointed him to a black leather couch.

Heather and Sam's solicitor were sitting in the two matching chairs. Peter Hann was the son of the veteran lawyer who'd handled (mishandled, more accurately, thought Jacko) the cases from both Roselands and the Forest Coaches depot. He was one of the newer legal breed – mid-thirties, dark, athletic, a carefully casual dresser, avoiding the pin stripes of his father's generation in favour of the sort of silvery suit that dodgy car salesmen wear.

They had spent the day with Sam. Heather flicked open her notebook. 'From the window, we let him witness you bringing out McPhain in cuffs. He began to shake and point. "Mac, Mac. It's him," he said. "That girl. Got me in trouble." We tried to find out if he was talking about the girl at Roselands or Michelle Robinson at Forest Coaches but he's still not making sense.' She shook her head, sadly.

Jacko nodded, not surprised, and told them of his day. 'Which means,' said Hann, ponderously, 'that Sam's conviction for the Roselands offence is bound to be quashed.' Jacko chose not to answer, even with a nod. 'And it throws new light on the evidence against him in the Michelle Robinson case. He was only arrested on the basis of a conviction which no longer stands up.'

'But we can't use any defendant's record, true or false, in any trial,' said Heather, po-faced.

'The defence can.' Hann explained how. Here was a sick man, he'd argue, who had already spent five years at the State Special on the basis of a confession to something he didn't do. 'Any statement he gave you about Michelle becomes worthless.'

'What about the scientific evidence against him in the junk room?' asked Heather, doggedly.

Hann said he had spent all night with his father going through the papers. 'Our case would be that the body was dumped on him. McPhain brainwashed him. Michelle was already dead when he told Sam to gag and bath her, share the bed with her. That could explain all the forensic evidence. We'll want disclosure of exhibits, by the way, for re-examination. The influence McPhain held over him explains the partial confession he gave to you two.'

A dagger twisted in Jacko's heart. He turned to the superintendent, listening and watching, impossibly still, behind his desk. 'Why do some people make false confessions?'

He smiled, amiably. 'Some to escape forceful interrogation. They hope that the truth will eventually come out. What we call coerced compliance.' Jacko stirred unhappily. 'Others because they are publicity-seekers, maybe living out fantasies of committing headline-making crimes. Some accept that they did do it, for a while anyway. They readily take in suggestions offered by an outside party. That's internalized coercion.'

He pondered for a moment. 'In this case, on the basis of what I've heard so far, I favour the latter with McPhain as the third party.' Jacko's pain abated, but only slightly.

'We had a lot of problems when he first came here. Roselands ran a stick and carrot regime. Own up to a misbehaviour, like a smashed plate, and you'd be rewarded – but you'd be punished and so would everyone else in your dormitory for keeping quiet.' There was detectable disapproval in his gnome face. 'He was always claiming responsibility for things, little things which he could not possibly have done. To curry favour with his peers and the staff. It took time to wean him off it.' Jacko concentrated to ward off a desperate desire for another cigarette. He'd decided he didn't want stress-related addiction diagnosed. 'Added to that, he was very disturbed by people in uniform. He used to cower from them.'

Heather broke in. 'But not khaki uniforms. He had a poster of them in his bedroom, pastes them in his book.'

'Black uniforms, then,' said Hann. 'Further evidence against McPhain.'

'Let's see first if he's got an alibi for the day Michelle went missing.' Jacko gave a defensive shrug. 'In any case Sam's not much of a witness, is he? If he's not mentally competent to give evidence in his own defence, we can hardly call him as prosecution witness against McPhain, can we?'

'Is that still the case, doctor?' Hann asked.

'Very much so. He's still clinically unfit to plead.'

Deadlock, thought Jacko, gloomily. A dreadful deadlock. Hann saw the impasse, too. 'Then he could die in here; an innocent man.' Heather sucked in her cheeks during the long, brooding silence that followed.

Hann collected his thoughts first, addressing the doctor. 'He's been locked away twice now. Five years on each occasion. There's proof now that he didn't commit the first crime and grave doubts, to put it mildly, about the second. Until that's all sorted out legally, is there a possibility he could be transferred to one of your outside villas or a hostel to prepare him for release?'

A solemn headshake. 'That's a matter for the courts. Sorry.' Playing safe, mused Jacko, and who can blame him? Imagine the uproar if he granted Sam a bit of restricted freedom and he went off and committed the most minor of crimes. 'Bungling Doc Frees Madman – Twice Over' would be the tabloid headline. And what about you, you hypocrite? You've been assailing this doctor for years. He'd kept his criticisms private so he didn't go public with an apology.

'So . . .' Hann was looking at him '. . . either you withdraw the murder charge or my advice to his mother will be to seek a judicial review.'

With all the publicity that would entail, Jacko groaned inwardly. He didn't want that yet. He didn't want it at all to be totally honest, but certainly not without catching the real killer first. He pictured himself going to see Michelle's family to tell them: 'By the way, we're letting Pattinson go because he's the wrong man but, sorry, we can't find the right one.'

It was going to take time to check McPhain's movements. His great fear was that with the closure of Roselands all work records would have been lost. Without a confession, he might never have a case against him on any of the murders.

'It will be a couple of months before we could consider that sort of recommendation,' he said, playing for time.

'It's been too long already.' Hann knew where his legal duty lay. With Sam Pattinson. 'A month.'

The doctor intervened. 'It's no argument to say that Sam's happy here because I take the point he shouldn't be here. And I am as anxious as anyone to see justice done.' A smile of mischievous pleasure. 'After all, I would like the public to know that this hospital didn't free a madman to kill, though I doubt we will get an apology from the popular press.' Or, for that matter, from me. Jacko rebuked himself, wallowing in secret shame.

'But now we're getting close to the truth. A couple of weeks either way won't hurt and it will give us a little extra time to find the right place for him. These days, with so many establishments overcrowded or closing, that may not be easy. We've minimized his episodic tantrums but they do need chemical control. He'll still require substantial supervision.'

He suggested a compromise: 'Six weeks.' Hann and Jacko nodded.

The conference seemed on the verge of breaking up. Hann half rose and Heather picked up her handbag from the fawn carpet beside her chair but Jacko lounged back. The doctor peered at him, attentively. 'Can I pick your brains on something else?' Jacko had tried to sound languid but he saw Hann start to sit again so he turned to him. 'It's not about Sam.'

Hann signalled his intention to stay anyway by settling back in his seat. Heather rested her bag on her lap.

'For the sake of this bit of research,' Jacko began, careful over each word in Hann's presence, 'let's rule Sam out of it. Let's assume he didn't do anything. Full stop. Maybe McPhain did. Maybe not. Let's not jump to conclusions. Let's rule him out by name for the time being, too. Let's call the killer Mac.'

The doctor slid open a drawer in his desk. 'Mind if I smoke?'

'Mind if I join you?' Jacko stood to take one of the doctor's Rothmans and a light. 'Now,' he said sitting down as he took a deep long draw, 'Mac killed Michelle and dumped the body on pliable Sam at the coach depot. Sam, after all, mentioned Mac in his interviews. Right?' Hann and Heather nodded.

'A year later, Mac abducted and killed Angie Stevenson and hid her body. To cover his tracks and head off any hue and cry, a card is posted to her landlady which mentions the name Mac.

'The following autumn, a man calling himself Mac dated Jill

Fisher at Goose Fair, kidnapped and killed her and again hid the body.

'Last summer the same man attacks Tracey Smythe in the forest but this time we do find the body.' He detailed the PM's gruesome findings and Hann visibly flinched. 'What have we got, doc?'

'A complete psychopath, I'm afraid,' said the doctor without hesitation. 'Sadistic, clever and manipulative. A formidable foe. He knows the difference between right and wrong but ignores moral judgement for his own gratification.'

'Will he work to a pattern?'

'Not necessarily. The intervals between the killings committed by the Yorkshire Ripper, say, conformed to no set pattern. Anything from ten days to eleven months between attacks. Dennis Nilsen waited almost a year between the first two, then did more than one a month for a time. It's not a predictable moon thing.' He looked down at his tiny folded hands which rested lightly on the desk. 'If you're right, he's killed four times in as many years, the last time almost a year ago. You must accept the fact that he is likely to kill again when his urges tell him to and that could be quite soon.'

Jacko felt his stomach grinding. 'What happens to him between killings?'

The doctor considered his answer carefully. 'He could be living a perfectly normal life, sleeping with a woman who hasn't the slightest idea what he's up to. Maybe she satisfies some of his needs, but not necessarily. Maybe a prostitute does. Or chatlines. Or magazines. His relief, most likely, will be artificially stimulated.'

Masturbation, he means. I'll not make a note of that. We've all done so from time to time, Jacko acknowledged in a rare moment of total honesty.

'Sometimes fear puts them off for a while. Not remorse over what they've done, though they profess such feelings when they're finally caught. I never accept it. Fear of being caught can produce long periods of inactivity. But the more he gets away with, the greater is the risk that he'll succumb to future urges. In your scenario, of course, he still holds two bodies. Who knows?' He peered mournfully round his audience. The room seemed to have gone cold. Heather hugged her handbag as if it was a hot water bottle.

As he tried to digest this dreadful diagnosis, Jacko sat so far back that he was perilously close to the horizontal on the psychiatrist's couch and he pulled himself up.

The doctor asked a question that showed his grasp on what he'd been hearing. 'Tell me, why are you linking the forest case with the others? I can see the thread of Mac running through the first three but then you lose me.'

'The black home-made candle which violated Tracey in the forest.' He grimaced, apologetically. 'I know it's tenuous.'

The doctor looked up and questioned the cream ceiling. 'A serial killer who's into the occult? Mmmm.'

The temperature in the room seemed to drop several degrees more. Jacko had been on cases before where vandals, bored juveniles mainly, had daubed pentacle symbols on gravestones and splashed animal blood around churches but only now did it occur to him that he'd never asked the simplest of questions. 'What is the occult?' A helpless shrug. 'I mean, can you give me a quick idiot's guide?'

A flush filled his face at the crassness of his phrase but the doctor smiled. 'Technically, it means hidden, secret things – astrology, for instance. You can argue that Freemasons qualify.' Jacko's relieved grin tried to tell the doctor he was not talking to a member.

'They can be no more harmful than a UFO society. Some are esoteric in a civilized way and believe that after death they'll all go off to somewhere called Summerland which sounds a very pleasant place.'

His smile vanished. 'The problem comes with what's popularly known as devil worship. We've had a few adherents in our care. Lethal when combined with mental illness.' He shook his head. 'It's when occultists take what's called the Left-Hand Path that things become dangerous.' Jacko was lounging again, absorbed.

'That's the path to black magic and Black Masses. Sabbats, they call them. They're loosely based on the witchcraft purges of the sixteenth and seventeenth centuries. Witches were supposed to be impervious to pain. Bounty hunters would look for some skin deformity, a birthmark say, and prick it with a trick knife, the sort used on stage with a blade that disappears into the handle.' He demonstrated with his delicate hands, pushing a clenched right fist into his flat left palm. 'No cry of pain so another witch was denounced to be burnt at the stake.

'Some of the surviving ceremonials are interpretations of confessions extracted from so-called witches about things they were supposed to have got up to – initiations, human sacrifices and so on.' He shook his head in rejection. 'They were having their nails drawn at the time or worse and said what their accusers wanted to hear. Complete balderdash, most of it, fabrications, but all good grist to the mill for the established churches. Coerced compliant confessions, I'd call them, non-internalized. Not worth a light.'

'Much of it still going on?' asked Jacko.

'You get the occasional child abuse ring where there's unconfirmed rumour of rituals. Mainly, I suspect, it's just to terrify their young victims into submission with the abusers concocting chants and ceremony to give some credence, some cover, to justify their outlandish sexual tastes.'

Jacko nodded his thanks. 'Hope that helps,' said the doctor. Well, only sort of, thought Jacko. They had found child porn hidden behind McPhain's cistern but nothing on black magic or S-and-M which might link him to the killings.

He pulled himself upright but now the doctor lounged back. 'Any other similarities – time of day, for instance?'

Heather took over, well versed. 'Two early morning. One late at night. The other unknown.'

'How about the victims – social backgrounds, physiques?'

'The first, working class; the last, decidedly middle; the other two under-privileged. Two virgins. Two sexually experienced. All white, mid-teens . . .' She broke off and Jacko could see an idea dawning, actually rising, in a face that changed from pensive to wonderment, but the thought did not form quickly enough to prevent her stumbling with the words. 'All of them not terribly well developed, physically, I mean, but they all reputedly had . . .' she hesitated again '. . . well, sort of, noticeable, nice, er . . . shapely rumps.'

Hann, silent for some time, suddenly spoke. 'Hope to God you're wrong about this, Inspector.'

'Well,' said Jacko forcing a smile, 'we've been wrong before.'

Hann leant forward in his chair, looking from Jacko to Heather as he spoke. 'I don't blame either of you for Sam's position. I did a spell in Crown Prosecution before joining the family firm and, to be honest, I'd have sanctioned the charge on that evidence at that time.' Heather perked her head round towards him. 'The fault's ours and my father's mortified. He believes now he shouldn't have consented to a rubber-stamp committal for trial and gone for a "no case to answer" before the magistrates. He wasn't to know then that there'd be no trial. He's deeply distressed by it all. I've tried to tell him it's a defect in the law. I know it was well-meaning, trying to be humane so that people like Sam, suffering from mental abnormality, would not have to go through the fearful ordeal of Crown Court. But in this case it's led to unjustified, indefinite custody. The result is a grave miscarriage of justice.'

He looked down, face in anguish. 'I just wanted you to know that. That's all.' Heather was smiling quietly at him when he looked up.

As if caught by the climate of the confessional, the doctor said: 'How do you think I feel, having someone like McPhain on our staff and not detecting him?'

And you two think you've got problems, thought Jacko, hiding his deep despair.

After a day filled with child abuse, black magic and soul-searching, the conversation magically moved on to soccer and England's World Cup chances ('Nil,' said Jacko, knowledgeably) and Heather, who hated sporting talk, drifted out of the office – to freshen up, she said.

When she returned her brown eyes were happy and bright for the first time that evening and gleamed behind contact lenses.

They said goodbye and thanks to the doctor, and the three of them walked in single file down the stairs and then, Heather and Hann shoulder to shoulder, out of the foyer, polished spotless, and across the road to the car park with Jacko dawdling behind them, beset by depression.

On the way, Hann suggested a stop at a nearby country pub he knew for a drink and an evening snack perhaps, because – he was mumbling awkwardly – there was no one waiting at home for him.

'Good idea,' said Heather enthusiastically.

'No thanks,' said Jacko. He wasn't going to be a gooseberry tonight. His soul cried out for solitude.

Driving home, he thought of Mrs Pattinson, widowed now, alone, her husband killed by a heart complaint. Every year, for ten years, with a year in between, she had made this trip on this road by service bus to see her son. Every month for a decade, spring, summer, autumn, winter. And he pictured Sam then, marching through the frozen mud in the dark, under escort, to milk the cows. He'd give them names, of course, but they wouldn't come when he called and they would never look at him with the devotion he had found but once in his pitiful life. And who took him away from Max? He cursed himself.

On every visit Mrs Pattinson would have seen those State Special sights he'd just put behind him – the high walls, the glass-roofed refectory block that was really a punishment block for some patients who couldn't tell right from wrong, the tall chimneys visible from the kitchens and laundry where they worked, child labour in Dickensian conditions, black-clad guards with jangling bunches of keys, inmates wandering like zombies. Dangerous, some of them; but not Sam.

How many years had he got left to live now? A dozen, no more. Yet she'd never stopped believing, never given up on him. Where do you find that kind of faith? He would have accepted the inevitable, abandoned hope. Misery overwhelmed him, maiming him.

He was on a long straight stretch approaching the forest, deep birch woods fronted by bracken on either side, and he pulled into a sandy picnic area, empty, tourists gone, the sun that had shone all day behind hanging purple clouds.

Dying, that sun, he thought, mournfully, as he switched off the engine. Like Tracey Smythe a few miles down the road from here. Somehow – and this, he knew, was an unprofessional thing even to think – he'd never regarded her as his baby. She'd been handed down to him through the police chain of command.

But Michelle Robinson was his baby; his case from start to finish and, on a beautiful summer's evening, his thoughts went back to winter and he saw virgin snow lying over her grave in the silent cemetery, never to be touched or

127

soiled by human hand until it slipped away to join her at rest.

He sighed from deep within an aching heart. He'd let her down. He'd let Sam down. He'd let justice down. He lit a cigarette, wound down the window and looked over a pine-scented scene so peaceful that it pained him. Out there, he knew, just knew, lurked a pervert, a sadist, a satanist.

He did those things to Michelle, things I saw with my own eyes. And I had to close them. He framed Sam and I believed him, bought it. What a thick, stupid bastard.

Four years later, I'm certain, he did those things to Tracey, things I wanted to close my ears to when the pathologist briefed us. And his ears no longer heard the bird song all about him.

In between, still missing, Angie and Jill, both linked with Mac. Back at the State Special, when the doctor raised that nauseating notion about him still holding the bodies, he had automatically assumed he was hinting at necrophilia. Now he was thinking it through with a heaving stomach.

The candle in Tracey was made from human fat. How do you get fat? By boiling animals down. He wasn't digging them up. He was boiling them down. Oh, my God, boiling humans down. How can anyone . . . oh, dear God, what sort of man . . .

He opened his eyes with a start. Stop this. Now. You're a detective. Your job is to catch him, not analyse him. He screwed out his cigarette in the tray, extinguishing this thought chain.

He leaned his head back against the cushioned rest. Wintry thoughts lingered, thoughts of death. Years ago, on a road which crossed the one he had just driven down, there'd been a traffic pile-up in thick fog. One lorry caught fire. The driver was immovably trapped by his shattered legs. His door was buckled and jammed. One by one the heat drove his rescuers away. One was left. 'Don't let me burn alive,' pleaded the driver.

The motorist knew what he had to do, punched him once, very hard on the temple, knocked him out and ran, his clothes beginning to smoulder. Medical evidence showed that the driver had been unconscious when he was burned to death.

The coroner rebuked the motorist at the inquest. An act of mercy, maybe, he ruled, but unlawful all the same. Outside the court Jacko saw (and, after all these years, could still see) the lorry man's widow as she squeezed the motorist's hand and said thank you. Jesus, such courage. Such certain knowledge of what was the right thing to do. He doubted whether he possessed it in that kind of quality or quantity and he prayed he'd never be put to that kind or Mrs Pattinson's kind of test.

He massaged his forehead hoping to coax out positive thoughts. None came. He longed to have the Little Fat Man at his side, to draw inspiration from him, but he was gone. What had he once said? 'If we've cocked it up, we must uncock it.'

How? Positive thoughts now. Rule out Sam Pattinson. Go back to the beginning. Who's left?

In his mind, he drew a frame. 'In the frame' is an old CID catchphrase. Someone in the frame is a suspect. He wasn't sure where the phrase came from. It had nothing to do with framing someone with faked evidence. He guessed it meant keeping the face of a suspect in mind with a frame round it, like a wanted poster, brushing in details until the picture was complete.

As there was more than one suspect he listed their names like jockeys against numbers in the frame of runners and riders down at Colwick Park racecourse. It took two more cigarettes, much mental juggling and rejigging until he was satisfied.

No. 1 in the frame, the top weight, was McPhain with lots of form from Roselands to make him firm favourite, if not the racing certainty. He would not jump to conclusions. He had made that error before.

No. 2 was Keith Bannion, the security guard who wore a black uniform. His job with TVE Securities had brought him into close touch with Forest Coaches and Pattinson. Strands of Michelle's hair had been found in his truck. His firm, albeit a different department, owned the house where Angie Stevenson squatted.

No. 3 was Norman Hollis. He wore a dark boilersuit for his work which had given him access to Forest Coaches and Sam. He drove a Nissan Patrol which had conveniently broken down.

No. 4 was Nick James who, like his boss Hollis, had access to Sam at his place of work. His alibi had been his mother and mothers are the least believable of all alibi witnesses.

No. 5 had no name, the hit-and-run driver, never traced, perhaps one of the four further up his ladder. The driver may not have stopped after knocking down that woman cyclist because he had Michelle's body in his boot, on his way to dump her on Pattinson.

On the other hand, the hit and run may have had nothing to do with Michelle's murder. A time-wasting diversion, like the one detectives hunting the Yorkshire Ripper took over those hoax tapes with a Geordie accent. Beware blind alleys, he cautioned himself.

No. 6 was Colin Bates, a rank outsider admittedly, no known access to Sam, no truck. Another cigarette while he worked out what had niggled him and should have been spotted when he was watching that *Crime Catchers* programme with Michelle's parents years ago. It put a big question mark against his name. A pacemaker, maybe, who would lead him to the winning post before another innocent girl became the next mutilated, lifeless victim.

And he saw then what he had successfully shut out – Michelle, as he had found her. I'll catch him, he told her.

He studied the ladder-like frame he had painstakingly built during that hour, completely alone, on the edge of the forest and saw himself walking slowly towards it and stepping on the bottom rung.

Watch your back, Mac, whoever you are. I'm coming, you homicidal maniac, you sordid swine, you fuck pig. I'm after you. And this time there'll be no mistakes, no escape.

He was in the habit now and then of talking to himself very loudly and obscenely and he wondered what the superintendent back at the State Special would make of him.

16

'What the hell's going on?' said Detective Chief Superintendent Sherman as Jacko padded across the new gold carpet. He hoped he hadn't picked up dog shit on his worn out black shoes. He was deep enough in it already, by the sound of the Olympic Torch's summoning call.

The carpet was not the only change to the office. In place of Scott's cartoons hung carefully posed photos of family and career events, presentation shots, Sherman both giving and receiving, framed commendations and certificates. Jacko cringed.

That day's *Evening Post* was handed to him across the desk on which the bank of trays, neatly stacked, stood next to the half-filled spike of saved notes. He took the newspaper as he sat on a hard, high-backed chair, now known throughout the CID as the bollocking chair.

'Well?' asked Sherman before Jacko had time to read the story beneath a single-column front-page headline: 'Tracey: Man Quizzed.' 'Where did it come from?'

'Dunno.' A lie. He had leaked the story to the paper's crime reporter, a taciturn man so secretive that often his bosses didn't know where he got his info.

'I've already had Colin Bates on, wanting to know why he wasn't given it and if it counts as a clear-up,' Sherman continued.

Jacko put the paper on the desk and briefed him on McPhain's arrest. Before he was half way through he was interrupted: 'Do you fancy him?'

For Tracey's murder, Jacko realized he meant, and, to be honest, he didn't know. The health authority couldn't locate his work records. He didn't hold a driving licence and claimed never to have owned transport, which would have made him an unusual abductor.

'He's not a racing certainty.' Then, casually: 'One thing's for sure, though. It was McPhain, not Samuel Pattinson, who abused that young girl at Roselands.' He summarized his confession.

Sherman dismissed it too hurriedly. 'Not our fault. Doesn't affect our case against him on Michelle Robinson.'

'That's not the way his solicitor sees it,' and Jacko told him of Peter Hann's rereading of the evidence.

'What?' The simmering Sherman came to the boil, face reddening. 'You've been discussing this case with defence lawyers without having the courtesy to tell me?'

'Hang on a mo, sir,' said Jacko, unruffled, his cover story well rehearsed. 'So far this year on the Tracey Smythe inquiry, I've interviewed almost thirty convicted or suspected child molesters, many in the presence of their briefs. I can't come running to you every time I set up a meet. No one could have foreseen this outcome.'

Sherman subsided. 'Where does that leave us?'

'With six weeks to decide what to do about Pattinson.'

'That's up to Crown Prosecution.'

Jacko quite enjoyed this next bit. 'Hann wants disclosure on our exhibits.'

'Why?'

'For re-examination.'

'They were tested at the time.'

'They matched Pattinson's type. But with this new DNA, Forensics will be able to tell whether any semen stains bore his genetic fingerprint.'

Sherman showed no sign of detecting the import of what he'd heard. Jacko suppressed a smile. He saves every scrap of paper that passes over his desk, he thought, but disposes of evidence in an untried case. Still, he was technically the officer-in-charge, so let him work it out. Meantime, try this for size:

'We have to face up to a real possibility that while Pattinson has been languishing in the State Special for something he didn't do, the actual culprit has killed again and again and again.' And, as he filled out the details of the Mac connection, Sherman was visibly shrinking in the swivel chair.

132

His eyes closed. His chin sank in the direction of his tie. 'Shit.' He clasped both hands on his receding forehead as if to shield himself from the fan's fallout.

Jacko knew the feeling. He'd suffered, too, when the enormity began to register over what Bev Beaumont told him. The palpitations of panic – how much of the shit is going to stick to me? The pangs of shame – should I have done better? The hurt professional pride – will I be a laughing-stock when it all comes out? A dreadful moment in a detective's life. Yet he was totally unprepared for his response when it eventually came. 'That WPC in Skegness has certainly handed us a poisoned chalice.'

Jacko should have said: 'She deserves a commendation.' He said nothing. He kidded himself afterwards that he was too shocked, lost for words, at the sight and sound of a man professionally dropping dead in front of him, but he knew deep in his heart that he had funked it.

Sherman recognized immediately that he had exposed himself, and babbled about collective responsibility and the buck stopping here, patting his almost empty desk. Jacko, burning eyes on him, still said nothing. The man had died for him.

'Should I recommend the chief to bring in an outside deputy to conduct an independent inquiry?' he panicked on.

'That might attract premature publicity. We don't want to tip off the killer. Do we?' Pause. 'If the theory's right, all we've got on our side is surprise.' Another pause. 'It's early days.' He could see the relief spreading over Sherman's face, so cruelly he wiped it off. 'No doubt, it will come to that in the end.'

'What battle plan are you proposing?'

'A pincer movement,' said Jacko, catching the military flavour. 'A team working backwards, checking the timetable McPhain gave for his day off when Tracey vanished, trying to trace the crew and passengers on the bus he claims to have caught home from Goose Fair when Jill Fisher vanished, seeking evidence that he was in Skegness around the time the card was posted to Angie Stevenson's landlady. A team working forward from Michelle Robinson's death, turning over the suspects again. Vice and Child Protection are shortlisting other weirdos for us.'

'All right for manpower?'

'Provided I can keep Sergeant Hurst.'

A curt nod. 'What shall I tell Colin Bates?'

'Invite him round. I want to see him.'

A baffled look vanished as Jacko explained that he'd gone back over the Michelle Robinson file, played videos of the two *Crime Catchers* items during the search and recalled the question that had troubled him in an undefined way as he watched with Michelle's parents; insignificant then, crucial now.

Sherman got up quickly, eager to please, and walked to a grey steel cabinet where he opened the bottom drawer. He always kept all his old papers, he said fussily, as he rummaged. Once a quarter he emptied the spike on his desk and kept the scraps in old Jiffy bags, carefully dated. 'Never know when they'll be useful . . . Ah.' A puff of pride. He had found the bag for the first quarter of 1985.

He sorted through it and studied all the jottings he had made at the time of the Robinson case. 'No,' he said, finally, 'I never told him that.'

He looked pathetically happy at being of some use. Jacko rose. He had padded back across the carpet, not caring any more how dirty his shoes were, and was opening the door when Sherman asked: 'What's your role?'

Half-turning, half-smiling, Jacko said: 'It's a simple case of rounding up the usual suspects, putting them in a bag, giving it a good shake and seeing whose number comes up.'

The Olympic Torch had finally seen the light. 'Maybe we should have done that at the time,' he said, deeply unhappy.

He'll never speak a truer word, thought Jacko, closing the door.

Keith Bannion, Suspect No. 2, had just walked in the rain, a blue mac over his black uniform, through the barrier at TVE when Heather's car pulled up alongside him.

Jacko got out of the passenger seat and blocked the footpath. 'A word please.' He opened the back door. 'Hop in.' Jacko slipped on to the back seat behind him and slammed the door. Heather drove away.

'Where are you taking me?' Bannion asked, paling.

'For a ride,' said Jacko, without a trace of humour.

This was the way they'd decided to work during all interviews, Jacko as Mr Nasty, Heather as Ms Nice. They had no legal excuse, no reasonable cause, to arrest any of them or search their homes. They hit them hard and often right throughout the month. Chase, chivvy and unnerve them. Shake them up. Force a wrong move. The classic tactic of a detective with no real clue, no time to spare.

She parked by a wide river beneath a dripping plane tree. Jacko fished out a typed list from a pocket. 'I want to know where you were on these dates.'

'What's this all about?' he said, reading the list.

Heather turned in the driving seat. 'Just routine. We're cross-checking someone's movements.'

'Is it about the forest murder?'

'What do you know about the forest murder?' asked Jacko, swiftly.

'Nothing. Only what I've read in the *Post*.' A bleached look. 'It's just that, well, you know, I, I . . .' The shock made him stammer. 'I saw you up at her old man's place, Forest Coaches.'

He had seen Mr Smythe at the depot several times, he said, but had never spoken to him and had never seen his daughter Tracey.

Jacko pointed to the top date on the list. 'That was the day she disappeared. Where were you?'

A lost look. 'I can't remember. I don't keep a diary.'

Yes, he agreed, TVE Securities had clients up in the forest he sometimes called on but he couldn't recollect, after all this time, what run he had been on that day.

Jacko pointed to the second date: 'Last night of Goose Fair. Ever been there?'

Most years, he stammered, but on Thursdays, never Saturdays which were always crowded and the rides more expensive. Sometimes he'd stroll round on his own, but mostly with a gang from work.

The third item, the month Angie Stevenson disappeared. 'Were you in Skegness around that time?'

He shook his head. 'Not been for yonks.' He went fishing on most of his holidays, he replied to a chatty inquiry from Heather, and, no, he didn't have a girl-friend, not a steady one anyway.

Bannion recognized the last date without prompting. 'I've

135

told you all about that.' He didn't deviate from his five-year-old statement. 'As though it was yesterday. I still think about it sometimes. Poor girl. Is that loony still inside?'

Jacko stared at him. Heather nodded and smiled.

'That'll be all for now,' said Jacko and he made to open the door.

'Oh come on, sir,' Heather protested. 'Have a heart. Look at the weather. Let's drop him off at the bus stop.'

When she did, Bannion smiled his thanks to her and ignored Jacko. She shuddered dramatically as she drove away. 'What a creep.'

The following week they were standing next to an empty milk bottle knocking on the door to his end-terrace home. His scowl for Jacko softened for Heather. 'What now?'

Jacko walked past him without invitation and led the way into the kitchen. Heather pulled a blank postcard from her bag, a pen and the photo-copy of the picture card from Skegness with Angie Stevenson's signature. 'Just for elimination purposes, we'd like a sample of your handwriting.'

He sat down, with a troubled frown, and wrote on the blank card at Heather's slow dictation. He scribbled so fast that he easily kept pace with her. She looked over his shoulder. It was a spidery scrawl, worse than Jacko's, nothing like the writing on the clock tower card and he spelt accommodation correctly.

'Is this about that chap?' he asked.

'What chap?' Jacko spoke sharply.

'The one in the papers. The one you're questioning about the forest murder. Is he blaming me or something?'

Jacko ignored the question to ask one of his own. No, Bannion replied, he hadn't thought any more about his movements on the day of that murder.

'Then we'll have to ask your boss.'

'I'm not sure they keep the logs this long.'

They called at TVE Securities next morning. Its director Luke Tyson obligingly handled their inquiry. He summoned his secretary. A few minutes later she returned with a print-out.

On the day Tracey Smythe vanished, Keith Bannion had been on a round that took him to a new pit well south of the river.

*　　*　　*

136

Norman Hollis, Suspect No. 3, was roused from his bed at six on a wet, misty morning. Blinking, his face creased, he opened his door in pale blue pyjamas. 'You again?'

He pinked, embarrassed, at the sight of Heather. Without a word, he turned his back on her, leaving the front door open and disappeared from the hallway into a bedroom. Jacko took it as an invitation to enter.

Heather picked up a pint bottle of milk from the step and followed him into the kitchen where Hollis, in grey flannels, white vest and barefooted, joined them. He had washed but not shaved and had only run his hands through his tousled hair. 'Tea?' he said, with forced politeness, looking at Heather.

She moved gracefully to head him off at the sink. 'Let me.' She held up the milk bottle like a trophy, put it on a yellow work-top and picked up an electric kettle.

Hollis slumped down at a round table where Jacko was already sitting with the list spread out in front of him. 'I'd like to know where you were on these dates.'

He looked down at the list, then up at Jacko. 'Why?'

'It's known as the process of elimination,' said Heather, above the gush of water filling the kettle.

He turned to view her side on. 'Elimination from what?'

'Our inquiries,' said Jacko, unhelpfully.

Hollis watched her replace the lid and switch on before turning back to Jacko. 'Last time I saw you I was co-operative because I was as shocked as everyone by that dreadful business in the forest.'

'On that date you mean?' Jacko's finger shot to the top of the list.

His eyes stayed on Jacko and didn't follow it. 'I told you then that I had been in the vicinity but saw nothing and that I'd had dealings with Mr Smythe at Forest Coaches but not recently. I can tell you no more.'

'You can tell us whether you were at Goose Fair on this date . . .' Jacko jabbed the paper. '. . . or at Skegness around this time.' Another jab.

Hollis looked at him in disdain. 'Are you joking?'

His eyes went to Heather as she spoke from the work-top. 'It would help us test the veracity of someone else's story – someone we've got in custody.'

He answered without referring to the list. 'I've not been to anywhere on the Lincolnshire coast in years. And I've not been to that fair since I was a kid.'

Heather asked where the cups were and he directed her towards a white wall cabinet. 'Nice place,' she said, admiring fitted units, steel-rimmed, white plastic. 'Lived here long?'

'Almost a year,' he replied, confirming what they already knew. According to his old neighbours in Moorwood, he made a tidy profit when he sold his house in the village bought from the council under a government scheme that gave tenants the right of cut-price purchase. He'd moved to this place, a three-bedroomed bungalow on a big private estate close to a golf course on the outskirts of the city.

They knew the answer to the next question, too. He'd once had a young wife who'd walked out on him after six months. She asked it anyway. This is how Jacko had been trained and had trained Heather – know the answers to most of the questions they asked and ask them anyway, as bait, to trap suspects into lies. 'Does Mrs Hollis . . .'

He turned his back on her sharply and addressed Jacko just as sharply. 'Now is that all?'

'Not quite. Let's go through this day again.' He had reached the bottom of the list, the day Michelle Robinson had disappeared. 'You'll remember that I spoke . . .'

Hollis stiffened. 'You treated me like a criminal, inspecting my vehicle in full view of everyone. I've nothing to add about that either. Now, if you'll excuse me . . .'

Heather poured the tea into three cups. 'We were hoping you'd give us a specimen of your handwriting.'

'What for?'

'To rule you out of a case we're investigating.'

Hollis stood. 'Have you a warrant?'

'No but . . .'

'Then my answer is no.' He took the tea, walked to the kitchen door and looked back at Jacko. 'Drink your tea while I change, then I must go to work, I'm afraid. If you want to see me again, arrange it through my solicitor.'

Jacko and Heather sipped in silence. He returned, clean-shaven and wearing a smart blue suit, ushered them out and locked the door behind them. Heather followed his Nissan

Patrol to a huge colliery. He looked repeatedly in his rear-view mirror on the half-hour drive and strictly observed all the speed limits. In the pit yard she parked alongside him.

They walked together, ignoring each other, to the main offices where Hollis went on ahead and Jacko asked at Inquiries for the manager.

In his office, after phoning regional HQ for clearance, the manager promised them handwriting samples from all his field staff to compare with non-existent booking forms from hotels which had filed non-existent complaints about unpaid bills. 'I'm sure there's some mistake.'

True, thought Jacko, who'd made the whole thing up. All he wanted was Hollis's. 'Probably a travelling con man but we have to check these things.' He rubbed his hands enthusiastically. 'Let's make a start. Anyone around now we can talk to?'

Jacko gave Hollis a friendly nod and tapped his fingertips together, wearing his silly smile, as the manager explained the reason for his summons. 'What day are we talking about?'

Jacko gave the date of Tracey's disappearance. 'That certainly lets you out, Norman.' The manager looked up from his records, beaming. 'That morning, we had breakfast together before a site meeting.'

Heather beamed back. 'Ah, the man we're looking for didn't check in, though he had booked in writing in advance.' She was already fiddling inside her shoulder bag. 'Perhaps Mr Hollis wouldn't mind, purely for elimination purposes, giving . . .

'I'm sure he wouldn't . . .' the manager looked from Heather to Hollis '. . . would you, Norman?'

He took a blank postcard, put it on the desk and wrote left-handed, pushing his biro quickly across the card as Heather dictated. 'Will that be all?' he asked when she finished.

'For the time being,' said Heather, head down as she read the result. He had spelt accommodation correctly.

'Sod it,' said Heather, as they drove out of the pit yard. 'I was rather hoping it might be him. He makes my flesh crawl.'

Nick James, Suspect No. 4, was picked up on a cold, wet evening after a game of cricket at a Miners' Welfare. He had drunk more pints afterwards than he'd scored runs or taken wickets, whistling as he approached his car, a battered Hillman Minx, fumbled to unlock it, climbed in, wound down his window and fumbled again to find the ignition.

'You're nicked, Nick,' said Jacko who appeared out of the twilight.

He turned his head, face stunned, then filled with resigned submission when he saw the warrant card Jacko held up. 'Step out, please.'

He followed him to Heather's car parked some distance from the long, low Institute, a busy place, the social centre of any pit village. She turned on the interior light and saw that shock had left him sweating in his black donkey jacket over his whites. Hands gripping his knees, he squeezed himself into the back seat in a cowed, defeated huddle.

Jacko pulled out his list. His hand trembled as he took it. Some time passed before he collected his befuddled thoughts, but eventually he was sure he'd been on duty the morning Tracey Smythe had vanished. He worked in the wages offices now at a colliery the other side of a big estate from the Welfare. He still lived with his mum at Moorwood and travelled here every weekday.

He was certain he hadn't been at Goose Fair the night Jill Fisher disappeared. He played cricket for his village every Saturday and the teams always had a few pints together afterwards in the local, a sporting ritual. 'I didn't miss a Saturday match last season.'

But he hadn't had a single game the season before and he'd spent a week during the month that Angie Stevenson vanished in a union-sponsored convalescence home in Skegness. 'Smashed meself up, didn't I? On me old Honda.'

He looked at the photocopy of the picture postcard. 'Never seen it before. That's nothing like me writing.' He took the test to Heather's dictation, writing clearly on a blank card pinned to a clipboard.

'You've spelt accommodation with one m,' said Jacko, smiling grimly.

James looked at it again. 'Always was better at maths than English.' He still maintained that he had not seen or spoken to Michelle for a week before she disappeared or been inside Forest Coaches for several weeks before that. 'You're not still on that, are you? I thought you'd got that cleaner years ago.'

Then he added something that had Heather making notes to his dictation. 'I clocked on just before seven-thirty. Hollis had already booked himself out on an inspection and gone. I only went with him on big subsidence claims with a lot of measuring to do; Forest Coaches, for instance. A small house, say, he'd handle on his own. I expected him to be out most of the morning. He was in a real paddy over his truck breaking down. He was carrying a load of papers under his arm and began stuffing them in various files. Odd that.'

'Why?' asked Jacko.

'Well, why not leave them in his vehicle? Why not wait for the breakdown truck? He could have skived off for an hour or two. I would have done, with an excuse like that.'

Me, too, thought Jacko. 'What was the panic, do you reckon?'

James shook his head, dumbly. 'Dunno.'

'Is Hollis married?' asked Heather, knowing the answer.

'Dunno,' he repeated. 'Used to be. She pissed off. They reckoned in the canteen that he used to knock her about. Wouldn't surprise me. He's a mean bastard. I never liked working for him.'

'Got a girl yourself?'

James seemed to roll his head on his neck, uncomfortable to be discussing women. 'Sort of. Don't see her very often.' The teenage daughter of a miner, he explained, who had taken redundancy and returned to the family's native Tyneside.

'OK. Thanks.'

'Aren't you going to breath test me?' A look of sheer misery.

'Oh,' said Heather, 'I'm sure you were just turning the engine over to make sure the battery wasn't damp. You wouldn't have driven it, would you? You were catching a bus, weren't you?'

'Yes.' He was nodding his head vigorously.

Heather made a detour to Moorwood to drop him off. On the way, he relaxed and talked cricket, lamenting the rains which had virtually washed away local hero Richard Hadlee's farewell Test Match at Trent Bridge.

They pulled up at the end of his road. He opened the door with his left hand and reached across to touch Heather's shoulder with his right. She looked round at him. 'He was always so bloody close, Hollis, I mean. I can't prove it but I think he was on the fiddle. Back-handers maybe or his expenses. He's not done badly since, has he?' He smiled at her. 'Thanks for the lift.'

'Nice guy,' said Heather as she drove away. 'What do you think?'

'Not quite sure.' Jacko knew that sounded guarded, pessimistic even, but he was growing restive. He was sure, positive, there'd be another victim, and soon, but the killer struck so randomly that there was no way of predicting when or where or his next target and that awful knowledge haunted him.

The only hope of catching him was to make him break cover and he was beginning to think with ever-escalating anxiety that all this chasing and chivvying wasn't working.

17

'Heather Hurst.' Makatiel, Angel of Punishment, the Plague of Gods, repeated the name, rolling it off his tongue. 'A lovely sound.'

'Yes,' said Adam, the heavenly man, the one who has not sinned.

'Must see her again.'

'Yes,' said Adam. Eyes closed, he tilted his head back on the pillow. 'But how?'

Makatiel didn't answer straight away and Adam suspected he didn't know. Instead he said: 'She likes you, doesn't she?'

A fire within had burned away all images of other women. He thought about her constantly – at work, driving, about the house, and, above all, here in bed. He felt the first stirrings and tried to fend them away. 'Yes.'

'And she's submissive, isn't she? Look at the way she reacts to that inspector. You can tell she likes dominant men.'

Every free evening he'd taken a roundabout route home via the divisional police headquarters. At first, he had just driven past, hardly daring to look away from the road ahead in case he glimpsed her. He parked round the corner and scuttled in front of the station, furtively glancing up at the windows, trying to picture her at work behind a desk.

He began dropping into the modernized Victorian pub nearest to HQ in the hope that she'd be there and he could gaze upon her. He would sit alone at a corner table, drinking a half-pint, and allowed an illusion to wash over him – of her walking up, smiling, sitting down, chatting.

Cleverly he would work the conversation round to the police service and would ask: 'Is the discipline hard?' and she would say: 'I like it that way' and they would give each other looks of absolute understanding and they would leave together and come back here, to the Dark Room.

This evening he'd been sitting for an hour outside the pub in the pale sun on a bench at a wooden table with a view through flowering shrubbery of the car park and his eyes darted from red Fiesta to red Fiesta but he'd never caught sight of her. 'Not working, is it?' A long pause. Then: 'So we must plan. It works best when we plan. What was the best?'

'The Stevenson girl, I suppose.' He wasn't sure because, in reality, she's only been best of a disappointing bunch. None had come near fevered expectation but she was infinitely better than the forest fiasco which had rendered his nights barren for months.

'That didn't work because we didn't plan.'

'Is there danger in this?' asked Adam, cautiously.

'That's part of the excitement.' Makatiel laughed but only briefly and, in a serious voice, added: 'They have got their man. Or they think they have. It said so in the paper. She may not be back. You probably won't see her again.' Pause. 'Unless you act.'

'But how?'

Another long silence. 'Give her a ring. Most detectives seem to come in the pub around six. So give her a ring just before that and say you have information for her.'

'What if that inspector comes, too?'

'Tell her it's confidential.'

'What if he comes?'

It took him a long, long time to work it out and he ended with a master plan and a fallback position.

He would ring at about 5.55 and ask for her by name. If she wasn't in, he'd hang up. If he got through to her, he'd put on an accent and arrange a meeting. In a public place. Where he could hide and keep watch.

If she came alone, he'd reveal himself and feed a bit of the information, not much, just enough to get her interested. He'd tell her about the other truck in Moorwood that morning and who was in it. He'd say he didn't mention it at the time because it would have cost him his job. Besides, they'd got that loony for the Michelle Robinson murder and he didn't think it was that important. But now they were asking questions about other missing girls he realized it was his duty to come forward. Then he'd say he had extra evidence, to back up what he was saying. Photos? That worked with Michelle Robinson. Yes, photos back home, and she would come with him.

If the inspector was there, he wouldn't break cover but would phone again, say something unexpected had turned up and arrange another meeting. Sooner or later, she'd come alone.

He wouldn't make the call at the weekend. He wasn't sure if she worked weekends. Next week. Early next week. He could wait no longer.

'How does that sound?' asked Makatiel.

'Will she co-operate?'

'You know she will. Can't you just see her taking the Test? She wants you. She needs you.'

'Yes,' said Adam, stiffening, so hot, so big. 'Yes.' Burning now. 'Yes. *Yes.*'

18

Colin Bates, Suspect No. 6, arrived at the reception desk ten minutes late. He did not apologize. 'Alec not about then?' he asked, glancing round the panelled foyer at HQ.

Jacko introduced himself but the PR in Bates made it impossible to tell if he remembered him. His date with Chief Superintendent Sherman was for lunch but he didn't look hungry. A light blue suit was impeccably tailored around his still considerable paunch.

Off screen, he looked smaller, older and more podgy, an anachronism in a TV age which, it seemed to Jacko, was now all shoulder pads and cheekbones. He smiled sickly sweet little celebrity smiles at women who did flustered doubletakes as they walked towards the PR suite. And he talked of the senior officers he knew and the cases he'd solved for them.

They turned off the corridor into a small room where Heather was waiting. Bates gave her his yes-it's-me-you-lucky-thing twinkle. 'Mr Sherman thinks you may be able to help us with a small matter first,' said Jacko.

'Anything to oblige the constabulary.' A brittle little laugh, more than it was worth, from Heather for a line she had heard from him before.

Jacko nodded him to a couch and sat beside him. Heather moved to a TV set in the corner and squatted to insert a cream cassette into a video player beneath it. She was wearing a tight black skirt and even Jacko, a tit man, wished she wouldn't crouch that way. Bates stared fixedly at the view. She rose and smoothed the skirt when the screen flickered into white life. 'We'd like you to take a look at a couple of old shows,' she said as she sat at a desk near the set.

'How awful.' A chortle, quaintly old-fashioned, not in the least modest.

'This is your *Crime Catchers* of 5 March 85,' said Heather as the blue lights flashed and the tin whistles played.

They watched in silence the items about the building society robbery and the missing Michelle. When he saw and heard himself again, Jacko knew what Bates meant. It was like looking at old family or army snapshots of which people who have come into your life much later have to ask: 'Which is you?' In half a decade he had changed and aged when he wished for neither and he began to fret over the wasted years and the too little time that remained.

'Now,' said Heather, standing up, 'a week later,' and she replaced the cassette, sitting again to operate the remote control and fast-forward the new film to: 'Now for our clear-ups.'

Michelle reappeared with Bates saying: 'Thanks to you out there, we have traced that white sports car and not one but two Land-Rover type vehicles in connection with the hit and run . . .' Bates nodded, relaxed.

Jacko turned to him. He went straight in, like a smart-arsed TV interviewer savaging a guest. 'Who told you we had traced two Land-Rover type vehicles?'

'That must have been my understanding,' he said, cautiously.

'From whom?'

He thought for several seconds, looking away and then at Heather. 'I thought you said that in our office when you were checking on our patrolman.'

She shook her head. 'No. If you remember, we saw you with Mr Luke Tyson. As a result of his search through records, we interviewed Keith Bannion.' She sorted among a pile of papers on the desk, picked one out and read Bannion's statement. She put it down again. 'I certainly told everyone in the room, you included, that we had traced the white sports car and, through that driver, found out about Mr Bannion. He obviously was in one Range Rover but no mention was ever made of a second similar vehicle.'

'I thought you did,' said Bates, his mind elsewhere. 'It must have been Alec, then.'

'No,' said Jacko, flatly.

'How can you be sure?' He spoke crossly, taken aback.

Jacko added to his discomfiture. 'If a fucking fly crawls across Mr Sherman's desk it runs the risk of being spiked and filed away for future reference. He's searched his diaries and his pads. Not a mention. Take his word for it.'

'Must have been one of my assistants.' He pulled himself up physically and mentally out of his slump on the couch. 'I'm not a one-man band, you know.'

Jacko gave his head a slow shake. 'No. Courtesy of their union we have traced both your assistants at the time – one to London, one to Birmingham. Both say they washed their hands of it on the second show because you objected to running Michelle in the first place. Why was that?'

'Rubbish.' He tensed his pink flabby neck with an angry peck.

'Runaway girls are for the Sally Army, you said.'

'That's merely a news judgement. They're too commonplace to run every week.' A short worried silence. 'What are you suggesting?'

Jacko stretched his legs out. 'What I'm saying, not suggesting, is that you know something that we don't. Sergeant Hurst told you nothing about a second truck. Mr Sherman didn't. The hit - and - run was never solved. Yet you know about a second truck. How?'

'Are you suggesting I made a mistake?' His stiff neck had reddened. 'Or made it up, like some bloody tabloid hack?'

'I'm saying you are in possession of information that may be useful to us.'

'And that I'm withholding it?' A crimson flush now and his voice was rising with his blood pressure. 'After all the help I've given the police?'

'Oh, come on now.' Jacko sounded appeasing but the phrase was, in fact, a come-on. He was gearing up to say something he didn't believe, but that wasn't going to stop him saying it, to rattle his cage.

Bates bit. 'What?' He twisted round to face him, head on. 'Come on. What?'

'The force has been pretty good to you over the years.'

'You can't buy publicity like I give you.'

'Balls.' Jacko spoke it very quietly.

'What did you say?' Bates almost shouted it.

'I said balls. You make a good living out of us.'

'How dare you say that? How dare you?' His tubby body rocked and twisted and wobbled in unconcealed rage. 'I'll be taking this up. Worry not.'

'I'm not worried,' said Jacko, easy-going.

'I'll have you know . . .' Bates was jabbing a finger at him '. . . that what I do is in the public interest.'

'Of public interest maybe. That's not the same thing. Any public good that comes out of it is purely coincidental to the main aim of increasing your viewers and making more money for your company.' Jacko was speaking very fluently. 'The media report crime not to catch the criminals but because it's good reading or viewing. Let's be honest here.'

An open-mouthed silence from Bates, so Jacko went on. 'Take Jill Fisher. Too commonplace, you say. You weren't interested in finding her for her orphaned baby. You were only interested in not boring your customers with the commonplace because that's bad for business.' A pause, well-timed, effective. 'Or was there another reason for you originally not wanting to run Michelle?'

Hostile silence from both now, so Heather chipped in, picking her words, careful not to disclose too much. 'You see, we are on an inquiry in which TVE's name keeps cropping up. First, a TVE security van driven by Mr Bannion on the scene of a murdered girl and a hit and run which may or may not be connected. Then your programme, TVE-produced, and you can't explain how you know about a second truck being in the vicinity. We have another girl, another runaway we're worried about, who lived in a TVE Properties house.'

'Who?' asked Bates, with can-I-be-of-help? eagerness.

'Too commonplace for you to bother about,' said Jacko acidly and he looked down to light a cigarette.

'Supercilious bastard,' hissed Bates.

'Her landlady and neighbours . . .' Heather continued as though the bitter exchange had never taken place '. . . have complaints about their landlords – overcharging, financial penalties when they're late with their rent, subsidence damage, running repairs, not carried out . . .'

149

'Rachmanism,' Jacko interjected, noisily blowing out cigarette smoke.

'Oooh.' Bates leant back with a dull smile. 'Now I get it.' Another finger jab. 'You've been listening to those two no-hopers I fired and their pub gossip about Glynn Tyson's enterprises.'

'Are they wrong?' A neutral question, not a clue what he was talking about, fishing.

'Of course, they're wrong,' Bates snapped. 'I'm surprised at you listening to their tales. Bloody union malcontents. Give them a decent contract and a house to go with the job and, when they lose both, they whinge and moan and manufacture stories to flog to gossip columns.'

'So tell us about Mr Tyson and his enterprises.'

'Now see here.' He was nettled, frightened almost. 'You are dealing with a major media player.' Spare me the PR bullshit, thought Jacko. 'A highly reputable concern with sound, sensible diversification. All you've got is shopfloor tittletattle and manufactured stories.'

'Talking of which,' said Jacko, 'where did that information about a second truck come from?'

Bates bridled, his face a bluish red, veins throbbing at his temple. 'The more I think about it, the more I'm sure it came from one of those two incompetent sods. I never trusted them and neither should you.'

Jacko called a halt then. He'd pressured him close enough to a heart attack. Time to throttle back and let Bates make the next move. 'Perhaps you would check for us among your old files, like Mr Sherman did.' A winsome smile, faked and forced, like a TV newscaster moving on from death and disaster to one of those royal baby stories. 'Now, maybe, you'd care to join him for lunch. I'll show you the way.' He rose.

Bates suddenly seemed to have lost his appetite and mumbled about having enough food for thought and taking a raincheck with apologies. Jacko showed him the way back to the foyer, having to walk swiftly to keep pace. He couldn't get out of the place fast enough.

Not a word passed between them, which suited Jacko. He needed time for analysis. Who told him about a second truck? The only other truck they'd traced belonged to Hollis who claimed it had broken down on the ring road; a fact that was never made public. Was there a third truck that only Bates knew about? Or had he used his programme to cover for someone, to take the heat off somebody? He got no answers; just more questions.

'What the bloody hell's going on?'

Jacko was back in the bollocking chair and this time the Olympic Torch was pushing a closely typed two-page letter across the desk towards him as if it was too hot to handle.

'Dear Sir,' it started, 'We act for Trent Vale Enterprises and its president Mr Glynn Tyson. We have to hand a report of a conversation which recently took place between one of the group's most senior and experienced executives and two of your officers – DI Jackson and W/Sgt Hurst.'

The letter then quoted verbatim slabs of the interview with Bates, including Heather's long interjection listing TVE tenants' complaints and Jacko's one-word summing-up: 'Rachmanism.'

It continued: 'Having taken counsel's advice, we are of the firm opinion that slanderous and malicious allegations have been made against our clients. Some of the statements made also raise serious questions about your officers' ethics and intents.' It cautioned against 'accepting the word of politically motivated ex-employees,' and concluded with a threat of 'proceedings against you and your officers'.

The letter was addressed to the Chief Constable who had initialled a black rubber stamp block to indicate he had read it and 'Action: Head of CID' was stamped in red.

Jacko went through it again because he always had to reread legal letters to understand them, so he was only half aware of some of the things Sherman was grumbling about across the desk: 'Dreadful publicity . . . We need the media . . . Costly litigation.'

He looked up into his melancholic face. 'He must have taped me.'

'You mean, it's true?' Sherman rocked forward, astonished.

'Oh, yes.' Jacko looked away in thought, then back at the letter. 'When you fixed that lunch, did you tell Bates I wanted to see him first?'

'Of course not.' An offended look. 'What sort of detective do you think I am?'

Don't answer that, Jacko urged himself but not quickly enough to stop a happy smile drifting across his face.

'What's so bloody funny?' snapped Sherman.

He changed his grin to grovelling. 'Have another look in the Jiffy bag of your spiked stuff from the first quarter of 85, will you?'

'Now, look here Mr Jackson . . .'

Get off your agoraphobic arse, he thought impatiently, but all he said, very servile, was: 'It is important, sir.'

'So's that bloody letter.' Sherman pointed across his desk. 'Have you any idea . . . ?' He patted his head. 'Do you realize . . . ?' He shook his head, unable to articulate his anger. 'What are you playing at?'

'Carrying out your instructions, sir.'

'What?'

'You told me to stick all the suspects in a bag and give them a good shake. I think a number's come up. Please, sir.'

Sherman rummaged in the bottom drawer, returned to the desk and felt inside the bag as Jacko talked. 'Remember me sitting here, while you were deputizing for Mr Scott, getting advice from you on how to conduct myself after a verbal complaint from Norman Hollis's brief . . .'

'Fat lot of good it did . . .'

'What was the name of that lawyer?'

Sherman slipped free his old note. 'A Mr Hill of Gemmell and Co.'

Jacko looked at the letterhead: Gemmell and Co. And the signature: J.E. Hill. He closed his eyes and breathed in deeply. At last, a link between Suspect No. 3 and Suspect No. 6 from TVE. It was coming together. A buzz ran through him.

He explained to Sherman who said dismissively: 'Could be a coincidence.'

'Let's think about it. We turn over three suspects – Bannion, Hollis and James. Only Hollis has ever screamed for a lawyer. Next thing we know Bates is in here taping me and we get this . . .' he held up the letter '. . . from the same lawyer. Hollis must have told TVE we were on the warpath, getting close, and Bates came prepared with a tape recorder. Acting, no doubt, on

152

Mr Hill's instructions.' A thoughtful pause. 'It was odd the way Bates, a big-time journalist, never once asked why we were so interested in an incident five years on. He didn't ask because he already knew we've reopened that investigation. He's made his mistake. He's given us the missing connection.'

Sherman showed no sign of sharing his enthusiasm. 'Bannion could have tipped Bates. He works in the same building.'

This, thought Jacko angrily, is like trying to motivate a side of beef. He's three ranks above me, earns twelve grand a year more and he's bloody useless. He seldom thought finance but, when he did, he had begun unconsciously agreeing with Mrs Thatcher's value-for-money philosophy.

'We gave Bannion the hardest time of all.' Sherman winced. 'Not a peep about any lawyer. Not from James, either. Hollis and TVE are running scared.' He waved the letter again. 'This is a holding operation. To slow us down. We're getting close and they want me off the case.'

Sherman looked at him for what seemed a long time and Jacko's heart sank to his testicles which began to ache in advance of the kick about to be aimed there. He was consumed with a passion, a complete compulsion, to see the job through to the end. Now, he feared, he was about to be jocked off, dumped. He decided on quick buttering up. 'You could, of course, be right about Bannion. The same questions remain. Why should he or Hollis talk Bates into putting out misleading information? What's going on at TVE? What secret is Bates protecting?'

Sherman, undecided as always, asked a holding question: 'What is the present position?'

Well, said Jacko, urgently, anxious to show off his expertise, to prove himself indispensable, James had been cleared by his workmates. That left Bannion and Hollis, both alibi-ed for the forest murder by their bosses. McPhain was looking more and more doubtful. 'No vehicle on any of the four dates.'

Sherman slid another letter from his tidy basket across his desk and Jacko read that the Crown Prosecution Service had decided – 'in view of the additional surrounding circumstances' – to discontinue the case against Samuel Pattinson.

What additional circumstances? he wondered. Sherman, he

guessed, had told them the exhibits were gone but was admitting his cock-up to no one else. He decided not to pursue it. He wanted, so desperately needed, to stay on this inquiry.

Pattinson, the letter went on, would appear in court next week for the formality of having the charge of murdering Michelle Robinson officially and publicly withdrawn.

Fair enough, he thought. We owe him that. A warm feeling for Mrs Pattinson immediately frozen by the thought of facing Michelle's folks. He'd tell them before it hit the papers and the airwaves. But not yet. There was time. Still time. One more break and we're there.

'Let me tell you this.' Sherman was talking again, hands folded on the desk, trying to look and sound stern. 'The only reason I'm keeping you on this is because of your intimate knowledge of it. If you're right – and I'm still not convinced – that we have a serial killer on the loose, time is of the essence and it would be unfair to field a fresh team. I want no more performances like that.' He nodded at the letter Jacko was holding. 'It's bad public relations.'

'Yes, sir.' His contrite face, the one he wore for Jackie the morning after a wild night out. 'I was only putting them all in the bag and giving it . . .'

'That's enough. You're on your last warning.'

19

'Perfect,' Makatiel declared.

He was leaning on a yellow railing on the fourth floor of a multi-storey car park a few steps off Maid Marian Way, a dreary dual carriageway, looking down on a bar next to a hotel.

He had wandered round the city centre surveying the access to a score of pubs and hotels. A medium-sized car park right in the centre had a good view of an old railway hotel across a main road which ran up to the Goose Fair site but round the corner was the central police station. To the north, near the BBC building, two promising pubs but the vast car park opposite was underground. To the south, beyond the slabbed market square with its stone lions, a perfect car park alongside a huge shopping complex but no clear views of pubs, only the pinkish cream brickwork of the new Crown Court.

An overcast day, cool for July, but he strolled in one of his brightly coloured short-sleeved sports shirts, so passing girls would notice him. When none did, not even a glance, he cursed them under his breath: 'If only you knew. If only you knew what I've done to bitches like you.'

Out walking like this, he would picture himself on trial at the new Crown Court, the centre of attention, the nation's spotlight on him. He was annoyed, puzzled really, that the police and therefore the press had not cottoned on to all that he'd done. It would have been a turn-on to have the city's women in terror of him, like the Ripper had held Yorkshire in his grip. He visualized empty streets and deserted pubs and he would smile to himself. Irked that he'd never received the recognition he deserved, Makatiel once drafted a letter to the press, a long, rambling confession written in red ink, with satanic symbols in the margins, but Adam confiscated it and filed it in the Dark Room.

Once or twice he'd discussed the hunt for Tracey Smythe's killer with workmates and he'd said: 'I'd string the bastard up.' And he'd laughed aloud as he drove home but at home, in bed, both Makatiel and Adam accepted that there would be no trial, no State Special, no strait-jacket. If capture looked certain, he'd set fire to his private writings in the Dark Room and jump from the altar with a chain round his neck, make the headlines that way. He wondered if his workmates would remember his quote about 'stringing the bastard up' and tell the press. He hoped they would because it was, well, clever, ironic really.

Sometimes he worried how long Heather Hurst would last. In the Dark Room she'd see the two ghosts of his past sex life hanging on the wall. And she was a policewoman. Where would her duty lie? To him, Makatiel was almost sure, ninety-nine per cent certain; once she got to know him and had been initiated.

'But' – Adam, typically, raised the lingering one per cent of doubt – 'what if she wants to leave?' And Makatiel would shrug those broad, oiled shoulders and Adam would know what was meant.

'Let's go through it once more,' insisted Makatiel, a stickler for detail. 'Phone at 5.55 p.m. on Tuesday. Put on the accent. Tell her to meet you outside there at seven.' He looked down at the glass double doors to the Mint Bar. 'Inside's no good; could be a trap. Watch for a few minutes to make sure she's alone. On the phone, say you've useful info about Moorwood, 1 March, five years back. Over there, say it would have cost you your job to have come forward before but you realize now it's your public duty. If she presses, mention the other truck and who was in it. That's all. Leave out the rest. Say there's photographic evidence at home. Right?'

'What if that inspector's about?'

'Abort and try twenty-four hours later.'

'That might be best.' Adam was weakening. 'If England get through tonight to the semi-finals, the streets will be deserted with everyone watching TV. No one would see us.'

156

Adam had felt his own cold feet.

'Make a decision on the spot. Wait and see. She and that inspector can't always be together. They don't live together. He's too old. Besides, she wants to be with you. And when we get her home . . .' Adam was warmed again, all over.

20

'Are we still into kinky sex?' Heather's face was filled with such anticipation that Jacko wondered whether to plead a headache, wished she would leave him in peace to dunk his Hobnob, undisturbed by such offers first thing on a Monday.

'Can I have a nap first?' he said, guardedly, and she laughed, as he gulped his strong, sweet coffee. He ran the back of his hand across his mouth, recovering his man-of-the world pose. 'What ya got in mind?'

Her ex-colleagues in Child Protection had been keeping an eye on the red-light district for new weirdos on the patch, bizarre incidents worth checking on, remember? she asked and he nodded.

On Friday night, she began, reading from her notebook, a pensioner in a two-up, two-down terraced house close to the Goose Fair site, phoned the police.

She'd heard noises from next door – a steady twack, twack, twack to the accompaniment of low moaning and stifled groans; suddenly, the screams of children. She suspected child battering and, after dialling 999, peered through the curtains and saw a well-dressed man, fair hair, thirtyish, leave the house and climb into a black Range Rover.

Inside the house police found a woman, also thirty, and her teenage daughter comforting each other. Upstairs, crying, was a two-year-old boy. The children were unmarked but their mother, wearing a dressing gown, looked distressed. She said her boy-friend had lost his temper and beaten her up. Her daughter went further. She said she'd heard noises and came downstairs to find her mother naked, tied to a coat hook behind the door, being whipped.

The mother declined to make a complaint, give details or see a doctor. 'No convictions but she does work nights for a sex chatline.'

'So?' asked Jacko, only marginally interested in what consenting couples got up to in private.

'So we checked on the number of the car the neighbour noted. And' . . . her eyes teased him '. . . it belongs to Luke Tyson, director, TVE.' Jacko whistled shrilly.

She gave him a low, throaty laugh, very dirty. 'What's that worth?'

'Sorry, sexy. I think we're both going to be tied up for the rest of the day.' He was smiling, thinking: Terrific, aren't they – policewomen? It was the old borough force down the road in Grantham which first allowed them in; years ago, long before a local shopkeeper's daughter became Prime Minister. One way or another that town had a lot to answer for, but it would only be half a service without them. And a lot less fun. He was a great believer in work being fun. 'Some other time.'

Heather put a size five foot in the door when Carole Pagett tried to shut it in their faces. 'We're not going away,' she said standing with the other foot on the scrubbed doorstep.

Only the pleading of her daughter, playing truant, desperate to avoid giving the nosy neighbour more to gossip about, persuaded her to let them into the front room.

Heather cooed and fussed over the toddler and eventually they sat down on a fawn sofa whose springs felt second- or third-hand beneath them.

Jacko looked around a room, thinly furnished, smelling of stale smoke, but, apart from one dirty ashtray, very clean, with new, plain cream wallpaper so amateurishly hung that it had blebbed badly.

'No one's taking my kids,' Carole was saying, defiantly. She had long curly brown hair partly hiding a face as worn as the sofa. 'I've had Social Services round.'

The children were as clean as the house, in the same sort of Oxfam-clothed, make-do-and-mend way, and Heather complimented her. Didn't work. The daughter, who hovered at her

159

mother's shoulder, was saying nothing, except mumbling about how happy she was at home. Carole was saying less, shaking her head determinedly on the subject of Friday night.

Jacko fished for a £5 note, gave it to the daughter and asked her to take her little brother to the shops in his pushchair to buy something nice. The girl looked at her mother who nodded silent approval.

'Bright girl,' said Jacko when the front door to the narrow street closed.

'It won't work, getting them out the way like that,' she said, bluntly. 'I'm still saying nothing.'

'How old is she?'

'Fourteen.'

Jacko looked at her with a steady, serious face and spoke with a voice to match. 'We're on the murder of that fourteen-year-old girl last year up in the forest. We think she was tied up and beaten. That's why we're here. Not to take away your kids. To catch him before he kills another fourteen-year-old. And the psychiatrists tell us he will.'

That worked and Carole Pagett told her story over two of Jacko's cigarettes.

She'd had that bright daughter when she was seventeen. The father left them when she was eighteen. Her parents didn't want her back, not with a screaming kid. For ten years there were other bedsits, other rented terraced houses like this, other men and a few pin-money jobs when the girl was old enough for school.

Then she settled down in this place with a man. She knew he'd been to prison but thought he was going straight until the local CID called. The boy was born a week after the father got a handful (she knew the jargon for five years). 'I just can't manage on state benefits.' She flicked ash nervously into the already well-filled tray. The fact that she smokes as many as me can't help, Jacko thought.

She heard that Blue Line International paid £2.75 an hour. She was on the overnight shift while the kids were in bed. 'Cash in hand.'

She worked in top-floor rooms in an old warehouse. There were five others on her shift; all from the same kind of background, some of them prostitutes hiding from Vice or their pimps. 'The lines are red-hot, non-stop, most of the night. You've no idea what some of them want to talk about.'

'Try me,' said Heather.

'Put it this way. I only had one regular caller who was genuinely nice. A shift-worker, I think. No woman. Lonely, that's all. He just wanted to talk to someone. I could have liked him.

'The rest . . .' she shook her head so that her long hair brushed her dry, ivory-white cheeks '. . . wanted talking through the most incredible scenes. Showering together and the things they got up to in their minds with bars of soap was the mildest.'

Oddly, she found, most callers wanted to fantasize about being dominated rather than being masterful. 'We had this character, fifty if she was a day. She called herself Miss Strict. She used to take her false teeth out and make smacking noises.' Heather started to giggle. 'One punter was ordered to put spring-loaded clothes pegs on his nob. She held out the phone so the rest of us could hear him screaming. You have to keep them on. That's the trick. It earns you a bonus. Some are on for an hour. Most are calling from work or they're kids whose parents are out.'

One regular, she was saying, Jacko lighting her second Benson, so liked being masterful that he insisted on being called Master.

He seized on it. 'Master? Never shortened to Mass or Mac maybe?'

'No.' Her dull, brittle hair wafted across her cheeks.

'I had to go through the whole bit for him on the phone – please, harder, again, that's wonderful, more. One night he asked for a date. Against the rules, I told him. Fifty pound for just a drink together, he said. What would you have done in my place?' She looked round her place with its hand-me-downs.

'He's not handsome but smart, well off, a bit of a Yank accent, not too obvious. He offered me £150 a session. He came straight out with it. Take it or leave it. That's more than I earn for a whole week of nights. So . . .' Her voice trailed.

Heather looked sideways at Jacko. Her lips and eyebrows were downturned, her get-lost look. He had seen it many times in the Fairways when drunks tried to chat her up. Woman's talk, he realized. 'Mind if I pop on the kettle?'

161

he asked. Carole nodded. He rose and walked into the kitchen.

'What does he like doing?' asked Heather.

She hesitated, then undid the front buttons of her loose green dress and slipped it off her shoulders. She turned in her chair next to a table that looked like a wooden carved sky at night, white cup ring shining on the dark stained polish.

'My God,' gasped Heather, frowning so deeply that she viewed her back through the tips of her black eyebrows. 'The sadistic bastard.'

Carole buttoned herself up.

'Ever below the waist, backside maybe?'

'Always back and shoulders. If he creams his pants quickly, it's manageable. The other night he was very slow. Woke the kids.' She sighed, more hurt by what her daughter had seen than by her own pain.

'We know who he is, you know,' said Heather, watching for her reaction, as Jacko rejoined them with three mugs of tea. 'Luke Tyson.' Carole nodded.

'Are TVE Properties your landlords?' Another billowing headshake.

'Does he know the police were called?'

'Yeh. He called round yesterday. He's still in a flap. Gave me double to keep his name out of it. He won't be coming again.'

Jacko smiled without mirth. 'What will you do now?'

'Back to night shift, I suppose.' She shrugged her sore shoulders, resigned, defeated.

'Welcome, Master Tyson.' Jacko walked into the interview room and looked down on the sand-blasted features of Luke Tyson with malicious amusement.

He sat opposite him, and a sergeant turned on the tapes. Heather was being excused this interview. Some men, Jacko had told her, shy away from sex talk, especially specialized sex talk, in front of women. He did himself and he was nothing special and she'd nodded ambiguous agreement. 'You're under arrest on suspicion of committing bodily harm on Carole Pagett and other matters. You can have a solicitor present.' A wicked smile. 'Mr Hill of Gemmell and Co., I presume.'

162

Tyson's hives flamed. 'Let's wait and see.' Jacko summarized Carole Pagett's interview. 'You've got no case.' A calm transatlantic voice.

'Oh, really.' Still smiling. 'Why?'

'Because you've got no complainant. Neither of us are discussing it because it's a private matter. No complainant, no case.' Simple, he seemed to shrug. 'Anything that may or may not have happened was by contractual consent.'

Jacko sat back in the lip-pursed concentration with which he greeted any legal conundrum. 'Not so,' he eventually said. 'A suicide pact might be described as by contractual consent but, if you had the misfortune to survive it, you'd be sitting there, nicked.'

Tyson was unimpressed and every question was answered with 'Private' or 'Nothing to say.' During this short session, the custody sergeant interrupted to announce that Mr Hill had arrived and was demanding to see his client. Tyson surprisingly signed a slip of paper waiving his right to legal representation but he added: 'At this stage' and curtly told the sergeant: 'Tell him to wait.'

Jacko guessed he didn't want Hill, his father's confidant, present while this embarrassing subject was being discussed and stuck to it longer than planned, softening him up. What did you use on her? How often? Private. Nothing to say.

Then he came to the point. 'You see, we're investigating two other cases where the victims were similarly ill treated and, on both occasions, fatalities resulted.'

His hives turned ruby-red. 'Wrong. Completely wrong. It's madness.'

'We'll see,' said Jacko and he pulled out the four photos he always carried in an inside pocket and reshuffled the pack.

He played Angie Stevenson's picture first. No, said Tyson, with a deliberate headshake, he'd never seen her.

'She was being evicted from one of your houses.' Jacko gave the address and the landlady's name. 'Ever visited those premises?'

'The company's got scores of them.' But soon Tyson was agreeing that he'd visited the street when pre-purchase surveys were being made. He couldn't remember the landlady by name, 'but, obviously, if she had a lodger, she'd be told she was in breach of her tenancy agreement and told to get rid of her.'

'In a personal visit – by you?'

An exasperated face, blotchy. 'I've told you. We've scores and scores of tenants. I never handle problems like that. We've staff, a big staff, for that.'

Jacko played Tracey Smythe next but Tyson said the only time he'd been to the forest was when his mother took him to see the Major Oak soon after the family had come from Canada to settle in Trent Valley. His one and only visit to Goose Fair, he said, looking at Jill Fisher without recognition, was around the same time.

Another headshake when Michelle Robinson was placed before him. Jacko gave him the date of her disappearance but again saw no sign of recognition. Then the place and date together – Moorwood, 1 March 1985 – and a cautious flickering of interest.

Jacko looked down to study the vehicle ownership record he had extracted from the national computer. 'I see you're fond of Range Rovers.'

'Useful, in my job.' Another shrug.

'Were you running one in 85?' Jacko asked, knowing the answer.

'Ya.' An involuntary concession, immediately regretted with a frightened face.

'Colour?' His lips tightened. 'Olive,' said Jacko, softly. 'Right?'

His mouth was so tight now that the point of his chin had moved up a vertical inch and the lower half of his face looked squeezed.

'Mr Tyson, were you driving that olive-coloured vehicle down the main road in Moorwood on that morning?'

His hives whitened and his face had the appearance of being stung by a swarm of bees. He audibly smacked his tongue to unlock his lips. 'I'd like to see Mr Hill now.'

'Mr Jackson?' The 'm' came out through a nipped nose as though the caller had heavy hay fever. 'Glynn Tyson. How long yer keeping my son in?'

Quite apart from the shock of being phoned out of the blue

by the president of Trent Vale Enterprises, it was a difficult question to answer. Luke Tyson had been held overnight. Not one word did he add during a long and tedious interview in the presence of Mr Hill who answered everything with: 'We note your question.' And Jacko knew that Carole Pagett would not press a charge unless he could link him to the murders. 'We'll be seeing him again today.'

'Is it necessary to keep him in custody?'

'Bail might impede my inquiries.'

'Hill says you have to release him today.'

'That's down to my boss.'

'What the hell are you trying to prove?' Impatient, aggressive. 'Whaddya want?'

'Information.'

'He's got none for you. Hill's been all through the dates you raised last night. When that girl was killed in the forest Luke was in London and can prove it. He's had no personal dealings with the property where that other missing girl lived.' A sudden change of tone and direction. 'This is worrying his mother to death, you know.'

'I know,' said Jacko, sympathetically, then, steely: 'Mrs Robinson and Mrs Smythe have suffered, too.'

'For christsake.' Anger, hand-wringing, anger again. Some performance this, Jacko decided. 'You've got nothing on him.'

'We have as far as Carole Pagett's concerned.'

'Not any more. Hill saw her this morning. She's made no official complaint.'

'Doubled her money, did he?'

'You listen to me, you smart arse . . .'

'No.' Jacko surprised himself by an icy coolness that kept his inner rage controlled. 'You listen to me. You have a son, no daughter. You don't understand parents of daughters. A father may think it's great fun when his son starts screwing around, a chip off the old block, but if anyone touched his daughter, he'd strangle him with his bare hands. If we tie Luke into anything, Carole Pagett, as the parent of a teenage daughter, will come in with us and all your millions won't stop that.'

A good little speech that, heartfelt, and Jacko imagined him sagging. Very quietly, Tyson said: 'I don't approve of his sexual tastes but that doesn't make him a killer. All the evidence points the other way.'

'On the forest job, maybe, if what you say checks out . . .' A pause for thought-gathering. 'But what was he doing in Moorwood on 1 March 85? All the evidence on that murder connects with TVE. One of your security guards, Keith Bannion, patrols the scene. Norman Hollis works at the colliery up the road. When we question him he screams for your lawyer. Not the duty legal aid lawyer, like anyone else. Right-to-Silence Hill, your lawyer. Luke had an olive-green truck – the same as the vehicle that bowled over that woman cyclist and didn't stop. What were your friends, relations and employees doing at the scene of that murder?'

Tyson spoke slowly, clearer than at any time. 'He was engaged in kosher commerce. No one else's concern. Nothing to do with any girl or any murder.'

'What kosher commerce?' No reply, so: 'Was your son driving on that road that day?' Still nothing, so: 'Know what I think? I think your son is either a murderer or a hit-and-run driver. Five years ago we were getting close, so you or Luke used Colin Bates to take the heat off. He planted an item in his programme to give the public the impression we had all the information we needed about traffic movements that day. When I prove it, I shall do you all for conspiracy.'

A short laugh, more of a nervous cough. 'You'll prove nothing without my help. Now.' Businesslike. 'I've come up with a name.'

'Whose?'

'I'm a businessman. What's in it for me?'

'What do you want?'

'Luke out now. All inquiries into that hit and run dropped. It's five years old; just a minor accident. Nothing to do with any murder.'

Jacko rounded on him, astonished, unable any longer to check his anger. 'We're dealing here with someone who's killed once for sure, maybe four times. He's also framed an innocent, harmless boy. And you're bargaining?'

'All I've got is a name. No proof.'

'Let's have it then.'

166

'Not without an agreement. Luke out. Extraneous inquiries dropped.'

'I don't believe this. You think you know a suspected serial killer and you're trying to do a deal before you give him to me. What happens if he strikes again while we're pissing about?'

'That would be on your conscience, not mine. Yes or no?'

'I'd need my boss's approval.'

'Get it and you get the name. Not before.'

'Mr Tyson, this is not the conduct of a responsible citizen. You are holding vital . . .'

'Don't preach to me, please.' The 'please' came out like a word foreign to him. 'You get what you want. So do I.' Then, tantalizingly: 'You're warm, but not yet hot. Close but not close enough. I can help.'

'If you want a deal, get your mouthpiece Bates to put it to his old friend Sherman.'

'Colin seems to have lost a little credibility.' A shallow laugh. 'You ordered Luke's arrest. You get him out.' Jacko fell silent. 'Mark this.' A menacing tone now. 'Fail and all bets are off. No name, not another word. Never again.'

The phone went dead.

'No deal,' said Sherman, walking into his office where Jacko waited, lounging, cross-legged, in the bollocking chair.

He'd referred it all the way up to the Chief Constable, he said, as he sat down wearily. 'He's expecting the sky to fall in on Thursday when Pattinson comes out. Demands from civil liberties, mental health pressure groups and rent-a-quote MPs for an independent inquiry. He's already in touch with the Complaints Authority over setting up an outside investigation. It's inevitable, isn't it?'

Jacko nodded. 'We had a prima facie case. The rest was up to the law. And the unfit-to-plead law is a bad one.' Sherman's look told him he was unconvinced so he added: 'Peter Hann, Sam's lawyer, sees it that way. They're campaigning to get it changed.'

The Olympic Torch drew in breath. 'How would it look if young Tyson's London alibi starts collapsing and we've let him go without a court order? Sex maniac son of millionaire freed to flee while sick innocent man is held for five years. Think what Paul Foot would make of that in the *Daily Mirror*.'

'Can't we take away his passport? Maybe his old man would trade in the killer's name for bail.' Jacko knew he was sounding desperate. Any deal was better than letting a serial killer roam the streets.

'Whose name?'

The question had preoccupied him all afternoon. 'It has to be Bannion or Hollis.'

'You admit yourself both are alibi-ed for the forest job.'

'But not Michelle Robinson.'

'Possibly he wants you to think that, to steer you away from his son, get him out and away from our jurisdiction. Anyway, Crown Prosecution have already been told to apply for the longest custody order they can get so . . .' an end-of-subject shrug '. . . it's not on. Chief's orders.'

Jacko wouldn't let it drop. 'Look, we can't prove this the old-fashioned way. After this time lapse, we're not going to get sightings of vehicles. Your mate Bates saw to that. We need inside info and old man Tyson's got it. Surely . . .'

Sherman pitched himself forward. 'The answer is no. Now, the chief wants you in court when Pattinson appears on Thursday. No off-the-cuff quotes to the press. Refer all inquiries to the PR who'll have something prepared.'

'Saying what?'

'Man in custody, looking at similarities with other cases but not saying how many. He doesn't want a panic. He's not convinced by the serial theory and neither am I.'

Jacko hardened his face and voice. 'We've got two bodies and two girls missing and every instinct tells me . . .'

Sherman broke in. 'Frankly, my instinct tells me your obsession with it may have clouded your judgement.' Jacko gritted his teeth. 'So, at noon after court we want you at division for a hand-over briefing.' Jacko stared hard, mouth hanging open. 'We're fielding a new team leader.'

'What?' Jacko uncrossed his legs and stamped his feet firmly on the carpet but could still feel, actually felt, it being pulled from beneath him.

'A PR exercise. Anyone associated with the original Pattinson arrest is . . .' He looked down to his empty pad as though seeking a compromise word and settled for 'compromised' but Jacko knew he really meant 'discredited'.

'For fuck's sake.' An angry throaty growl. 'I've been working seventy hour weeks . . .'

'You . . .' a stiff horizontal finger pointed at him across the desk '. . . are confusing effort with result. We needed a result and you haven't come up with one.'

'We're close.'

'You've been saying that for five weeks.' He dropped his finger and voice. 'You're overdue for some leave so take some.'

Jacko still pretended he hadn't heard. 'We're very close. Give me a deal with . . .'

'No.' His finger was up again, vertical, wagging. 'Listen to me. You're a throwback, out of fashion. Policing today is about being sensitive to public pressures and perceptions, not Ramboing around, setting up deals, making intuitive judgements and . . .' he lowered his voice and head '. . . political statements.'

A long memory, five years old, unforgiving and unforgivable, thought Jacko. He folded his arms but not with defiance. 'It's about catching killers and . . .'

'And,' Sherman interrupted, 'working within the system. You're always bucking my system. Look how you made a present of our case on Pattinson to his solicitor. You have no respect for conventions.'

'Respect has to be earned. It's not a God-given right. Conventions have to be questioned; otherwise, we'd still be doffing our helmets to drink-driving squires while nicking their servants for biking without lights.'

Sherman flushed. 'What are you saying?'

'What I'm saying is that if Pattinson faced trial tomorrow he'd walk free because we've disposed of all the exhibits. And that's not down to me.'

Sherman stood, white-faced, quivering. 'Out of my office.' And he added a thunderous: 'Now.'

Jacko, shaken, rose but still faced him. 'What are my orders?'

'Fill in the next thirty-six hours on loose ends. Take some leave after the briefing. Spend some of that time considering your future and we'll discuss it when you get back.'

Jacko walked briskly to the door and turned. 'Any ideas?' He was smiling his malicious smile. 'I mean, have you or the chief any ideas for cracking this case?'

'Just shut the door,' said Sherman, quietly, looking down at his blank pad with a blank face. And a blank mind to match, thought Jacko bitterly. He closed the door.

21

Two messages awaited him when he got back to the incident room soon after six. 'Hill of Gemmell and Co. phoned. "All bets are off," his client said.' Heather looked up from her notes. 'What's that mean?'

In too much of a turmoil to stand still, he paced as he told her of Sherman's decisions. Shadows fell over her face. 'I don't believe it.'

'Neither do I.' Exhausted now, he lowered himself on to his swivel chair and sat forward, round-shouldered. He'd never felt so gutted, such a failure.

She sighed and shook her head, groaned, cursed and finally fell silent.

'What's the other message?'

'Eh?' She was lost in thoughts. 'Oh. A phone call just before you came in. Odd really. Refused to give his name and said he had info about Moorwood, 1 March 85. I'm seeing him at seven.'

Jacko frowned. 'Recognize the voice?'

'No.' She looked away. 'Geordie accent but . . .' she chewed her lower lip '. . . a bit phoney somehow.'

He asked for a verbatim and she closed her eyes behind her red specs to recall all she could as she'd only made a note of the time and place.

He: 'Sergeant Hurst, please.'
She: 'Speaking.'
He: 'I've some information that may be useful to you.'
She: 'What about?'
He: 'Moorwood, 1 March 85.'
She: 'Who's speaking?'

171

He, evasively: 'It's a bit difficult to talk.'

She offered to see him at work or at home but he said: 'Outside the Mint Bar, next to the Albany. Seven o'clock.'

She: 'I'll be wearing an almost black suit, frilly white blouse and red spectacles. How will I recognize you?' But he rang off.

A distracted headshake, thinking. 'Could be someone from inside TVE who's heard we have locked up Luke Tyson. The first worm coming out of the woodwork, perhaps.' She looked at the clock on the cream wall. 'I'd like to stand you a drink, but . . .' She stood.

He sat still, head hanging, a small bell ringing within it. Go home. Get out the holiday brochures. For a second he saw himself snoozing on a beach but the alarm bell rang loudly. 'Hang on. I'm coming with you.'

'He asked for me.' A touch of petulance.

'Listen. Whether Sherman believes it or not, we've got a homicidal maniac out there. It's one thing to chat up a known snout. You don't need anyone else around. But an anonymous caller? And you a woman?'

'A policewoman.' Definite petulance.

Christ, he thought, irritated, it must be quicker to train those Brooke Bond monkeys than some policewomen. 'We don't know who he is. The Robinson case hasn't had a mention in the papers since Pattinson was sent down. And this guy knows the date? After all this time?' His voice was rising. 'I said I'm coming and that's that. I'll stay out your way.' A sly grin, a low voice. 'I'll watch your back.'

She gave him her get-lost look, very petulant now.

'Where is she?' He had been in position for fifteen minutes and she was five minutes late. His hands gripped the yellow railing on level four of the multi-storey car park looking down on the entrance to the Mint Bar. His other self was beside him, at his shoulder. 'Where the hell is she?' On the very brink, Adam had always been the most impetuous.

'Wait,' said Makatiel, the calmest in a crisis. 'Just practise what you have to say. Introduce yourself . . .'

'She knows me,' Adam snapped. 'She likes me.'

'Say you're sorry for tricking her into a meeting but you're very worried. Look very worried.'

'I am very worried.'

'Tell her about the truck and who was in it. Admit you should have owned up before but you were scared of losing your job. If she wants to take you to the police station, say there's photographic evidence back home that she should see. Suggest you both go to collect it first. If she takes you to the station, just make a statement about the truck and the men. Don't mention the woman cyclist. Not yet.'

Adam mentally nodded, stone-faced. 'Where . . .'

Heather rounded the corner from Maid Marian Way, walking leisurely up an incline, back erect, hips rotating. 'Oh, my God.' Rainforest heat forced open every pore, like stepping into a Turkish bath. He felt, saw, his body glisten. His penis rose within his Y-front, a snake up a tree.

Heather stopped in front of the glass doors and looked up the gloomy narrow street, shaded by a bridge linking high buildings either side.

'Make sure she's not followed,' whispered Makatiel, urgently.

'Is it safe?'

'Wait.'

Heather turned and faced the main road, a side-on view. She planted her black shoes two feet apart, bowed her back, fingered the small of it, then ran her hands down her buttocks to smooth her creased skirt.

A volcano in the depths of the steaming rainforest erupted. He squeezed his eyes shut and turned abruptly away from the wall and ducked into a squatting position behind a car. He threw his head back and clasped his stomach with both hands. 'Oh no. No. Now look what she's made me do. With all this waiting. The bitch.'

Jacko had circled the block twice, stopping at each end of the short, steep street. Second time round he browsed for a moment at the touristy T-shirts, mugs and wicker baskets in the windows of the Tales of Robin Hood exhibition and smiled at a notice warning children of an adventure they might find scary.

173

He turned into St James Street, ignoring Heather on the opposite pavement, walked up the chilly, echoing stairwell of the car park, opening the spring-loaded door at every level, glancing over the bonnets along the walls. No one, nothing suspicious.

He echoed his way down and crossed the street, prettied up with young trees and black old-fashioned lamp standards. 'Let's knock it on the head.'

Heather nodded. 'I'll stand you that drink.'

She led the way down two flights of steps to the bar. He peeled off, heading for a corner table where blue lights and a juke box video screen hung from a low ceiling. She joined him with a white wine and a lager. 'Sorry,' she said, handing him his glass.

'Probably some crackpot.' He didn't want to think about it, just drink up and go. To be with Jackie, his son and his dog. They'd have him home soon – for good.

He looked at Heather. Keen as a spring wind still, he thought, dropping everything for this wild goose chase. Maybe she had nothing to drop. The red specs were back. She hadn't mentioned Peter Hann for a couple of weeks. On the shelf again, he feared. These days he often found himself worrying about her with almost parental concern.

'Come on, Jacko. There's still time. Let's think.' Pause. 'What do you make of tonight's little episode?'

'Pointless to speculate.' A shrug, unenthusiastic. 'Whoever it was got cold feet. But remember this. Never meet an anon tipster without back-up. A known informant anywhere, any time, but not an anon.'

She nodded, apologetically. 'Whose name did Tyson want to give you?'

'Hollis or Bannion, I think. Who else has TVE got to trade in?'

'What have we got on Bannion?'

'On Michelle, her hairs in his truck and that shaggy dog story to explain them. On the forest, alibi-ed by Tyson.'

'And Hollis?'

'Again an alibi on the forest. On Michelle, he claims to have been given a lift from his broken down vehicle on the ring road by some Good Samaritan who, thanks to Colin Bates, never came forward.'

'What's the connection between Hollis and TVE?'

Jacko lit a cigarette. 'In Glynn Tyson's entrepreneurial world, kosher commerce equals swindle.'

'A swindle involving Norman Hollis.' Heather theorized. 'Which, in his job, would make it a property swindle. Selling off unwanted NCB housing stock to TVE Properties at under value. Turning a blind eye to inflated subsidence claims. Something like that?'

Jacko got up, went to the long bar and returned with two more drinks. He'd been thinking on his feet and resumed the speculation when he sat down. 'Something that Michelle Robinson spotted at the estate agents where she worked. She could have seen a lot of confidential paperwork. Maybe a neighbour or a friend had recently bought or sold a property and she had an idea about true market prices.'

'Maybe,' said Heather, uncertain.

They sipped in silence and Jacko felt the shot of zest that Heather had injected ebbing away. She started the next line of thought. 'What did Michelle tell her young sister that morning? What was the last thing she said?'

'I'm seeing someone. It might be some good news.'

'What's good news to a girl of sixteen?' asked Heather and she answered herself, a woman's answer: 'An admirer.'

He shook his head, instant rejection. 'She had a steady and was turning down other offers from the likes of Nick James.' Silence, then speculatively: 'A job?'

'She'd got one. She was happy and doing well.' Heather wrinkled her nose. Her nostrils twitched. 'Her dad's job.'

Jacko leant back and looked at her in admiration. 'That's it. Her dad wasn't going to get his job back after the strike because he'd damaged Hollis's car while he was picketing. She knew Hollis. He lived round the corner then. She went to see him and said: "Either you save my dad from the dole or I'll blow the whistle on your swindles."'

He was speaking fast, buzzing, revived. 'He killed her to silence her. It wasn't a sex crime at all. It was made to look that way. To fit Sammy's past. He killed her at home, not in the junk room. We read it wrong from the beginning. He was driving the truck with the body in it when he had that accident. He couldn't stop. Not with Michelle in the boot. He dumped the body on Sam. He knew him and the dog. He had access to the depot from handling the Forest Coaches subsidence claim.'

The wonderment on Heather's face slowly drained. 'How does Luke Tyson fit into all of this?'

She left him in meditation and fetched two more drinks. 'Blackmail.' Heather answered her own question again as she sat down. 'Luke was Hollis's paymaster on behalf of TVE Properties. Hollis went to him and said: "I killed to keep her quiet, to protect you as much as me. The police are closing in and I need your help."'

'Makes sense, I suppose.' Jacko was depressed again. It meant, of course, that Sherman was right and he was wrong. There was no serial sex killer. Michelle was a one-off. 'But how are we going to prove it? It will take Fraud months to work out any swindle. I've got a day and a bit before the Home of Rest.'

Heather patted his hand which rested on the table. 'We need to sweat him.'

'He'd ask for Right-to-Silence Hill and we won't get a word out of him.' Doubts flooded over him, drowning hope. 'Anyway, I'm sure Luke Tyson was the hit-and-run driver. His Range Rover is the perfect fit on the description.'

Heather's face was slowly refilling with that wondrous Eureka look. 'Let's assign two officers to see Luke at, say, two-fifteen. At Central nick, not our place. Let's pull in Hollis at the same time. Both will demand Hill. Who will he rush to first? Who pays his salary? We could have Hollis to ourselves for hours. Divide and rule.'

Good thinking, thought Jacko, but only for a second. 'He won't talk unless we can scare him. We need an arrestable complaint. If he is on the fiddle, who might he have put the bite on? There must be a way in.'

That evening they broke the law. Both had extra drinks which took them over their limits when they eventually drove home.

But over that unlawful one for the road they worked out a way in. He wasn't sure about it. But, if it worked, he saw himself walking into Sherman's office, telling him he'd got Michelle's killer. Maybe not the forest killer. Maybe not a serial killer. But Michelle's, and she was his baby. And now Sherman could stick his job. He'd go out in style.

* * *

'Sorry,' said Adam. A shamed voice.

'It's all right,' said Makatiel, very understanding. 'But she came, didn't she? And she came alone.'

Moments now, long moments, without a word, without a thought.

'Tomorrow's much better,' said Adam, anxious to make amends. 'The streets will be deserted because of the big match on TV. Hardly a soul will be out. Let's think.'

Silently, a new plan, a better plan, was forming. 'Phone at the same time. Give her your name. Your proper name. Tell her you've got some good stuff. Here. She'll come in her car. No one will notice. Nobody will be about.'

'And then?'

'We know what will happen then.'

'But if she won't co-operate?'

'Kill the brazen bitch.' He hated women who touched private parts in public places and where she'd touched herself was his property, very private indeed. 'Kill her. Then let's get out. Go. Anywhere. Start again. A spree. A killing spree. Kill. Kill. Kill.'

'Yes. Yes. *Yes.*'

22

MOORWOOD, said the roadside sign. Jacko looked at the dashboard clock and pointlessly worked out that it was five years, four months, three days and two-and-a-quarter hours since Michelle Robinson was last seen alive by anyone other than her killer. He felt ancient.

'Blast,' said Heather, nodding to the trip meter. 'Just inside the lunch limit.' They could only claim a meals allowance if they were outside a set radius from HQ, a rambling old manor on the Fosseway south of the river.

'We'll say we had a call further up the road,' said Jacko. 'Bung in a few extra miles, too, to reclaim last night's booze.'

A cold, grey morning, more like January than July, and Heather's streaked Fiesta splashed through swirling rain. Just before the landscaped slag heaps it turned off the main road into Forest Coaches.

Mr Smythe was waiting for them in his first-floor office which looked down on the wired compound. His face was a waxy grey, like the clouds outside, his neck too thin for his unbuttoned collar. He had withered ten years in ten months and seemed to have missed out on his forties, which Jack looked upon as his finest decade when experience gained and enthusiasm retained combined to produce his best work. 'Some news?'

'In a roundabout way,' said Jack as Heather sat down. He carried on to the window and looked out. 'You'll remember we arrested your young cleaner after we found the girl from the village down there five years ago.'

'I've always felt bad about hiring him.'

Jacko turned. 'Well, don't. He didn't do it. We're releasing him tomorrow.'

'Good Lord.' His face was immobilized as Jacko explained how the impending quashing of Pattinson's previous conviction had led to a review of the evidence.

'Always thought he was harmless,' said Smythe. 'I'm delighted for him.' The cloud lifted briefly to let in a glimpse of warmth, then descended just as quickly. 'Awful though, for him and his family. All those wasted years. And for that poor girl's parents.'

Jacko stood over him. 'Whoever killed Michelle Robinson may also have killed Tracey.'

'Who?' Smythe lifted his head and his voice, a demanding voice, wanting information, his right. 'Do you know who?'

'We've got someone in custody and are interested in a second man. But between them they are alibi-ing each other and we need your help.' He took the easy route in and, no, Smythe said, while he'd heard of the Tyson family, he'd never had any business dealings with TVE or any of its companies, apart from that *Crime Catchers* interview with Colin Bates before Tracey was found.

'But you do know Norman Hollis?'

'Yes.' A nod, a long sigh.

'Tell us the circumstances.'

Forest Coaches, he said, put in an application for subsidence compensation when the old prefabs cracked and crumbled. Hollis came from the colliery to inspect the buildings. About this time Sam Pattinson joined Forest Coaches, under a charity-sponsored scheme to find jobs for the mentally handicapped.

'We know you had a row on the phone with Hollis,' said Jacko. 'What was that about?'

'I thought he was dragging his feet. The buildings were an eyesore. I wanted to replace them.'

'How did it resolve itself?'

'I had to wait eighteen months before I got a settlement and then it was only moderate.'

Jacko lowered himself on the edge of a chair by the desk and leant forward, speaking softly. 'Was that all there was to it?'

'What do you mean?' A soft voice, cautious.

'Yesterday someone in this case offered me a deal, a bribe almost. I had to report it because that's my duty as a law officer.'

He had rehearsed that line carefully, conscious that Smythe was a magistrate but anxious not to labour the point.

Smythe looked down at his papers, silent.

'We do need your help,' said Heather, smiling encouragement, on cue, part of their strategy.

'What if you're wrong?' He didn't look at her.

'What if we're right?'

He looked now, still dubious. 'I don't see how it fits.'

'You remember that about the time Michelle vanished there was a hit and run just down the road?' He nodded but only vaguely. 'We never found that truck. What if it was his?'

'I see,' he said, eyes back on his papers.

He blew out, as though smoking, and began to talk with his chin on his chest. 'After that row over the phone, he came to see me here one lunchtime. He said there was a big backlog of work on claims but there was a way of expediting it. He offered to put in a report that the buildings were in a dangerous condition, a safety hazard. He'd lose my original claim form and bump up the price a bit. He wanted half the difference.'

'What did you do?'

'Told him to get lost.' He was facing Heather now. 'How could I, in my position, condone that sort of thing?' A slight shrug. 'Besides, I'd decided I was in no hurry. Some of those militant pickets were damaging property. Why build a new place to have it burned down?' Another shrug, uncomfortable. 'I waited till it was all over. I got it. Eventually.'

'But you didn't report it?' He shook his head. 'Why not?'

'All he'd have to do was deny it. I had no proof.'

'But you're a magistrate. People will believe you.'

A hunted look, trapped. 'I was on good money from the board at the time, a big contract. I didn't want to rock the boat.'

The truth of his own words hit him then. He'd bottled out of his civic duty for business reasons. Guilt swamped his face. 'Everybody's at it these days. MPs on their freebie foreign trips. Civil servants retiring to their lucrative consultancies. Trade union leaders with their overseas conferences. Company golf days for clients. Tax fiddles ...' Hindsight, Jacko diagnosed smugly; self-justification. 'Bumping up out-of-pocket expenses.'

Jacko's wrinkled face filled with guilt too.

'You've been arrested on suspicion of corruption,' said Jacko and he cautioned him. 'You have the right to a solicitor.'

Hollis, thin lips pressed together, nodded towards a cream phone on the interview room desk.

'Be my guest,' said Jacko, pleasantly.

Hollis picked it up and tapped a number. Lips hardly moving, he asked for Mr Hill. Then: 'Where?' and 'When?' His face purpled. 'As soon as possible, please,' he said and put the receiver on the cradle. 'He's busy,' he said, still looking at the phone.

'I could have told you that.' Jacko used a taunting tone, his clever dick voice.

'I'm saying nothing till he gets here.' A determined face, eyes hooding, bringing down the lids, drawing a blind.

Jacko ignored him, addressing Heather. 'Hill's representing Luke Tyson at Central nick.' Hollis stared vacantly across the desk. 'What a busy man.' He was giving the impression of talking to himself. 'So we'll just sit and wait.' Wait they did, in silence, a long silence, broken in the end by a constable bringing in a tray of hot mugs. Jacko drank his as he smoked a second cigarette.

Between sips Hollis held his mug close to his face as if in need of its comforting warmth. The sips became gulps as the tea cooled and he put the mug down on the desk with a bang. 'What's this about?'

'Subsidence,' said Jacko, quietly.

Silence again. Hollis began to fidget in his chair and asked to go to the toilet. Jacko nodded again, couldn't-care-less, and the constable went with him.

When he had gone out of the room Jacko surrendered to his mounting tension, wringing his hands so tightly that his shoulders caved. 'Shit.'

Heather gave him a confident smile. 'Patience, Jacko.'

He looked relaxed again, all-the-time-in-the-world, when Hollis resumed his seat.

Another wordless five minutes, half way down a third cigarette. Hollis's knees broke into slight spasms as he jerked his heels off the floor, fractionally but rapidly. He stilled himself.

'I'm not carrying the can for all of this, you know.' He licked his dry lips.

'No one's asking you to.'

'Leery bastard.'

'Who?'

'Tyson. I knew we'd never get away with it.'

Over the next two and a half hours it came out in dribs and drabs and he spent a long time on the events of 1 March 85 because he regarded clearing his name on a hit-and-run crash as far more important than back-handers which he saw as perks of his job.

Towards the end Heather walked out with exasperation on her face, exhaustion in her step. She was replaced by an inspector from Fraud, who would take over the investigation and, for his benefit, Jacko summarized what had gone before.

'So it amounts to this, does it, Mr Hollis? And correct me if I'm wrong. You first met Luke Tyson when you were inspecting one of TVE Properties. You agreed to speed up and increase his subsidence claim?'

'It was his idea. I went along with him because I was in money trouble.'

'Right through the strike, you took money from him?'

'Never more than a few hundred. Just to get me settled after my divorce. I wanted out but he kept coming back. He'd got me by the short and curlies.'

'But you did try to put the bite on Mr Smythe at Forest Coaches?'

A helpless sigh. 'Talk about messing your own doorstep. I felt sure he'd turn me in when I found out he was a JP.' He collected himself. 'But it came to nothing. I didn't make anything. Anyway, the damage was worth more than he was claiming.'

'Meantime, you and Tyson were getting slack with the paper-work. Right?'

'Head office had their hands full.'

'Let's go over 1 March again.'

The night before, he said, Region phoned to tell him to get the documents out for a snap audit. He was short of several altered papers. He arranged to meet Tyson at 6.45 a.m. in a layby on the ring road. He drove in his brown Nissan Patrol to keep the appointment. Tyson was waiting for him and handed over the documents.

'My truck wouldn't restart. Flooded, I suppose. I had to leave it there in the end and jump into his Range Rover. I wanted to be back before my assistant started so I could file the stuff. He drove like a bloody lunatic. Coming up the main road he clipped that woman on her bike. She flew over her handlebars into a hedge. He didn't stop. Reckoned he couldn't. If we'd been seen together, someone might have twigged us.'

Hollis phoned Tyson to tell him that the CID had linked the missing Michelle Robinson with the hit and run and had examined his vehicle. Hill phoned back and ordered him to say nothing to anybody. 'I told him I was worried that Luke's vehicle would be traced. He said they'd make sure TV publicity was kept to a minimum.'

'When did you find out that we had arrested Luke Tyson?' Jacko asked.

'Hill phoned me yesterday.'

'Did you call our police station last evening and arrange to meet Sergeant Hurst?'

'Why should I?'

'To get your side of the story in first, before Luke blamed the lot on you, perhaps?'

'Is he?' Jacko kept very still. Hollis shook his head. 'No. Not me.'

'Now,' said Jacko. 'You knew Michelle Robinson as a near neighbour. Did you see her that morning?'

'No.' Very positive.

'Could Luke have seen her?'

'No.' Less positive, followed by doubt. 'Not unless he picked her up after he'd dropped me off and turned back towards the ring road.' Certain again. 'But I never saw her. I would have recognized her. The last person I would have wanted to see when I was with Tyson would have been Red Robbo's daughter. No, I'm sure he couldn't have seen her.'

'Did you see a white TVE Security van?'

'Yes.'

'Where and when?'

'It came to the colliery about ten minutes after I got back. That's its routine. Forest Coaches first, then us.'

183

'And you're sure Bannion didn't see you and Tyson together?'
'I don't think so. Tyson or Hill never mentioned him.'

Jacko went in hard, Mr Nasty. 'I put it to you that you and Tyson picked up Michelle and you killed her because she had seen the two of you together.'

'That's crazy. If Luke is telling the truth, he'll back that.'

'Did she ever call at your home and plead for her dad's job and ask you to drop your complaint?'

'Never. No. Never.' He was shaking his head, furiously. 'Her whole family was giving me the cold shoulder. They weren't talking to any strike breakers. We hadn't spoken in a year. Anyway . . .' a confused frown '. . . that cleaner at Forest Coaches killed her, didn't he?' A shocked pause. 'Didn't he?'

Tired eyes, sad eyes, the eyes of his team latched on to him as he slumped down in his chair; defeated, depressed eyes, the dressing-room eyes of a World Cup team which had just run their legs off for their country, played their hearts out, strained every muscle and still lost.

He took off his spectacles and rubbed his own. 'Knock it on the head for the day.' He replaced his glasses and explained that he was being taken off the inquiry and why. He'd dreamt of quitting on a high, a big celebration, a trophy held high, with a happy farewell speech but, in the end, it came down to this: 'Thanks very much for all your efforts. No one could have had better workmates. Stick with it under your new governor. I know that you'll get there in the end.'

There were groans and obscenities. Computer screens were switched off and covered. Raincoats were collected from a stand by the door. In twos and threes they shuffled out with forced smiles and half-hearted waves and only Heather was left.

She got up, walked behind him, bent and rested her chin on his right shoulder. She clasped her arms in front of him, squeezing, bringing the left side of her face so close that the frames of their spectacles clashed. 'Good try.'

'Not good enough.' He shook his head so that hers had to move in time. 'I was hoping for something for the Robinsons.' A poignant pause. 'I'll drop in on them on my way home.'

She released her grip and straightened. 'What about the England game?'

He glanced at his watch: 5.50. 'Should be home for seven.' He twisted and raised his head towards her. 'What are you up to?'

'Got a date to watch it, too.' An agonized face from her, a puzzled one from him.

'You hate football.'

'There's always half-time for a romp on the sofa.' She laughed and hugged him again.

'Fifteen minutes? I run into extra time these days.'

'Boasting,' she said and kissed him lightly on the temple.

'Who's the lucky man?'

'My Peter of course.'

'I thought that was on the blink.'

She pulled away, surprised. Then she smiled her understanding. 'Oh, these.' She tugged her red specs down her nose. 'He likes them.' She shrugged, nonplussed, no accounting for tastes, she seemed to be saying. She picked up a pile of statements and walked on to a steel cabinet. 'Sod 'em. They're all idiots at HQ. Let them do all the work and worrying for a change. I'd settle for regular hours.' She turned towards him, smiling, comforting him. 'And so should you. Jackie will be pleased to have you home for a while.' She lowered her voice, switched off her smile. 'But I'll tell you what. I've loved every minute I've worked with you.'

He was watching her without really listening to her. He had seen this see-if-I-care bravery before. She wore it when love affairs ended to hide her private hurt. A hard, wasted day and she still looked and smelt lovely in a simple, pale yellow dress, not thick enough, really, for a cold day like today, fastened at the back so that when it was unbuttoned Hann would see the best view of her first. A twinge of anxiety gripped him, a father's feeling for a daughter who had grown up too fast. 'Me, too.' He rose, walked to the door and put on his raincoat over his grey suit. 'See you tomorrow.'

He closed the door and walked down the corridor. He heard a phone ringing behind him. Not my case any more, not my baby, he told himself. Fraud will take the corruption;

Traffic the hit and run. He had nothing left. Let Heather answer it. She was still on the case, not him. He was washed up, finished, a has-been without a case. He did not turn back.

23

'Mr Jackson there?' A man's voice when the der-derring of a public box stopped as the coin dropped.

'Just gone,' said Heather. 'I may be . . .'

'Heather Hurst?'

'Speaking.'

'It's Mr Keith Bannion.'

'Oh, hallo.' She didn't like men who introduced themselves as Mr and she didn't like Bannion but she was pleased the call wasn't to cancel her date with Peter Hann, so she sounded pleased. An awkward pause. 'Can I help?'

'I have some information for you.'

'What about?' Rapid breathing, so she repeated the question, adding his first name. 'What's the information about, Keith?'

'I'm very worried.'

'No need to be.' Syrupy smooth. 'Is it about TVE?'

'Yes.' He sounded surprised.

'Have you heard about Luke Tyson?'

'Only gossip at work. This is more than gossip.'

'We might be interested in that.' She wasn't sure how much more they needed. 'Let's talk.'

'Not at work.' Alarm in his voice.

'Of course not.' Syrupy still, for she could fizz for a man, even a man she didn't like. 'After work. When? Tomorrow?'

'I'm away tomorrow. I could make it tonight.'

'Won't you be watching England?'

'Not interested.' A speedy explanation. 'I'm going night fishing a bit later.'

'When, then?'

He ignored the question, speaking hurriedly again. 'I'm not on the phone.'

'Here or at your home. When?'

'I've got some good stuff at home.' Pause, then softly: 'Pictures.'

Heather perked with interest. 'Of what?' No response, so: 'Of documents?' Still nothing, so: 'When can we see them?'

'I shouldn't be doing this.' Anxiety followed by calm. 'But you were decent to me and what's happened's wrong.'

'Whatever's convenient.'

'I'll be home for an hour from seven. It won't take long, will it?'

Heather calculated quickly. It was 5.53. She could drop in on Peter at the Playhouse Bar where they were meeting for a quick drink, put the order for take-out Cantonese lemon chicken on hold, double back to Bannion's house for a quick look and listen, just to get a feel for his info, and still be free by half-time. 'Seven then. And don't worry, Keith. We won't allow anything nasty to happen to you.'

She wondered about ringing Jacko at the Robinsons. Best not to disturb a delicate meeting like that, she decided. Besides, Bannion was known to her. It wasn't as if the call had been anonymous.

She collected her brown trench coat and striped brolly from the stand. She'd go alone.

'He's out on his rounds,' said Mrs Robinson, ushering Jacko into the empty lounge.

'This weather?'

'Chasing slow payers. He'll catch 'em all in tonight.'

They gossiped until Mr Robinson came in at the back door, waxed coat dripping. He called a greeting from the kitchen. He changed into grey slacks and a white T-shirt before entering the lounge, the best room. He'd lost weight climbing his window cleaner's ladder and looked fitter than Jacko had ever seen him.

'Here,' he said, ripped a can of lager from the plastic bindings and handed it to him. He walked barefoot to the TV, carrying his own can, and switched on. The old pros on the studio panel were warming up with clips from earlier rounds.

'There's something important I've got to tell you,' said Jacko from the couch. Mr Robinson turned down the sound and walked in front of Jacko over the half-moon mat to his easy chair in the corner. 'I wanted you both to know this before it's on the radio or in the papers.' He breathed in deeply. 'Samuel Pattinson is being released tomorrow.'

'What?' Mr Robinson gripped his green can so tightly that lager bubbled out of the hole where the ring had been pulled back.

'He didn't do it.'

'Oh, Lord,' gasped Mrs Robinson, eyes shut.

Her husband groaned. 'Hell fire. You're all bloody mad, man. You let the sod out before and that cost my daughter's life.' He was frothing like his drink and his wife gave him a withering look.

Jacko quietly explained why Pattinson shouldn't have been in the State Special in the first place and how the evidence against him could no longer sustain a charge.

'You made a mistake, you mean,' said Mr Robinson. Jacko nodded, barely noticeable.

'Which means the real culprit's still out there,' said Mrs Robinson. She flicked her head towards the window and the wet, dismal street, and Jacko knew she was thinking of her daughter who would walk home when it was dark.

'We've reopened the case.'

'After five years,' snorted Mr Robinson. 'The trail is as dead as our Michelle.'

'Don't say that.' His wife snapped at him. 'Don't you ever say that.'

All three looked at the TV, not hearing it, not really seeing it. Jacko ended the silence, doing the PR bit, half-heartedly telling them of the number of people they had questioned, the new operation that was planned, the hopes for an early breakthrough, the expected reawakening of media interest.

'Those ghouls will get no help here,' said Mr Robinson, sourly.

Wasting my breath, thought Jacko, but who can blame him, having to go through all that unspeakable agony again? 'I'd best be making tracks.' He nodded at the screen. 'I want to see this.'

'You'll not make it,' said Mrs Robinson. 'Watch a bit of it

with us.' A warm invitation, greeted with an icy look from her husband.

'Oh, no . . .' He started to push himself up.

'Please.' She placed a hand on his arm. She looked at him pleadingly, buying his time, and he suspected she was not quite ready to handle her husband on her own.

'OK. Thanks.' He sat back. He'd make a run for home at half-time, he decided.

'Turn it up, then.' She spoke sharply at her husband who heaved himself morosely out of his chair.

'You know, I've always fancied our chances a bit,' lied Jacko, anxious for sporty chat.

Mr Robinson said nothing and didn't look at him again. They listened to the national anthems of England and West Germany in silence. Not out of respect. It was just that they couldn't find the right words for each other.

The teams lined up. At 7 p.m. a whistle blew in Turin to start the World Cup semi-final.

'You're in,' said Heather, brightly, when Bannion opened the door on her first knock. 'Good.'

'Just.'

'Couldn't see your truck.' She stepped inside but turned and shook her brolly over the empty milk bottle on the doorstep. Each side of the narrow street was lined with parked cars. She had driven past his house, first on the left, and found the only vacant space towards the end of the road. As she walked back in the rain, every uncurtained window danced with rainbow reflections from coloured screens. She bent to put the brolly by the door, which Bannion clicked shut behind her.

'Told you,' he said, rather sharply. 'I'm off tomorrow.' She followed him into a kitchen which had a hospital smell, tangy and clean. A rusty steel tool-box stood on the sill next to a red screw-top canister labelled 'Drain Clean'.

She put her shoulder bag on the table and turned. He stood at the door. He looked small, out of uniform, in a loose blue towelling shirt and baggy black trousers in which a pocket bulged. 'Now.' Smiling. 'What's this about, Keith?'

'Told you.' Nervous, truculent almost. 'Them goings-on at

TVE.' He spoke with a croak, oddly high-pitched, eyes ranging over her.

'Nothing to worry about,' she said, reassuringly. 'What have you got for me?'

'Pictures.' Pause. 'Of something you've been interested in for a long while.'

'May I see them?'

'In the Dark Room. Just dried. Everything's ready.' He vanished in the hall. She followed again. He was standing half way between her and the street door, opening another door outwards. On it was taped a handwritten sign in black block capitals: DARK ROOM – PLEASE KNOCK.

He stepped out of view again and a block of light lit the hall. He reappeared and shuffled to one side. 'After you.'

She hesitated, looking down on a set of stone steps, a dozen or so, bowed by wear at their centres, a corroded metal handrail running down a bare brick wall.

She looked at him, uncertain. He smiled weakly. 'Turn left at the bottom.'

Don't go. A woman's intuition combined with a police officer's hunch. She swallowed a fraction of a second's fear. The balls of her feet in leather-soled shoes tapped a slow beat, a funeral march, louder with every step.

The door shut behind her. Below her a black pleated curtain on a ringed rail billowed briefly on the down draught and flickering yellowy-orange light came and went.

The air was dank, not stale, a bitter, woody, burning smell, like a blown-out match. Three steps from the bottom now. Hot as a hothouse. White cotton briefs sticking to her. Tapping feet burning. Don't go. She froze, back foot on a higher step than front. Light footsteps behind, quickening, closing. She tried to turn her head.

What the hell? Whiteness, wetness on her face, forced forward by a hand pushed against her neck. 'Bas . . .' The word was strangled by an arm round her throat, pulling.

Bastard. Bastard. Bastard. Kick. Kick. Use your hands. Punching, scratching, clawing. A phantom. The curtain. You're caught up in the curtain.

What is it? Get it off. Get that pad off your face. Pull. It's coming down. Pull.

She could see whiteness below the bridge of her nose, blackness above. Blackness with whiteness. A double-headed monster, half-man, half-beast, in shaded charcoal on white paper on a black wall. Bare backsides, sturdy, turned towards her, black ink on white paper on black walls. Candles, lit, smoking, burning; pitch-black stems.

White skulls and bones on a black background. The Killing Fields. That's in Cambodia, stupid. This is . . . This is . . . Where am I? Black on white. White on black. Blackness. Whiteness. Whiteness. Blackness. Where am I?

England on the attack, white shirts sweeping forward with precise play, but Jacko felt no purr of pleasure at their performance, no national pride.

All they want are those streets safe for their surviving daughter. That's all. How can I help achieve that? What have I got? If Tyson confirms Hollis's movements, they alibi each other.

That leaves Bannion. What have I got on him? The hairs in his patrol van, certainly. He knew Sam and his wolf, had access to the huts. But Sam showed no reaction when they came face to face at that ID parade. No fear, nothing. A blank mind, but only for a second. Because Bannion was in gaudy civvies, not his black uniform.

A pleasurable purr now. Let's not get excited. He's alibi-ed on the forest murder. Maybe Sherman's right. Maybe there is no serial killer. Each case, a different killer. Stick to Michelle, your baby.

What have you got on Bannion re Michelle? Forest Coaches was his first call at 7.30 but what was to stop him being out and about in Moorwood earlier? We've only got his word on the time he left his home. No neighbours confirmed it.

Snatched her off the street, you mean? Eyes on the screen, he shook his head with dismay as if at a misdirected pass. Doesn't gel. Michelle had a date with someone – someone who had good news. She was meeting somebody she knew.

Bannion never had any contact with her or her family. He doesn't live in the village. The office where she worked wasn't on his rounds. What possible connection could there be? He prodded and probed his mind, a ball playing winger seeking an opening.

West Germany, in turquoise, regrouped and came out on the attack with fast, flowing football. Robinson ohed and ahed and occasionally added his own commentary. 'The daft bugger's running into a blind alley.'

Me, too, Jacko brooded. He felt no apprehension for his country, under great pressure now. A tiny chink was opening up, a way out of his blind alley, and when the half-time whistle blew, with the game goalless, he made his move.

The panel was back and, over their chatter, he said: 'We knocked off your old neighbour Norman Hollis today for back-handers.'

A muted stare, but Mr Robinson's hostility had gone. He rose and turned down the sound. 'You don't think he's involved with our Michelle?'

'He could have a cast-iron alibi, sorry to say.'

'Marvellous, isn't it?' A mocking voice, hostile again, as he sat down. 'You can catch fiddlers, but not our girl's killer.' His wife let it pass without rebuke.

'We're holding him anyway, while we check.'

Curiosity overcame him. 'On the make, eh? How much?'

'Hard to say, yet. Enough for a few of life's bigger luxuries. His house, for instance.'

Mr Robinson blew air through his teeth into a hiss. 'Wonderful, eh? While we starved. And all over a lousy ten-quid headlight.'

Jacko had worked his opening. 'Who shopped you on that?'

'He did.'

'But he didn't witness it.'

'A security guard did.'

'Who?'

'Blimey. I can't remember all this . . .'

'It will be in those union papers,' said Mrs Robinson, quickly. 'From the industrial tribunal. You've still got them upstairs. Is it important?' Jacko nodded urgently. Robinson made no move. 'I'll fetch them,' she said.

Jacko sank in his cushion as she stood. Mr Robinson turned up the sound after she left the room.

The match had restarted when she got back, carrying a buff

wallet folder. 'Sorry,' she said sitting down beside him again. 'It's a tip at the bottom of that wardrobe.'

She handed Jacko the file and he flicked through it on his knee. 'Rejected' said a rubber stamp on the top page which listed the parties to the union's action for unfair dismissal.

The second statement from the bottom was headed TVE Securities and described how Mr Robinson was caught in the act of smashing the headlight glass on Hollis's Nissan Patrol.

It was signed: K. Bannion.

Jacko got Mr Robinson's nodded consent to take the file. As he stood at the lounge door, West Germany scored a fluke goal with a high, looping deflection. 'Lucky Krauts,' said Mr Robinson. He did not look from the screen to say goodbye.

Heather was in Paphos on a hot day. Cool hands caressed the nape of her neck and worked their way across her shoulders. Ah, that's better.

She liked to doze in her bikini bottom with the sun on her back. He always did much more than slap on protective cream. He made a massage out of it. Fingers on her spine. Palms on the small of her back. Paradise.

Sticky hands began kneading bare buttocks. That's not on. Not in public by the hotel pool. What's the randy sod doing? What am I doing with him? It ended months ago. Get your greasy hands off me. I'm with Peter. I want Peter. She was beginning to wake up.

'Stop it,' she murmured but the massage went on, vigorously now.

'I said, *stop it*.' She raised her voice angrily, tried to throw her arms back but her wrists were strapped to the lounger's frame. The bent bastard. She tried to back heel him. Her ankles were bound to the foot of lounger which, she realized with panic, was vertical, not horizontal. 'What the hell do you think you're playing at?' She opened her eyes. 'Where am I?'

'You've been sleeping.' A man's voice behind her. The rub-down stopped.

She turned her head and tried to squint away the blur. Bannion came into fuzzy focus at her shoulder.

'Oh, God, no.' A whisper to herself. Without contact lenses

194

or her red specs she thought at first that he was completely naked, very dark at the crotch, but then she could make out a black G-string, shiny leather, very, very full. On a black cord round his muscular neck hung a five-sided star.

His body glistened in the dancing light of three black candles. One was on a square jutting out from a wall, waist high, covered by a black cloth. On the cloth was a silvery sort of bow, flecked with golden glitter. An upturned cross hung on the back wall above. Another candle, much thicker and brighter, was in the centre of the room on a stand. The third was somewhere behind her.

'What the devil do you think you're doing?'

He held up a jam jar for her inspection. She could see the marks of fingers which had scooped out what looked like soft lard.

'Our unctions,' he said. 'Sacrifices were made for this.' And he turned from her towards the black-clothed square. Her eyes followed. Each side of the inverted cross a skeleton, tinged with yellow in the candlelight, hung with outstretched arms from a thin steel chain which ran slackly from wall to wall. A gloating grin filled his face when he turned back.

Icy cold then. Goose pimples rose and froze solid. Fine nape hair broke free from the grease and bristled. 'Get away. Get away from me, you sick bastard.' She twisted her body, bucking. Her bonds held firm.

'It's necessary,' said Bannion, out of view again, resuming the massage, roughly, harder.

'Get away.' A thin voice, higher, not quite hysterical but close. 'Leave me alone.'

'Anointment. For the Sabbat.'

'Stop.' What's this weirdo talking about? 'Leave me alone.' She struggled, twisted, bucked and all the time the bindings held and the anointment went on.

'Magnificent.' He seemed to be panting. 'What a magnificent birthmark.'

'Get your fucking hands off me.'

A warped smile. 'Language like that only increases the price you will have to pay.'

Appease him. Open communications. Talk, girl, talk. 'Listen to me, Keith . . .'

195

His hands stopped work. He was at her shoulder. 'Address me as Makatiel.' A snarling voice. 'I am your Angel of Punishment.'

Jacko turned on the car radio but paid no heed as England hunted for the equalizer.

It's a start, he mulled; something to toss into the melting pot tomorrow. Prove the link. How?

Well, Bannion's first call was 7.30 at Forest Coaches, then 7.40 at the old colliery. Michelle caught the bus from the main road. He could have made contract with her any morning. Chatted her up. Found out about her father. Conned her that he could help get him reinstated. Sweet-talked her into a meet.

He took a roundabout at a crawl and headed south on the ring road. His was the only car on that stretch of dual carriageway but he didn't top forty.

It's possible, you know. Could all fit. He decided he wouldn't wait for the noon conference. He'd pick up Bannion at dawn and search his place.

More roundabouts and lights. One set showed red. He stopped and lit a cigarette.

Jesus. It hit him then. A thunderbolt.

Bannion's alibi on the forest job wasn't worth two pennyworth of cold piss. TVE was a nest of thieves and liars.

The lights turned green. He moved off.

Bannion was on the main road when the boss's son was bowling over a cyclist while rushing Hollis and their doctored documents to work. If he'd come forward with that info, we'd have wanted to know what Luke Tyson and Hollis were doing together. He traded his silence for an alibi.

And old man Tyson was going to trade him for an amnesty for Luke. Bannion could have done the forest job. And he could have delivered Angie Stevenson's eviction notice. There is a serial killer. And he's Bannion. It fits. That Mountie's my man. It fits. Perfectly.

Fetch him in. Now. What did you preach to Tyson yesterday? How would you feel tomorrow if they found Michelle's sister dead? What would you say to her mother? 'Sorry, Mrs Robinson, but I wanted to get home to see the rest of the match.' Come on, dumbo. Stop at a phone box and call it in. Now.

First, let's check. See if he's in. Flood his street with uniforms while he's out and he could get wind of it, do a runner and kill all over the country. Call 'em out if his truck's parked outside.

He took the next left, a main road for the city centre, then into a maze of side streets, a short cut towards the Goose Fair site.

'This is silly.' A reedy, quavering voice, unrecognizable as her own. 'Think about it.' Firmer, more natural. 'I'm a policewoman, for christsake. For *Christ's sake, a policewoman.*' Heather was shouting now.

'No one can hear you.' Bannion spoke softly.

'*What do you want?*'

His response was to stroke her left buttock. 'Always knew you'd have a birthmark.'

'I haven't.' She wriggled in her bonds.

'Virgin white. Beautiful.'

'Because there's no suntan there. That's all.' Her face was as greasy as their bodies but with sweat. Her black hair felt sodden. 'Please.' A pleading voice. 'That's enough. Please. Keith. That's . . .'

'Makatiel.' He hissed the name, repeating it louder. 'You will learn to call me Makatiel.' He moved away from her.

She glanced sideways. He was standing in front of the black clad square, lifting the silver bow, offering it in both hands towards the inverted cross.

He turned back towards her and the bow parted into strands in his right hand. The ends reached the floor. Here and there the strands glinted and the tips of them made a tinkling sound when he dragged them on the concrete.

'Time for the Test.'

'Please.' Begging now. 'Let's just talk for a minute.'

'Of your fitness.' He was close, whispering distance. He lay the loose strands across his left hand, ten or a dozen, like curtain cords. The other ends were wrapped round his right hand. She could see that what glittered golden at a distance were small fish hooks threaded in at intervals of about two inches. 'The Silver Cord will test you.'

'Wait. Wait.' Trembling, sobbing. 'Wait for just a minute.'

'It will be applied to your birthmark. Don't scream. Don't murmur, and you pass and join me at the Sabbat.'

The Sabbat. She knew what it was. The Black Mass. She felt herself fading away, dizzy, sickening. She breathed deeply, fighting off apoplexy. 'They know I'm here.' She spoke with eyes shut, head hanging. 'They'll be coming. They know where I am.'

'Don't waste your strength. Don't tell me I need help and you can get it for me.' He strode away, back towards her. 'Look.' A commanding voice, shrill, shouting. '*Look.*'

He was standing facing her in front of the skeleton which hung from the chain on the wall to the left of the cross. 'This one . . .' He flicked his right hand back, no harder than a defensive shot at table tennis, and the cords lashed the bones, making them jingle like wind through Oriental door charms that warn of and ward off evil spirits.

He strode silently in front of the cross to the other skeleton. 'And this one . . .' a harder flick and the skeleton latched on to the hooks, snagging them, refusing to let go, so that it reared from the wall, dancing violently, crashing back '. . . said exactly the same.'

He addressed the skeleton, back to Heather. 'This one, I thought, had passed. She fooled me. Fooled me with her drugs.' He struck it again, angry, and it danced again, almost alive, in mid-air. 'No one will fool me again.'

He stepped into the brighter light of the big candle, five feet high on its stand in the centre of the room, and stood there, looking at her, flames reflected in wide, wild eyes.

'They all said I needed help, but it was they who needed it and it never came. They all say someone will come. No one ever does.'

He paused, staring fixedly at her. 'There should be more. Two more.' A smile now, slow, a long time forming.

He stood with feet wide apart. A snake's movement, quick, deadly, inside his G-string which strained to contain it and seemed about to burst. 'Let me demonstrate the Silver Cord.'

He turned into the narrow street. He passed the first house on the left. No TVE truck outside. No light from the front window.

He switched off the radio so he could think; decide priorities. A place to park as close as possible, then a phone.

So many stationary vehicles on either side that he had to drive in the middle of the street. Left, packed. Right, no spaces. Left, a red Fiesta, streaked with dirt, like Heather's. He glanced at the number on the index plate.

Heather's.

An emergency stop. He abandoned his car at right angles to the line of parked vehicles, keys in the ignition, driver's door open.

He ran back along the centre of the street. Hang on, girl, I'm coming, and if that pervert has touched one hair on your head, he's dead. Hear that? He's fucking dead.

He braced his feet, threw his right arm back, his left shoulder forward.

A singing, whistling, slapping sound. Dimness, not blackness. No pain; not physical pain.

She strained to look over her shoulder. The cords were wrapped round the big black candle, lit no longer, vertical no more.

It sagged and snapped when Bannion tugged the lash back to his bare feet. The brittle bottom scattered in bits as it hit the floor. The top half, softened by heat, was forming small, stagnant pools on the concrete.

Small chunks of it, black and cream, baited the hooks on the cords in Bannion's hand.

She tensed every muscle, filled her lungs and she screamed then, shaking her head, arching her back, loud and louder and louder, long and longer and longer. 'Silence,' he howled but she could hardly hear him.

Silence came, finally, apart from her breathless sobs. Exhausted. Extinguished like the black candle.

Above, the sound of breaking glass; no louder than a milk bottle snatched by the wind from the doorstep. Then, across the cellar's ceiling, fast footsteps.

Heather looked up, towards heaven.

*   *   *

199

He hurled himself at the cellar door, shouting, screaming both their names.

'Hang on, Heather.'

'Jacko.'

'You're dead, Bannion. You're dead.'

He hammered at the lock with the empty milk bottle he had used to break the front window. It shattered in his hand, slashing two fingers.

He ran to the kitchen and tipped out Heather's bag. Nothing better than a nail file and eyebrow pluckers. He looked in the sink. Nothing stronger than a spatula.

He opened the lid of a metal box on the sill and feasted on the sight. He took out a heavy screwdriver and ran back to the hall. He rammed it in the gap just below the Yale lock and pushed and pulled, a frantic oarsman rowing for dear life. The door sprang back.

He took the steps two at a time, bleeding hand on the rail, the other holding the screwdriver. He tore aside the curtain.

He saw Heather first, just a glimpse of her, spreadeagled, struggling.

Then Bannion. Like something out of Dante's *Inferno*. Glistening black hair, white gleaming body, black thong, white legs, a backdrop of arses and multi-headed animals, heinous, merging together in the shadowy half-light.

What the f. . . ? Silver threads snaked through the air towards him. They pitterpattered harmlessly on his spectacle lenses. Didn't hurt, he thought in the two-thirds of a second it took for the cords to wrap themselves round his face and hair.

And, oh by Jesus, fuck me, Mother of God, it hurt then as the hooks embedded themselves. Oh. Jesus. Sweet Jesus.

They bit deep into his ears, lips, hair, skin. Arghh. The stings of a shoal of ray fish. Arghhh. The bites of a million mosquitoes. Arghhhhh. A shotgun seemed to have peppered pellets into his face.

He screamed, louder, much louder than Heather, in agony, in pain that numbed his brain. He dropped the screwdriver in paralysed shock.

Four feet away Bannion tugged, hauling him in, lassoed. The paralysis had reached Jacko's legs. He stood firm.

Divots of skin, the size of maggots, hair by the roots, the size of lead shot, were torn out of him. Blood rushed through a colander of holes down his chin and neck and into his shirt collar.

Screaming, swearing, he charged forward to slacken the cord's tension, to ease his pain. Bannion jumped back, right arm up, landing his catch, tightening it.

Jacko forward, Bannion back. Forward, back, until Bannion was against the black-clad square.

Jacko saw the candle which stood on it. Now. He swept it up left handed and, in the same sweet movement, rammed it into Bannion's exposed armpit.

Different screams, fiendishly high. Different smells. Of burning hair and flesh. Jacko's thumb blistered and peeled as the tar coating melted over it. He held it there, screaming, pushing. The armpit became a cauldron of bubbling black pitch.

Bannion's left arm wrapped round his right shoulder as Jacko took his hand away. Bannion sank to the floor, holding on to the cords and Jacko's head followed, had to.

Bannion was trying to turn his back, to pull him down, beside him. Jacko threw out his left hand for balance towards the cross. He grabbed something as firm and cool as the branch of a willow tree stripped of its bark.

He pulled. Nothing came. Another tug, sharper, and something fell free from the wall.

Blow upon blow he struck with it. Over the back of Bannion's head and shoulder. White splinters flew. Blow after blow. The weapon seemed to be shrinking in his hand. Bannion let go of the cord, wrapping his arms around the back of his head, elbows tight to his ears, a child frightened of the thunder, screaming at first, then crying, begging, finally whimpering, 'No more. Please. No more.' The blows rained down on him. Without mercy. Blow after blow and splinters flew.

As Bannion lay still, Jacko collapsed to his knees, spent, and the only thing that hadn't surrendered, that wasn't shattered, was the calcified hip bone of Angie Stevenson which he held in his bloodied hand.

He had no clear memory of crawling across the floor and unbuckling Heather and certainly he was never to recall her nakedness. Her dress, bra and pants had been ripped, so she slipped on her raincoat and sat beside him with their backs to the black wall for a long time.

Then she knelt before him. His face looked like the flesh of a water melon – reddish pink with small pips of black tar. She stemmed the flow of blood from his cut hand with her torn underwear and blew softly on his burnt hand. The cords hung down his back like pigtails. Gently she lifted them over his shoulder so he could hold them at his chest, to take the weight. In the dim light of the remaining candle she could only see to disentangle a few hooks from his hair.

A line of them were embedded in his lips, zipping them together. He was desperate for a cigarette.

She helped him to his feet. With a final look at Bannion who lay still but breathing, he climbed the stairs, slowly and painfully, holding the cords loose in front of him.

He slid down the hallway wall to his haunches facing the opened cellar door. He cupped a hand close to an ear and made a dialling motion with his right index finger. She stooped and touched his shoulder. 'Won't be long.'

'Get up,' said Makatiel. 'You must get up.'

'I'm hurt,' said Adam.

'Don't let them take you. Do you want a strait-jacket? Do you want a padded cell?'

Bannion opened his watering eyes and pulled himself into a sitting position against the black cloth. Every movement wracked his battered body. 'What shall I do?'

'Get up. Burn your books. No one must read them.'

Bannion slid upright, staggered to a pile of exercise books and note-pads on a shelf, picked them up, held them over the remaining candle until the edges of the paper yellowed, curled and blackened. He dropped them on the floor.

'Climb on. Quick. No time to lose.'

Bannion held his left hand tight across his burnt, bleeding shoulder and, wincing, rolled on his altar.

'Stand up.' He pulled himself up against the wall. 'Put that chain from the ceiling round your neck.' He stood rock still.

202

'It's better than the State Special in a padded cell and a strait-jacket for the rest of your life, isn't it? You were going to do it before. They've got you now. There's no escape this time. Besides . . .' Makatiel paused '. . . they say it gives you the greatest erection of your life. The last orgasm but the greatest. Come on.'

'Will it hurt?' asked Adam. 'Will it be quick?'

'Take off your thong.'

Bannion pulled down the G-string with his left hand and stepped out, side footing it away.

'Put the chain round your neck.' He looped the chain round his neck. 'And again.'

What's that? Jacko listened. And again. What is it? A chain rattling?

Is there a trapdoor leading to the back garden? We didn't check.

Oh, shit, not again.

He slid up the wall and walked to the cellar door.

'Jump,' Makatiel ordered.

Bannion jumped from the altar. The jolt started in his toes and jerked through his body to the crown of his head which crashed back against the wall.

His hands shot to his throat. 'I can't breathe. I'm throttling.' He tried to force his fingers between the chain and his neck but flesh and muscle bulged over it.

'Nothing,' screamed Makatiel. 'No hard. No horn. Nothing. It's not working. Dance. Dance. Pull down. Asphyxia's what does it. Weight. We need more weight.'

'I'm strangling. I can't breathe.'

'Bounce. Bounce yourself.'

Gurgling now, slaver running out of the corners of his mouth. 'I want to die. Quickly,' sobbed Adam. 'This must end.'

'It's not working. That smoke is choking me. It's slow suffocation. Dance. Down. Pull down. Snap the spinal cord. Oh, God help me.'

'I can't. I can't. Please God help me.'

Jacko heard the rattle when he pulled back the curtain. Smoke with no heat in it smarted his eyes. Head down, he stamped on the burning paper with both feet, then kicked the pile apart.

The flames died. The smoke cleared.

He saw him then. His glassy eyes were almost out of their sockets. His lips twisted grotesquely. His blackened tongue stuck out from his foaming mouth, further, much further and stiffer than his penis, shrivelled to the size of a fat girl's thumb. His hands and feet twitched, the St Vitus's dance of death.

Jacko let go of the cords at his chest. He stepped forward, placed both arms behind his thighs, till his hands gripped their opposite's elbows. He pulled down. Just once.

Crack. No more than a finger being pulled out of joint. That's all. Crack. A vertebra snapped at the neck.

His head flopped. Motionless now.

Late but surprisingly light. A racing ambulance can't keep pace with the racing clouds above and beyond a racing window. Patches of light blue, splashes of crimson in the sky. A wind bends the treetops and dries the rooftops.

One-one after extra time but lost on penalties,' says a voice from somewhere above. 'Played their hearts out, though.'

'Ah, well.' Heather is smiling down at him. 'We can't win 'em all.'